Left for Dead

Left for Dead

Howard Jencks

Library of Congress Control Number:		2012905561
ISBN:	Hardcover	978-1-4691-9094-5
	Softcover	978-1-4691-9093-8
	Ebook	978-1-4691-9095-2

This is a work of fiction. Names, characters, places and incidents either are the
product of the author's imagination or are used fictitiously, and any resemblance
to any actual persons, living or dead, events, or locales is entirely coincidental.

This book was printed in the United States of America.

To order additional copies of this book, contact:
Xlibris Corporation
1-888-795-4274
www.Xlibris.com
Orders@Xlibris.com
112192

With special thanks to my wife,
whose encouragement and support made this possible,
and my mother for always being there when I needed her.

PROLOGUE

South Lake Tahoe was a little warmer than usual for August. With average temperatures in the high seventies to low eighties for the month, this year was an exception with most days in the low nineties. The ninety-three-degree Thursday afternoon was almost a record. The heat did strange things to people. Tempers were shorter, and for those people prone to outbursts, violence was more likely. And at 6,260 feet above sea level, ninety-three degrees was downright hot.

The area's primary industry was tourism. With seventy-two miles of shoreline, six casinos, and 182 ski trails, it was an adventurer's dream. People came from all over for some of the best skiing in the world during the winter months at resorts like Heavenly, located near the California-Nevada state line in the heart of the city, or Kirkwood, just a short jaunt over Luther Pass to Highway 88. Not much changed in the summer; people still came from around the world to hit the slopes and trails. They just did it on full-suspension downhill mountain bikes or with a pair of hiking boots. Of course, there was always the draw of the Lake itself. Locals and tourists could see anything from classic wooden 1947 Chris-Craft Runabouts to half-million-dollar Donzi ZR luxury performance boats on the cerulean water almost every day, not to mention the plethora of sailboats, fishing charters, and rentals heading in and out of the marina.

The casinos, just across the state line, provided plenty of options for nightlife, keeping the city going twenty-four hours a day. They had all the requisite banquet rooms to host conventions, private parties, and weddings. They kept people coming year-round. Although it was also the casinos that brought some of the less savory element to the area, they were the biggest moneymakers. Rain or shine, hot or cold, people could be found at the tables and slots trying to win big. Everyone knew the odds were against them, yet they kept trying, telling themselves that someone had to win, and it might as well be them.

It was transient populace that made for a small but lucrative prostitution and call girl business. There weren't many streetwalkers; most found their clientele within the casinos and hotel bars. The better-looking women had the luxury of working as call girls, meeting clients in their hotel rooms. These arrangements were generally made by their handlers. They would hang out at the casino nightclubs like the Lavish Green in Montbleu and watch for the guys who just couldn't seem to get it right. They would strike up a casual conversation with the man and, when the timing seemed right, offer to help him out with his troubles. If interested, the handler would signal a couple of his girls to come over. They were always on the dance floor, dancing and mingling but watching as well, waiting for the signal. Brief introductions were made, and the client and his newly found date would then be left alone to discuss any further arrangements. If an agreement was reached, sooner or later, they would make their way to the client's room to seal the deal.

Nicklaus Walkley knew how the system worked. He'd taken advantage of the high-priced hookers on more than one occasion. He wasn't a handsome man by any standard, nor was he what women would describe as homely either. He was just an average guy with an average build. At 5'11" he wasn't so tall that he stood out, but he wasn't short either. He had light brown hair that just fell flat to his head and hazel eyes that looked more green or brown depending on his attire. He kept his hair long enough that he could change the style from one day to the next, parting it on either side down the middle or just combing it straight back. He made it a point to do this, just as he often wore different styles of nonprescription cosmetic glasses for the same reason. He didn't want to be recognized from one day to the next as a local or regular patron to any establishment he frequented.

Nicklaus was paranoid for a reason. He was thirty-two years old and had moved five times since his twenty-eighth birthday. It was on his birthday four years earlier when he met his first prostitute. Her name was Star, or so she said. He met her at Wild Woolly's, a bar in Chula Vista just seven miles from downtown San Diego and seven miles from the Mexican border. She approached him and initiated a conversation that quickly became very flirtatious. Nicklaus enjoyed the attention; he wasn't used to it. He told her it was his birthday, hoping it might help. He was already anxious to get lucky. It had been—He couldn't remember how long since he'd been with a woman. They talked for nearly a half hour, and soon the talk became sexual. Star told him what she would do to him if he would only give her the chance. She was very explicit and promised to make this birthday one to remember. Nicklaus felt the excitement in his stomach. He hadn't felt this way in a long time.

He couldn't believe what was happening; he never had such luck. That was when Star dropped the bomb. She told him she would do everything she said but needed to know he had the cash. Nicklaus couldn't believe it. He felt stupid for not realizing she was a prostitute, but she had gotten him so aroused he didn't want to go back to his dumpy apartment alone. He told himself he wasn't spending another birthday alone, shit, not another night alone; it just wasn't going to happen. He found himself starting to negotiate with her. They finally reached an agreement and headed out. He fully intended on taking her back to his place, but while they were walking back to his Toyota, something happened.

Nicklaus was overcome with fear, fear of getting caught and having to explain to his mother why he was with a prostitute. He told Star he was too nervous, and the deal was off, but she insisted everything would be okay and kept saying, "Just relax. I'll make it worth your while."

They kept walking and were soon behind the bar, still headed toward his vehicle. Nicklaus told her to forget it, starting to get angry that she kept following him. It was then that she grabbed him, calling him a pussy, telling him that if he couldn't seal the deal, that was his problem, but he owed her fifty bucks for the time she wasted on him in the bar. Nicklaus remembered the instant rage he felt; the nerve of that hooker bitch to say he owed her. She hadn't done anything but trick him. That was when she tried to grab his wallet. He pushed her back as hard as he could. She tripped in her ridiculously high heels; he remembered thinking that should have been the giveaway. She started to scream.

Nicklaus didn't know why he got so angry, only that he had to walk away. Even if someone stopped him, even if it was a cop, all he had to do was explain how this fucking prostitute tried to dupe him into taking her to his place, and he'd be done, and she'd be going to jail. But he didn't; he looked around to see if anyone was looking. There was not a soul in sight. He couldn't remember what she was saying, just that she was calling him something fowl, challenging his manhood. It didn't matter; he didn't care. He knew he could get it up. In fact, his dick was harder than he could ever remember.

He stepped toward the hooker, who apparently recognized the change in his demeanor. She must have seen something in his face, something he had never even seen in himself to that point. Her words turned from an all-out assault on his manhood to terror-filled pleas for mercy. He remembered the fear in her voice; as it had fled his body, it must have entered hers. She was sitting up on her butt when he started toward her and began pushing herself backward, trying to get away, but the worthless slut was too slow, and he was on her. He didn't intend on fucking her anymore; it was much more than that.

9

He grabbed her throat and squeezed with all his might to silence her screams. No one had heard her yet, and he didn't need that to change now. He trapped each of her arms, placing his knees on her biceps as she collapsed beneath him. He remembers thinking how all the years of sitting at home alone, watching the Discovery Channel, helped create the killer he was at that very moment. Just like a lion from the Serengeti, he grabbed his prey by the windpipe and clamped down, cutting off all breath and silencing its screams.

Nicklaus kept squeezing and felt her trachea completely collapse in his grasp. He never felt more powerful as he watched the whore's face go flush as she tried to draw in a lifesaving breath. The blood vessels in her eyes ruptured under the pressure, and the whites of her eyes disappeared, turning dark as the night. When she stopped struggling, he held on for another fifteen seconds, just relishing the power he felt. His manhood throbbing between his legs, hard as a post.

He finally let go and stood over her. He remembered how perfect her body looked at that very moment. Legs draped one over the other, with her short skirt having ridden up to where he could almost tell whether or not she was wearing panties. He knew she wasn't. Her spaghetti strap shirt stretched out just enough to reveal her right breast, with her arms up as if submitting to him. That's what was wrong, he thought to himself; she needed to put her arms down. Nicklaus bent down and grabbed her left arm, pulling it down, positioning it at her side and bending it at the elbow so her forearm and hand rest provocatively under her exposed breast.

"There," he said to himself. "Now she's perfect." He took one last look, wishing he had a Polaroid to capture the moment. He had never seen a more perfect picture than what lay before him, and he created it. He knew at that very moment he would have to do it again. He also knew he had to leave. He walked to his Toyota, not looking around anymore, got in, and drove away. He could hardly wait to get home to take a shower and masturbate. He had never felt so alive.

That was four years, five moves, and twelve prostitutes ago, or at least he figured they were prostitutes by the way they dressed. If they weren't, they were stupid for being out at night walking the streets. Any respectable woman would stay home with her family or have a car.

Today he wasn't nearly as nervous as he had been back then, but he still found nothing aroused him more than the kill. It had been too long, and it was needed; he had to feel that rush, the adrenaline that came with the hunt, the predation. It let him know he was at the top of the food chain. He had to find someone, and it had to be tonight.

ONE

She looked at the clock; it was nearly seven thirty at night and still a sultry ninety degrees outside. It was unusually hot for an August evening in South Lake Tahoe and most people hated it. The local residents were drawn to the area for the beauty of the Lake, which was only enhanced by the surrounding Sierra Nevada Mountains that jet into the sky around the basin. Summers were mild, with the high temperatures generally in the 80s. Winters were cold, with average daytime highs in the mid-30s, dipping into the teens or even single digits at night. Mild if you were from Minnesota, but out-and-out glacial if you were from the low deserts of Southern California.

Rosa Jimenez hadn't been there long enough to experience the winter weather yet. As far as the summer and tonight's heat, she was indifferent. Rosa didn't look at the Tahoe area and recognize the beauty the region had to offer. Where others, new to the area, would be in awe of the majestic granite mountains visible to the southwest with peaks reaching 10,000 feet, or the lush green of the surrounding national forest the city was nestled in the middle of, Rosa simply existed.

Despite the many natural and man-made resources within a stone's throw of her tiny dwelling, she never ventured outside the incorporated area of the city. The hundreds of lakes and reservoirs, river canyons carved through granite bedrock, and miles of trails including a portion of the Pacific Crest Trail, were lost to Rosa. She did nothing more than what was necessary, what was demanded of her by her "employer."

Rosa was watching television, not really paying attention to what was on. She drifted away in thought, thinking about what her life had been like before. Before she had been taken and forced into a line of work she never fathomed to pay back a debt that her father could not. She loved her father deeply but hated him at the same time for what had happened to her. Her father had taught Rosa and her older brothers, Javier and Daniel, the value of family. They were supposed to take care of one another help one another no matter what. Never in a million years did she think helping her family would come to this. She told herself, "This couldn't be what he meant."

At twenty-four, Rosa was the youngest of three children. Her parents, Enrique Jimenez and Martha Jimenez Lopez, had immigrated to the United States after the birth of their first son, Javier. They had been living in the country illegally for years but decided it was necessary for their family's future and became naturalized citizens.

As Rosa was thinking of better times, her cell phone rang, bringing her back to the reality of her life. She looked to see who was calling. When she saw it was Carlos, her "employer," she thought of just letting it ring but knew she couldn't. The last time she decided she would make him wait, she ended up in the emergency room at Martin Luther King Hospital, peeing blood after the beating he gave her. She hit the Accept button on the touch screen of her Samsung, sliding it over to answer the call.

"Hello," she said with no enthusiasm.

"You are working Vex at Harrah's tonight. I'll pick you up in half an hour," Carlos said and then hung up.

"Vex," she said to herself as Carlos had already signed off. It was a high-dollar nightclub at Harrah's located on the Nevada side of Stateline. Vex ran nightly shows of its own on Friday and Saturday with sexy Vegas-style women performing high-flying aerial stunts in flashy costumes. Rosa knew she would have to dress the part to make the men think that she might just be one of the performers.

Rosa looked at her phone to see what time Carlos had called. It was already eighty thirty. She had to hurry if she was going to be ready by nine. It was one thing when she had to work floors; she could throw on just about anything and play the part to get the guy. Vex was a different story. She knew she had to put on something special if she was hoping to trick the men into thinking she was a performer, especially one they could take back to their room. Her trousseau would have to fit the part, and it was a high-paying part. She also had to be careful she did not end up looking like a cocktail waitress trying too hard for a tip.

Rosa got up and went into her bedroom. She pulled a teal-and-purple sequined dress from the closet. It was a low-cut gown, which gave Rosa ample opportunity to tease potential customers by bending over just enough so they could see more of her breasts than she really wanted. It draped below the knee, ruling out the cocktail waitress theory; although a slit that ran up her left thigh would leave no doubt that she was looking for a good time. She had used it with great success before, bringing in $3,500 for the night.

She hung the dress over the bedroom door and went into the bathroom to put on her makeup. She didn't have as much time as she would like, but it was sufficient. She matched her eye shadow to the dress and applied a lipstick that complemented her naturally tan skin. She grabbed the dress and slipped it over her face, making sure she didn't get any makeup on it. She looked in the mirror and decided to add a few curls to her normally straight black hair. She didn't have much time left, but a little on each side would give her the look she was going for.

She finished what she was doing and took one last look. For the briefest of moments, she thought of how she used to enjoy the thought of getting dressed up for a night on the town. It was something girls liked to do once in a while. Now she despised the fact that she had to do it at all and swore that as soon as she was done, and her father's debt was paid, she would never wear a dress again.

There was a knock at the door; Carlos was there. Rosa grabbed a small black leather purse that she carried with her everywhere. It went well enough with everything she wore and gave her a place to put the money. She also carried a small fixed-blade karambit knife in it. The knife had a three-and-one-fourth-inch razor-sharp blade shaped like a tiger's claw. She had sewn its KYDEX sheath into the liner of her purse and carried it with her everywhere since she had been raped by a John in Los Angeles. She swore that would never happen again. Her only comfort in the matter was that Carlos found the man before he got away and dealt with him. Not because he raped Rosa, but because nobody had her for free.

Rosa had witnessed the ordeal. It only lasted a few seconds. She couldn't believe the efficiency Carlos demonstrated with the knife he carried. It was the wickedest knife she had ever seen, exactly like the one she carried now. Carlos had walked up behind the rapist, grabbing him by the right wrist with his left hand. Carlos jerked the man around, pulling his right arm up and away from his body. All in the same fluid movement, Carlos brought the blade of the knife up under the man's arm, drawing the blade swiftly through the fat, muscles, tendons, and blood vessels on the underside of the arm where it attached to his body.

The man instinctively tried to reach across his body to grab his wounded arm, which was now dangling like a limp noodle at the side of his body, when Carlos slashed at his left arm, slicing into the *V* created on the inside of the elbow. The rapist tried to pull his arm back, but it was too late; it happened so fast the pain hadn't even set in yet. His left forearm hung toward the earth with the pull of gravity as Carlos had severed the muscles and tendons in it as well. Pools of blood began to form on either side of him as the blood drained from his body with every beat of his heart. At that, Carlos turned and walked away, returning to Rosa. He told her never to let that happen again. In the only gesture of kindness he had ever shown, Carlos told Rosa he would get her a knife and educate her in the art of how to handle a blade.

She opened the door, and Carlos walked in. He looked at her, eyeing her from head to toe. He nodded, giving his approval. "That should get 'em hard. Now let's go, I've got to be somewhere."

Ignoring his comment, Rosa simply grabbed her things, locked the door on her way out, and followed Carlos to his vehicle. She looked back at the fourplex she currently lived in. It was a dumpy little place nestled in some trees near the corner of Pioneer Trail on Fern Rd. She looked to the east and could see Harrah's from where she stood. She was less than a half mile from the casino and Vex and was starting to wonder what the evening held in store. She climbed into the passenger side of Carlos's 2009 Buick Regal. She wondered how much of her earnings went to pay for his car. She let it pass because there was no need in getting more upset before she even started.

"Are you coming up to Vex with me?" she asked.

"Not tonight. I have other business I need to deal with."

"Okay, then. I'll talk to you tomorrow."

"Send me a message when you hook up. I want to know where you're going to be," he said hardheartedly.

"Okay," she said as Carlos pulled into the drop-off area at the front of the casino.

Rosa got out of the vehicle. She had hoped Carlos would not follow her around tonight. Going to Vex really meant she only had to pick up one client. Men paid top dollar for a woman like her in the high-end clubs. She could make enough for the entire night, even if it only took the client ten minutes. So she hoped to spend a little time on her own before she went up to the club. Eat a nice dinner and have a drink to try and relax. It always helped her cope with what lay ahead.

Rosa walked into the casino's main entrance. She walked across the floor, heading for the west exit. She hated the smoke-filled atmosphere of the Nevada casinos but took her time nonetheless. Of all the things that were wrong with California, one of the few things the state did right in her opinion was ban smoking in public buildings. Once she reached the west-side door, she hesitated for a moment before exiting onto Stateline Road. She was nervous Carlos might see her; consequences for deception were harsh, but Rosa had reached a point in her life where death was welcome despite her hopes of someday returning home. She took a breath and peaked out the door. She checked to make sure Carlos wasn't anywhere watching and then casually walked out and across the road into the Heavenly Village shops on the California side.

She was casually walking through the village, enjoying the eclectic mix of shops and eateries, when she came upon the Fire & Ice Bar and Grill. It looked promising, and she was getting hungry. Rosa stepped inside and was met by a smiling young girl who asked, "How many tonight?"

"Just one."

"Right this way," the hostess called as she led Rosa to a small table near the large cooktop in the center of the restaurant. Rosa thought the place was pretty busy for a Thursday night. She took it as a good sign.

"Here's your table. Your server will be with you shortly."

Rosa looked around, enjoying the fact that she was free for the moment. The environment looked like fun, and she wished she could stay longer but knew she should eat and get over to Vex before she missed the prime time. There was a knack to picking up men, and Rosa knew it. Despite her hatred and revulsion for what she did, she had become very good at it and was a top earner for her handlers.

Rosa needed to get to Vex before the men got too drunk, and all the other women began to look good to them. She needed to get there while they only had a few drinks, were getting horny, and would be loose with their money. This would allow her to slide in with her sequined dress and play the part of the showgirl, providing the allure of what every man who went to such places wanted, bragging rights to say they banged a Vex girl. And once they thought they had a chance, it was time to talk money. Rosa was great at sealing the deal.

"Have you ever dined with us before?" came the question from a young man with a buzzed head and small black framed glasses.

"No, this is my first time."

"Great, you're gonna love it. We have a wonderful menu. You get to mix and match anything you'd like," he said. "My name is Nate, and if you'll come with me, I'll give you the tour."

Rosa got up and followed the waiter as he led her to what was referred to as the marketplace. "This is where you can work your magic, make a masterpiece of a meal. We have fresh vegetables, seafood, chicken, beef, udon noodles, pasta, and more. All you have to do is take a bowl and pile it high with whatever you want, add a little sauce, and you're golden." Nate grabbed Rosa by the hand and led her back to her table, pointing at the large cooktop that was surrounded by a bar full of people waiting for their food. "Then all you have to do is bring it over here, and one of our chefs will prepare it any way you want it. Now, can I get you started with something to drink?"

"Do you have any recommendations?"

"I'd go for the Frozen Raspberry Lemonade. It's a sweet little blend of rum, Chambord, and lemonade. Perfect for a hot summer night."

"Okay, I'll take one."

Nate was off to get the drink while Rosa went back to the marketplace to pack her bowl with fresh vegetables and chicken. Her job required she look good, so she tried to eat healthy most of the time. She splurged once in a while but not often. She also worked out regularly. It not only helped keep her figure, she also found it to be a tremendous way for her to relieve stress from day to day.

She gathered her meal, took it to the chefs, and, by the time she had it back, Nate had delivered her frozen drink. Dinner was good, but the drink was better. She contemplated having a second but decided against it. She needed her future client to be tipsy, not herself. Rosa asked for her bill and left enough cash on the table to cover it and the tip before heading back to Harrah's.

Two

It was turning out to be a beautiful night in the Tahoe basin. The mercury had dipped a tad since the sun settled behind the Sierras. It was perfect, Nicklaus thought to himself. He needed to be able to blend in, or so he thought. The reality was that nobody ever really paid much attention to him anyway. His paranoia told him different; as a result of which, he had become a master at being inconspicuous over the years. He would study people at his various jobs to see what he could do without drawing attention to himself. When someone would notice his quirky behavior, Nicklaus would just tell them he had a muscle spasm or thought he saw a wasp. It never made sense, but then again, most people didn't really give a shit anyway.

Nicklaus was prepared for the hunt. He was wearing a pair of loose-fitting cargo pants with a lightweight Western-style button-down shirt. The clothes were brand-new, resembling nothing he had in his closet. He had a pair of cotton workout shorts on under the pants and an in-vogue T-shirt with a little smiling stick figure on the back under the button-down. His Merrell cross-trainer shoes went well enough with either outfit. He wanted to be able to change his appearance quickly in the event someone saw him before he could get away cleanly, not to mention be able to run if needed.

He owned a four-by-four dark green 2004 extended cab Toyota Tacoma. It was one of the most common vehicles in the area, slightly trailing Subaru in popularity. Nicklaus left his rental home on Knox Avenue and drove down to Raley's grocery store on Lake Tahoe Boulevard at Park Avenue, a couple of blocks west of the state line. He parked in the grocery store parking lot and walked over to the Starbucks on the corner. After ordering a tall Americano, Nicklaus took the cup of Joe and headed out. He wanted to make sure he didn't get reported for parking in the lot without visiting one of the shops. The local business owners kept a keen watch for people using the parking lot as overflow when the casino lots were full.

Nicklaus headed east toward the state line. He made it as far as the Heavenly Gondola at the center of Heavenly Village. The gondola was a conveniently located ride that took tourists and locals to the Smokehouse Grill at Adventure Peak. They could catch the lift from there to anywhere else in the 4,800-acre park. Nicklaus was checking out the shops in the village and decided to see what they had to offer. The crowds weren't overwhelming, but there was enough of a variety of people to make it interesting.

He strolled through the village and was a little disappointed. He had expected more. He was cutting across the back of the village headed toward Harrah's when he noticed the shimmer of a sequined dress in front of him. Nicklaus surveyed the woman wearing it. She was far too dressed up to be alone, yet she didn't appear to be moving toward anyone. He began to follow her, watching how she moved so comfortably and gracefully despite her high heels. Nicklaus sized her up instantly. This woman—dressed the way she was, alone, and headed to the casinos—had to be one of the local call girls. Women didn't dress like that and go out on the town alone on a Thursday night.

He didn't have much time. She had reached Stateline Avenue and was starting to cross the street. If she made it to the casino before he could catch up, it could make things much more difficult. Nicklaus tossed his coffee cup into a nearby receptacle. He retrieved a $10 bill from his wallet and then began to jog.

"Hey, I think you dropped this," he said in a friendly, nonthreatening tone as he held out the money, but the woman just kept walking. "Excuse me, I think this is yours," he said a little more loudly but not so much that he would draw the attention of others.

Rosa slowed but kept moving as she was in the middle of the road when she heard something she couldn't quite make out. She looked back and saw a man hurrying toward her, holding something in front of him. "What is that?"

Nicklaus saw her slow; he was nearly upon her. *Perfect,* he thought to himself. "I think this is yours," holding out the money.

"I don't think so, but thanks anyway."

"No, here, I saw it fall out of your purse back there."

Rosa knew this guy was full of shit. She always placed her money into her wallet and zipped it shut before putting it back into her purse. There was no way anything fell out. She kept walking.

They were walking nearly side by side. This man claiming to have picked up her money was to her right when he finally put the money into his front pocket. "Okay, okay, you got me," he said as he reached up and grabbed her by the shoulder. "You didn't drop it. I just wanted to get your attention."

"Why is that?" Rosa asked as she took a slight step to the left, causing him to take his hand off her.

They had reached the sidewalk next to Harrah's. Nicklaus knew he was running out of time. He hated to rush, but he couldn't let her go into the casino; surveillance was too much there, and he hadn't worn a hat to conceal his face. She was too perfect. Her corpse would provide him with a mental picture he could relish for months to come. He had to have her, and he knew it.

"Look, you and I both know why you're out here dressed like that." His comment stopped her. He was in.

Rosa looked at this man. She wanted to slap him but didn't because she knew he was right. She just didn't know how he could have come to such a conclusion so quickly. She wondered if he could be a cop. Maybe they had been watching her and were setting her up. She had been in the area a little while now, and it was possible, but she had been careful. She had been arrested once before in Los Angeles by a young Hollywood Vice detective and had learned enough since then to avoid the setup. "Oh really? Why don't you tell me what it is you think I'm doing," she said seriously.

"I've got a room at Harvey's on the sixth floor with a king-size bed and a view of the lake. I had a good afternoon at the tables and don't want to spend the night alone." He thought he could see her expression change when he mentioned the tables. He knew he was right; this bitch was just another whore.

Rosa looked at him for a moment. "If you won big, you won't mind having a couple drinks. I was headed to Vex, you can come with me." She wasn't about to volunteer anything until this guy brought up money. That was the one way she would know he wasn't a cop. Until then, it was just drinks.

"Look, I've got a full minibar in my room. If you need a drink, you can have one up there. What do you say? Two grand and a little Belvedere should be enough."

Bingo, she thought. Entrapment is illegal, and he just made the offer. She was in the clear. "Okay," she said. "So you do know what I'm looking for. Twenty-five and you have a deal." She had to try to up the price a little. Rosa had discovered that the first person to bring up money always gave a little. If it was her, she inevitably had to come down. On the other hand, if it was the client, he would come up.

"Fair enough, but you're mine for the night." Nicklaus grabbed her hand and began walking. They hadn't been standing on the sidewalk very long, but there was a couple headed toward them. He knew if he didn't take the lead, this whore would, and she might want to go inside. He started toward the back parking lot of Harrah's.

"I thought you said your room was in Harvey's?" Rosa asked as they headed in the opposite direction. The client explained they could take the underground passageway from inside Harrah's. He was referring to a tunnel that connected the two casinos. Rosa had used the tunnel before, and it still didn't make sense to her why they were heading to the back. "That's fine, but where are you going?"

Nicklaus could feel her start to pull her hand away. He casually tightened his grip. "Don't worry, this way is faster. We can hit the back door and then make our way to the passageway. It's closer to the rear. You know how the casinos are? They make you walk past all the slots first."

He had a point. Rosa relaxed as the two walked around the corner to the back of the casino.

THREE

The town of Gardnerville, Nevada, is situated on the east side of the Sierra Nevada mountain range just over twenty miles from South Lake Tahoe. Despite the short distance, it's nearly a forty-minute commute on the meandering mountain roads. It's a small high desert town approximately 4,750 elevation with a population of 5,394 according to the welcome sign posted on Highway 395 at the city limits.

Michael Garrett lived just south of the city in a small house on Walker Street in the Pine View Estates. It was a modest three-bedroom two-bathroom home just over 1,300 square feet with an attached two-car garage. Michael's favorite part about his home was the view. The house was set on an incline with the backyard slightly higher than the front. As a result of this, Michael had an unobstructed view to the west, looking back toward the Sierras.

At twenty-eight, Michael had already been in law enforcement for seven years. He started his career with the Los Angeles Police Department and had gotten off to good start. He attended one of the last academy classes at the historic Police Academy located in Elysian Park. It had been in operation from 1936 until 1995, and every man and woman of the LAPD who preceded Michael had gone through that academy until the department opened the recruit training center in Westchester. Despite moving recruit training to the Westchester location, the Los Angeles Police Revolver and Athletic Club continued to maintain the facilities in Elysian Park for use by officers and their families. The department continued to use the historic academy for in-service training as well. Michael was number 1 in firearms and physical fitness and graduated as the honor recruit of Class 6/94.

Following his graduation, Michael was assigned to complete his probation at Southeast Division, which covered the Watts area. He spent the next year on patrol, working a variety of assignments as he was bounced between training officers until he completed the field training program. Then it really got fun as Michael was paired up with P2s, other officers not on probation.

Michael's performance never wavered. He completed his training in four months, when it took others six. He was a hard worker who shied away from nothing. He did his best to jump calls as much as his training officers would allow. This impressed his TOs, who were used to having to kick-start their trainees who simply wanted to lie low, handle their calls, and cruise through probation as quietly as possible. Of course it irritated those trainees who were made to look bad, and more than once they approached him and asked him to knock it off. It never worked because Michael loved what he did; it was who he was, and he had no tolerance for the lazy.

The year flew by. When Michael completed his probation, in accordance with LAPD protocol, he was wheeled to a new division, which meant he was at the mercy of the LAPD. It seemed as arbitrary as throwing darts blindfolded at a map of the city. Wherever it hit was where you ended up. Surely there had to be a reason for the assignments, but when Michael got the news he was headed to Central Traffic Division, he was stunned. He couldn't believe the powers that he would take an energetic young gunslinger and put him in traffic. It had a horrible stigma of being a place people went to retire. No respectable patrolman wanted to go to traffic, especially right off of probation. Once you got there, you were on training all over again. Now, instead of being called a "boot," you were a "pinky."

Pinky was the term used for new traffic officers regardless of time on the job. It was not a glamorous or affectionate title. Fortunately, ridding yourself of the title was easy; you simply had to get through the traffic training and take the basic collision investigation course offered by the department and complete the final exam successfully. Once that was done, you were a full-fledged traffic cop or, as Michael and many others liked to refer to them, Triple A with a gun. Michael protested his transfer as best he could without crossing any boundaries. However, it was to no avail, and his transfer remained unchanged. He was to report to CTD the week after he completed probation.

He went to work at CTD and was doubled up with a thirty-year veteran working graveyard. *Fucking great*, he thought to himself when he learned of his assignment. This was exactly what he didn't want. Everything he'd ever heard about traffic was about to become his reality. His new partner was probably some over-the-hill, overweight cop just hiding out on graveyard until he could pull his pension. Getting the graveyard shift at Central Traffic was the worst; everyone knew downtown Los Angeles was a ghost town as far as traffic went in the middle of the night. The only thing human roaming the streets were seven thousand to eight thousand homeless people on skid row.

Skid row actually had official boundaries established by the Ninth Circuit Court of Appeals. The area between Third and Seventh streets to the north and south and Alameda and Main Streets to the east and west was where commuters would see large numbers of cardboard boxes and camping tents lining the sidewalks. If you traveled through at the right time in the morning, you would catch thousands of people huddled together shoulder to shoulder on the west side of the north south running roads, trying to catch the morning sun as soon as it peaked over the skyline. This was the best they could do, or all they were willing to do. Regardless, they were not the primary responsibility for a CTD officer. They were a patrol problem, one that Michael wished he had at the time.

To this day, Michael vividly remembers his first night and meeting his new partner. It began just as he envisioned it would. He was changing in the locker room when a shorter stocky fifty-something man with a belly, grey hair, and a motor cop mustache walked past his locker aisle. He stopped and said, "So you're my new pinky?"

Michael looked at him with disdain, proud to be off probation and not wanting to take any more of the hazing. "I guess, but do you think we could work on names Jurassic?" he said confidently and with a smile, providing just enough voice inflection to let his new partner know he wasn't pleased to be there or with being referred to as a pinky.

"You got it, Homer. Mind if I call you Homer?"

"No worries, Santa, works for me."

His older partner began to laugh. He walked up to Michael, slapped him on the back with his left hand, and put his right hand forward for a more traditional greeting. "Mark Summers."

"Michael Garrett," he responded and took his new partner's hand. He instantly realized his first impression was wrong. This shorter seemingly overweight fellow clamped down on his hand with a grip like a vice. Michael tried to return the grip, but it was too late. Summers already had the drop on him, and it was all he could do not to let his face reveal the pain he was in.

"I'm big on tradition, so on second thought, I think I'll stick with Pinky, and you can call me partner, sir, or Summers. Got it, Squirt?"

"Got it, sir."

Summers released his grip and slapped him on the back again. "See you in roll call."

The rest of the night played out much differently than Michael expected. Following roll call, Summers helped him load up their black and white. Once they had the vehicle loaded up, Summers took Michael to the original Tommy's Burgers located on Beverly Boulevard between N. Rampart and Coronado Street. They both ordered one of Tommy's famous chili burgers with chili cheese fries and ate over the trunk of their patrol car. Summers filled Michael in on his expectations of him as a partner and told him to get any preconceived notions he had about traffic out of his head. Michael learned over the months to come that Summers was a black belt in judo and an amateur power lifter. They spent more time backing up patrol units from Central, Rampart, Hollenbeck, and North Hollywood than Michael could recall. He had a blast and learned a lot.

He was pulled back to reality at least twice a shift when they were called to handle a "deuce" (police jargon for *drunk driver*) by a patrol unit who didn't want to or for a traffic collision that occurred in their beat. It was during these times that Michael gained experience investigating fatal collisions, the likes of which were the equivalent of a homicide investigation on many counts.

Despite the fun, Michael knew his luck wouldn't hold. Sooner or later, Summers would get a new partner, and he would be assigned to someone else. So he started looking to the future. He decided he didn't want to live in Los Angeles forever, and there was no time like the present to start looking for work elsewhere.

Michael remembered a trip he took with a friend in high school to help his friend's family move. They moved to Camino, a small mountain city in El Dorado County near Lake Tahoe. He remembered how pretty it was and thought it would be a good place to start. He contacted the local sheriff's office and ended up speaking with the sheriff's secretary, Carol. Shocked he didn't get forwarded to some human resources robot, Michael spoke with Carol about applying to the agency. Carol sent him an application, and six months later, he was starting over again.

It had been four years since then, and he never regretted the move. His experience in Los Angeles paid off, particularly his time with Summers and his skill in investigations, which were a direct result from working traffic. Michael hated to admit it, but it had been a good experience. He had spent a couple of years working patrol at the El Dorado County Sheriff's Department and then made detective. El Dorado County was broken into two main geographic areas as far as the sheriff's department went. There was the West Slope and the Tahoe Basin, which were separated by the summit of the Sierra Nevada mountain range. It was likely the sheriff would have run the entire 1,700-square-mile county from one office except for the fact that the Tahoe Basin was cut off frequently from the West Slope due to snow.

As far as Michael was concerned, it was perfect. He loved working in the Tahoe area, and due to the fact that he was the only detective in the small office, he got to handle all of the cases that exceeded the capabilities of patrol. He had handled six homicides since making detective and had already closed four with arrests that led to conviction. As a result of his success and the close proximity, his counterparts across the state line in Douglas County, Nevada, had requested his assistance with a couple of homicide cases they were investigating. The cases were so similar there was no doubt they were related.

However, this weekend, Michael was off until Tuesday and was currently preparing for a three-day trek along the Tahoe Rim Trail. He had already loaded his pack and was currently double-checking his maps. He was planning to start at the trailhead located along the north side of Highway 50 at Spooner Summit in the morning. He was a minimalist backpacker, priding himself on carrying just over twenty pounds of gear, including the clothing he was wearing. It allowed him to move faster, which was important if he was going to accomplish his goal of reaching Brockway Summit, a forty-two-mile hike at a minimum elevation of seven thousand feet.

Michael was just finishing up when the phone rang, pulling him away from the topographical forest service maps.

FOUR

Michael grabbed his phone and glanced at the caller ID. The fact that it registered *El Dorado County* could mean one of two things—someone was either calling for advice on a patrol investigation, or he was getting called out. He hoped it wasn't the latter; he had been planning his hike for some time, and a callout would definitely put a damper on his plans. He answered the phone, "This is Garrett."

"This is Sharon with Dispatch. Hate to be the bearer of bad news, but we have a request for assistance from Douglas County for you. They have another homicide, behind Harrah's this time, and they think it might be their guy again."

"Where do they want me to meet them?" Michael instantly realized he would not be doing any hiking this weekend. Homicide investigations had to be worked nonstop until all leads were followed up. It was paramount in homicide investigations to identify, collect, analyze, and process information quickly and effectively and then act just as efficiently on that data to achieve maximum results. It was his willingness and tenacity to keep chasing down leads that were developed that led to Michael's success. Where others would break for the night, Michael always carried on. He told himself he'd get all the rest he needed when he was dead; because of this, he often maintained the element of surprise. This prevented suspects, or potential suspects, from getting their stories together and deterred the interjection of attorneys.

"At the substation in Stateline. Detective Cook is already there, standing by with the suspect."

"Holy shit, they already have the guy? What do they need me for then?" It was a rhetorical question, and Sharon knew it. Michael started to get his hopes up, thinking he may get to go on his hike yet.

"I don't know, but they asked for you and said it was critical. Detective Cook is waiting for you to call. His cell is . . ."

"I've got his number. Let 'em know I'm en route, I'll call shortly."

"Roger that."

Michael hung up his phone and walked into his bedroom. He was wearing a pair of khaki cargo shorts and a Life is good T-shirt, comfortable but definitely not appropriate for the crime scene. He changed into a pair of coyote brown 5.11 covert cargo pants and a button-down, short-sleeve olive plaid shirt. He liked the pants because they offered the storage of a traditional cargo pant, but the side pockets didn't stand out as much since there was no flap over the top, just a vertical zipper that kept them almost unnoticeable. He put on his black Danner work boots, threw on his belt, and ran it through the loops on his Sidearmor holster, securing it over his right hip. He opened the gun safe in his bedroom closet and grabbed his Kimber CDP Pro 1911 semiautomatic .45 caliber pistol, instinctively checked to ensure there was a round in the chamber, and then holstered the gun. He grabbed his wallet, badge, and keys out of the tray he kept on top of the safe; put the wallet in his right hip pocket; clipped his badge onto his belt in front of his pistol; and dropped his keys into his front left pocket. He always kept his keys opposite his gun side in the event he had to go for his gun while digging for his keys. It was just one more way to ensure he didn't have his gun hand occupied, which would slow his response to a potentially lethal threat.

Now that he was dressed, Michael grabbed his go bag. It was a small tactical bag where he kept several extra loaded magazines, a Benchmade folding knife, a small LED flashlight with a couple of extra batteries, his digital recorder, a digital camera, a legal pad, pens, pencils, and his police radio. He reached into the bag and withdrew two extra loaded magazines that he kept in a clip-on magazine holder and clipped it to his belt over his left hip. It had only been five minutes since dispatch had called, and he was already walking out the front door.

Michael retrieved his keys and hit the Unlock button on the key chain, unlocking his county-owned white Ford Explorer. He looked toward the Sierras, taking in the night skyline of the mountains silhouetted by the rising moon. He opened the driver's door and tossed his bag onto the front passenger seat while climbing into the vehicle. He started the Explorer, backed out of the driveway, and was on his way to the Douglas County substation. He was leaving the Pine View Estates subdivision heading north on Highway 395 when he called Detective Cook.

* * *

Detective Jonathon Cook was sitting at the sheriff's substation, making small talk with the homicide suspect who was seated across from him at a small table in the interview room. The room was only six feet square and would feel cramped even if you were in it alone. It had a small table that was permanently attached to the wall directly across from the only door into the room. On one side of the table was a short metal bench, also affixed to the wall. This was the side reserved for interviewees. It was uncomfortably close to the table and prevented them from being able to push away to gain comfort. Not that it would have helped much as the seat had no cushions and was at a ninety-degree angle to the wall. This was done by design.

The psychological manipulation required to get a suspect to admit the truth or confess to a crime begins before anyone ever speaks a word. The room's design was perfectly crafted for this. By manipulating the suspect's comfort levels, or rather maximizing his discomfort, police start with the upper hand. It was working; the suspect seated on the hard bench was already stressed over the night's events, and even though a person had lost his life seemingly at the stroke of a hand, the powerless feeling coursing through his veins at this moment was palpable.

Cook could see the room was working its magic. He was getting ready to make small talk with the suspect in an effort to develop a rapport with the person. It was textbook strategy for interrogations. You make people think you have something in common and get them to start talking about things that are insignificant but true. The theory was that once you got them to start telling the truth, it was harder for them to stop talking and start lying. It was then that his cell phone rang.

Cook pulled his phone from his breast pocket. He opened it without looking at who was calling. "This is Cook."

"Jon, it's Michael. What's going on, man?"

"I can't get into it right now. I'm sitting with the suspect at the substation. What's your ETA? I'm waiting for you, but don't want to push it. I'd hate it if Petey showed up." Cook had worked with Michael on a couple of cases before and knew what he brought to the table, not to mention the two had become close friends. So giving him a little time to get there was worth the wait.

"I'm coming from my house, but I can be there in thirty minutes or less. If you can stomach it, try to work your magic, and become this guy's best friend. I'll be the hard nose." Michael understood Petey (or PD) was the public defender, and if they could keep the lawyers out, things would go much smoother.

"I was just about to get started. I'll see you when you get here."

*   *   *

Michael hung up and activated the emergency lights on the Explorer while accelerating to ninety miles per hour. He wanted to get there as fast as he could, but he also had to drive with due regard for public safety. Even though his Explorer would go faster, he had found that anything over ninety could be a little precarious and presented risks he was only willing to take when someone was in danger. Besides, he knew he would get there in plenty of time. If Cook was just staring to work on this guy, he had at least half an hour before they got down to business.

Michael turned left off Highway 395 onto Waterloo Lane and followed Waterloo to Highway 207. He was thinking about the case while he ascended Kingsbury Grade, wondering what was going through someone's mind that was so serious he would kill over it, or if this could be the suspect he still sought for the two cases he hadn't closed.

He started his descent down the west slope of the mountain toward Stateline when he finally turned off the emergency lights. Traffic was light, and he'd made good time. Michael was going to be there in twenty-five minutes, five minutes before Cook expected him. If he was any earlier, Cook wouldn't even have had time to really develop the necessary connection with the suspect to work the interrogation. The fun was about to begin.

It only took a few more minutes, and Michael was pulling into the substation parking lot. He parked next to Cook's unmarked dark blue Chevy Tahoe. Michael could never understand why El Dorado County bought Explorers instead of Tahoes. The Chevys had more room, more power, and a lower center of gravity compared to the midsized Ford that always seemed to present a rollover hazard at higher speeds.

He grabbed his bag off the passenger seat and walked to the door. Because it was after hours, the door to the substation was locked, and Michael had to be let in. He pressed the Call button on the intercom next to the door. It was like the kind used outside the gates to private communities except instead of entering the person's name you were coming to visit, you just pressed the button. A buzzer went off on the other end, letting anyone inside know you were there, if there was anyone inside.

Cook heard the buzz and figured Michael must have made it. He excused himself from the conversation he was having with the suspect and stepped out of the interview room. He shut the door on his way out, locking it behind him. He walked to the front door and let Michael in.

"You made good time. I'm glad. I was starting to run out of things to talk about."

"You? How can that be? You have a doctorate in the art of bullshit," Michael joked. "So what's the deal? Dispatch said you think this might be our guy?" Michael was excited; he knew how important this case could be if this really was the suspect in the other cases. One more body on either side of the border and they would have to go to the press and advise the public they were dealing with a serial killer. Nothing hurt the tourism industry like a good serial killer, and South Lake Tahoe and Stateline were both driven by tourism.

"It's possible. That's the interesting part. Come on, it's time to meet the suspect."

Michael's interest was piqued. "Okay, well, what are you waiting for? Let's get this show on the road," he said as he began walking back toward the interview room. He'd been there before and knew exactly where to go.

Michael reached the door a step ahead of Cook. He retrieved his digital recorder, the legal pad, and a pen from his bag and then set the bag on a nearby desk. He activated the recorder and then unlocked the door and pulled it open. "Age before beauty," he whispered as Cook walked in front of him, entering the room. Michael stepped into the room behind him and was dumbfounded.

"Ms. Jimenez, this is Detective Michael Garrett with the El Dorado County Sheriff's Department. He'll be joining us."

Michael realized he must have looked like a fool with his mouth partially agape. He was caught completely off guard at the sight of the woman seated before him. He had assumed the suspect was a man and instantly realized Cook had never referred to the suspect as he or him. Michael quickly gathered himself. He placed the digital recorder and legal pad on the small table. He looked at the woman closely. There was something vaguely familiar about her, but he couldn't quite place what it was at the moment.

FIVE

Carlos had noticed the activity behind Harrah's and thought nothing of it. Carlos was no stranger to the police or their tactics and couldn't care less when they were busy. He wasn't a rubbernecker on highways trying to catch a glimpse of accidents, and he usually didn't give half a shit what reason local law enforcement had for scurrying around, unless it involved his business.

Rosa was supposed to have been at Vex. Carlos doubted she had anything to do with this, but he had been curious enough to go up to the club to make sure she was there. He had wrapped up his other business sooner than expected, and since he hadn't heard from Rosa, he thought he'd go back to the club and check on her anyway. He expected to find her trying to work the crowd until someone picked her up. Besides, he liked to make unexpected visits so she never got too comfortable or forgot to whom she worked for.

He had to valet park his car since the back lot had been closed off with yellow crime scene tape. When the valet opened the door of his silver Buick, Carlos asked, "What's going on? Is there anything to be concerned with?"

"I don't really know, mister," replied the valet. "I have been stuck up here, and besides, I'm not supposed to talk about stuff that happens around here if it's not good. Casino rules," yammered the young man.

"Keep it close," Carlos said. "I don't want to get caught up in whatever is going on. I just need to cash in some chips." He handed the valet a $20 bill to ensure it happened.

"Yes, sir," replied the valet with renewed zeal as he pocketed the jackson.

Carlos went inside and noticed the casino seemed to be business as usual. He went up to Vex, paid the cover charge, and went in. There was a good crowd. No reason Rosa shouldn't have already been cozied up to some poor bastard willing to part with his money for a little romance. Even if he wasn't, she could change his mind.

When he hadn't been able to find her, he figured she had already hooked up and was either on her way to the client's room or just forgot to send him the message, letting him know like he had told her. If he didn't get a message soon, he would remind her in the morning just where her place was in the scheme of things. Either way, he wasn't going to stick around. He headed back downstairs.

He spotted the same kid who parked his car and flagged him down. Carlos handed him the parking stub and told him it better not take long. The young valet assured him that it wouldn't and took off at a fast jog. While Carlos waited for him to bring his car around, he stood, watching the continuous stream of traffic pass by. That was when he spotted Rosa sitting in the back of a dark blue Chevy Tahoe that was coming out of the back parking lot. Judging by the look on her face, she was involved in whatever had the local cops all stirred up; and from the looks of the man driving, he was one of them. Carlos was furious. If she got busted by some vice cop again, she was going to pay back ten times what it cost him to get her out of jail.

Just as the Chevy pulled onto Highway 50, the valet pulled up in Carlos's Regal. Carlos all but pulled him out of the car and jumped in; he had to follow Rosa to see where she ended up. If she went to jail, he'd deal with it in the morning. If he was wrong and this guy wasn't a cop, he wanted to know who he was and where he was taking Rosa. He followed the Tahoe eastbound for just over half a mile when the vehicle pulled into a business parking lot.

The lot was fairly empty, and Carlos noticed the sign in the marque that read *Douglas County Sheriff's Substation*. He was right; the guy was a cop, and Rosa was in custody. He just needed to figure out why. Was she a witness or under arrest? Whatever it was, Carlos realized it was bigger than just a prostitution bust; the look on her face had revealed that much.

Carlos drove to the next intersection and turned right on a green light onto Lake Parkway. He made a quick U-turn on Lake and stopped on the side of the road. He wanted to let some time pass to ensure that the cop was able to get Rosa inside and get settled into whatever he was planning. He watched from the distance, waiting to see if the Tahoe pulled out of the parking lot. The vehicle hadn't left.

Believing he had waited long enough, Carlos pulled up to the intersection, waiting to turn left back onto Highway 50. When the light changed, he made the turn and fell in behind a white Ford Explorer then all but ran the red light. He was following the Ford, approaching the substation when he realized the driver was pulling into the parking lot as well. That was when Carlos noticed the low-profile light bar that ran across the top of the back window of the Explorer. He hadn't noticed it at first due to the tinted windows and it being nighttime, but as the driver of the Explorer was turning into the parking lot, the headlights from a vehicle approaching from the other direction gave it away.

"What the fuck is going on?" Carlos thought aloud. He drove past the substation again and went up to Stateline Drive. He turned right on Stateline and then took another right on Lake Parkway, which made a big loop. He followed Lake back around to Highway 50 where he was just minutes ago. He turned right onto Highway 50 again and drove back up to the substation parking lot. This time, he pulled into the lot.

Carlos parked on the west end of the parking lot next to a late-model Jetta that was in front of a real estate office across from the substation. He settled into the seat and waited, reckoning he might be awhile. He figured if someone came out and approached him, he would just tell him he was sleepy and had pulled over to take a quick nap before continuing on his way.

Six

More than an hour had passed, and Rosa could still feel her heart pounding in her chest; her dress was uncomfortably wet from sweat, and she was still shaking, although not nearly as bad as she had been. In addition to all that, she had been arrested again, for the second time in her life, and was sitting in some stuffy ridiculously small interrogation room. She was frightened and couldn't get the smell of the man who had tried to kill her out of her mind.

It was the smell of blood, fresh from the kill. Anyone who had been around death recognized it immediately. It wasn't a smell that could be forgotten. To a hunter, it was the smell of success; to a soldier, it was the stench of battle, won or lost, and it was not pleasant. As Rosa was neither a hunter nor soldier, it was going to be the cause of nightmares and flashbacks for the rest of her life. It didn't help that the lower half of the front of her teal-and-purple sequined dress was saturated in it.

Detective Cook had allowed her to wash the blood off of her legs after the crime scene investigators had photographed her, first with full body shots from every angle followed by photos of every part of her body. Had she not been so terrified at the time, she would have been humiliated. As it was, she was in a mix of emotions, both happy to be alive and terrified of what would happen next.

Rosa had so much racing through her mind. Would she be charged with murder? What would Carlos do if she was released? Would he try to bail her out if she wasn't? What would happen to her family if she went to prison? Who would they make repay her father's debt then? She was working herself into a frenzy, wondering what was going on. How long was she going to have to wait before they would start asking the real questions and stop with the casual conversation? She was starting to get irritated when the door to the little room opened, and Detective Cook stepped back inside, followed no doubt by the man he'd been waiting for.

"Ms. Jimenez, this is Detective Michael Garrett with the El Dorado County Sheriff's Department. He will be joining us."

Rosa looked at Michael and recognized him immediately. Michael hadn't changed much since high school. He was a little bigger and looked more mature, but he hadn't gotten fat like so many other men do. Rosa thought he had aged well. He was a rugged man but currently had a pensive look on his face. She couldn't tell if he recognized her or not because they had not been in the same grade. Michael was a senior when she was a freshman. He stepped forward and set some items down on the table.

"Not who you were expecting?" Rosa asked.

"I'm sorry," Michael said, quickly regaining his composure. "I had only been given partial details and, for some reason, thought you were a man." Michael glanced over at Cook and could tell he was holding back a smirk.

Rosa realized he had not recognized her. She wasn't sure if she should say anything or not. She knew it wouldn't help her situation, but it might make her feel more comfortable. She was thinking about it, but before she had a chance to fully decide, Detective Cook began the interrogation.

"Okay, Rosa, I know we have been talking, but there are some formalities I need to cover before we go any further."

"Okay."

Cook stated the date and time for the record and then identified each person in the room by name. He continued, "I need to advise you of your rights. You have the right to remain silent. Anything you say can and will be used against you in a court of law. You have the right to speak to an attorney. If you cannot afford an attorney, one will be appointed to you. Do you understand these rights?"

"Yes."

Michael was watching Rosa while Cook covered the basics; it was when he stated her full name that it clicked. Michael instantly knew why she looked familiar. He hadn't seen her for ten years, but it had to be her. "Did you go to Holtville High School?"

Rosa looked at Michael. She was wondering whether or not to tell him they grew up in the same town. He had just made the decision a little easier. "Yes, I was a freshman when you were a senior. I didn't think you recognized me."

"I didn't at first," he admitted. "You look a little different than you used to."

Rosa was embarrassed, and Michael could tell. He didn't want to ruin the chance she might talk to them without a lawyer. All lawyers did was muddy the water and milk the system of every penny they could squeeze out of it. The system was no longer about justice; it hadn't been for some time. It was about money these days, and people who had it bought their justice. OJ was a perfect example of that; he got away with murder when he was rich, only to get convicted of a robbery and be sent to prison when he was broke.

Michael didn't let another moment pass, fearing she was about to ask for counsel. "If you're uncomfortable with me being here, I'll step out. Detective Cook can get someone else."

"No, no, please don't." She looked down and began to cry. "You're the first person I've seen from Holtville in . . . I don't know how long."

Michael and Cook exchanged glances, not certain what was really going on. Michael motioned to the door with his head. "Detective Cook, can you grab us some coffee and a box of tissue?"

"Yeah, no problem. Rosa, do you take cream or sugar?"

"A little of both would be great," she replied.

Cook stepped out to get the coffee. Michael left the recorder going; regardless of what was currently happening, he wasn't sure if Rosa was trying to play games or not. Either way, they still had a homicide case to close. It wouldn't be the first time a woman had tried to cry her way out of something, and Lord knows it wouldn't be the last.

"So it's been awhile since you've been home, I take it?"

"You could say that," Rosa responded. She was still crying but getting herself back under control.

"So what happened to you? What are you doing up here?"

Rosa wiped the snot that was starting to drip from her nose with the back of her index finger. It was a good sign as far as Michael was concerned; it was an indicator that she wasn't faking it, or she was a really good actor. Some people could fake tears, but a runny nose was pretty much impossible.

"It's a long story," she said. "Besides, it doesn't really matter right now, does it?"

"That depends on your answer. If it's relevant, then yes, it matters. If it's not, then no, it doesn't." He wasn't going to lie to her. One thing he tried to avoid was lying to people, regardless of their guilt or innocence. All it did was give them cause not to trust the police in the future, which made the job that much more difficult.

Rosa's shoulders slumped forward, and she sighed. It was useless, she thought, embarrassed and ashamed of what had happened to her; she figured what could it hurt? "I really don't know where to start. My dad owed some people some money, and when he couldn't pay them back, they threatened to kill him and the rest of my family."

"How does this have anything to do with you being up here?"

"I was there when they came for the money. They told my dad there was another way. I could work off his debt, or they would kill me first. Not really much of an option." She started to tear up again.

Michael looked at her in disbelief. This was the kind of shit you hear about on the news happening in other countries, not in the United States. He listened intently as Rosa's story unfolded in detail. She explained how she later came to find out that these men her father borrowed money from belonged to the Mexican Mafia (or La Eme as she referred to them).

Her father had worked for Roy Armstrong the entire time he had been in the United States, almost thirty years now. Armstrong was a landowner, and her father worked on his land as a farmer, making next to nothing for the backbreaking labor he performed six days a week. He and her mother saved as much money as they could, but it was hard to do with five children to support. Their dream was to save enough to buy land back in Mexico to start a family farm of their own. After nearly three decades, it became clear that they would never be able to save enough money to fulfill their dream, so her father tried to take out a loan to buy the property.

He found the land he wanted in a small village a couple hours south of Mexico City in the southern region of Cuernavaca. The city itself was a gateway of resources and tremendously popular to foreign students who desired to study Spanish abroad. However, it was also perfect for farming year-round. With a temperate and moist climate, the southern regions of the area were ideal. He located sixty-five acres of farmland for seventeen million pesos or $1.3 million dollars, and he needed $130,000 for a down payment to buy the land.

Rosa continued, explaining how her father had gotten the family together and told them of his plans. He explained the financial situation and asked if they would be willing to help with the down payment. In return, they were all welcome to move to the farm, and together they could work the family property and make it their business. Only Daniel, the middle child, was willing to move to Mexico though all of the children were willing to donate money to help with the down payment. Unfortunately, even with the kids' help, Rosa's father was $45,000 short. He contacted a number of banks, looking for one that would accept the terms with money he had. He was met with one rejection after another.

He finally went to Cuernavaca and attempted to contact the landowners in person to see if they would carry the loan themselves. Although they seemed to get along, the owners were unwilling to work with Rosa's father. They had plans of their own and needed payment in full; however, they did offer one suggestion. They knew someone in Mexicali they believed may be able to help and gave Rosa's father the information.

Rosa said her father was desperate at this point. He was willing to try anything; he couldn't bear to see his lifelong dream slipping away. He was eager to contact the people in Mexicali to see if they could help. It couldn't hurt to try. He figured he had nothing to lose.

"My father is a proud man," Rosa said. "I hated to see how desperate he had become." She explained that she tried to talk him out of meeting with these unknown people. "I told him if he couldn't get the money through regular channels, then it just wasn't meant to be. The stress was consuming him, but he insisted on making one more attempt to get the funds together."

Mexicali was just across the U.S.-Mexico border, about ten miles south from Holtville. Mexicali is a large city surrounded by small boroughs. Although the Mexican census claims the city has a little over 650,000 residents, a more realistic estimate would have the municipality easily over a million. It has the largest concentration of people with Chinese ancestry in the country. They own and operate most of the casinos and bars in the city, some of which host an extensive network of tunnel systems connecting to Calexico, Mexicali's sister city on the U.S. side of the border.

"I didn't know their names, but my father contacted the people he was told about in Cuernavaca. He went to Café Nueva Asia," Rosa continued. The café is a trendy Chinese restaurant less the five hundred yards south of the border. A journey more easily accomplished by parking in Calexico and walking the distance, rather than trying to find parking along extremely congested Mexicali streets. "He hadn't told anyone what he was doing, but when he came home that afternoon, he called the whole family and invited everyone over for a barbeque that evening. When everyone got there, he told us he had found a way to get the money and was going to buy the land. We were going to celebrate.

"The next day, my father contacted a land broker in Cuernavaca to make the deal." Land sales didn't take long; unlike the real estate in the United States, it was simple in Mexico. There were far fewer laws governing the transfer of property, and there was no need for inspections. It was about the land, not the structures, and buyers knew that property was sold as is. The sale was complete in a couple of days, and the money was transferred.

Rosa told Michael that her father made a deal with the sellers; that they could stay there for another couple of months while they packed up in preparation for their move. They would pay a modest sum for the extra time (Rosa didn't know how much), and it would give her father and mother time to make all the necessary arrangements they needed as well.

All seemed to be perfect for the next month. Rosa said her parents were getting things situated to make the move. They had to get their finances in order as they were going to be transferring their remaining funds into a family trust. Her eldest brother, Javier, was going to be a signer on the trust as well so he could handle any financial issues that arose from the states once they made the move. Everything was coming together perfectly. Javier and Daniel painted the inside of the small home her parents had rented off of Alvarado Street; Rosa had helped her mother shampoo the carpets and clean the house. It was spotless and ready to be rented again. More importantly, her parents would get their deposit back.

The turning point came with the posting of the For Rent sign. As her parents would be gone by the end of the second month, the landlord posted the sign in hopes of getting the house rented as soon as possible. Rosa said it was only a couple of days after the sign went up that two men showed up at the door. She was there having dinner with her parents when they came.

"They just walked in," Rosa said. "We were sitting in the kitchen eating chicken molé when they showed up. I thought it was my brothers at first."

Michael just watched Rosa as she told the story. He was learning more about her than she realized. Watching her mannerisms and emotions, listening to her voice inflection as she became excited, he noticed the change as she became frightened again. Her story gave him everything he needed to establish a baseline on Rosa. He would be able to use this to judge whether or not she was being honest when he and Cook began questioning her about the homicide.

Rosa continued, telling Michael how these men joined them in the kitchen. Her father lunged to his feet, demanding to know what was going on, when one of the men punched him in the solar plexus. He crumpled onto the kitchen floor, gasping for air. Rosa went to his aid, screaming at the men to leave when, very calmly, the other man told Rosa to get back in her seat, and nothing else would happen.

She helped her father to his chair and sat back down herself. Her mother began to cry. Her father demanded to know what was going on. One of the men said they were sent by Señor . . . She couldn't remember the name. Her father said that he didn't understand; they must have the wrong home. The man said they had the right house. They had been there before checking on him.

Rosa remembered the next part vividly. He said, "You didn't think we would just give you the money, did you?" It was then that her father seemed to understand. Baffled, he asked, "Fernando sent you?" He kept saying he didn't understand. It had only been six weeks since he had got the loan, and Fernando had told him he didn't have to make a payment for three months. The man said yes Fernando; he had changed his mind about the loan and would require payment now since they were packing up and moving and hadn't bothered to tell him about the move.

"My father agreed to make a payment. He asked how much money they wanted and told them he would give it to them. He just wanted them to leave. They just looked at me and then at my father, and told him they would need at least $30,000. I couldn't believe it. My father was stunned. He said there was no way he could come up with that kind of money. He told them he had only borrowed $45,000 and had put it all down on a piece of property. He pleaded for understanding."

Michael watched intently as Rosa continued. He realized there was no way she was making this up. Her story flowed too smoothly for her to be making it up as she went along.

Rosa went on to explain how the man who had hit her father the first time stepped toward him again and slapped him harder than she had ever seen someone hit another person, knocking her father out of his chair. The man told him he should have been more forthcoming with Fernando about his plans. He had done this to himself. Rosa said the other man stepped closer to her and then reached out and grabbed her by the hair at the base of her skull. He snatched her to her feet and then jerked her head back. Her father, still dizzy from being struck, struggled to get up; her mother started to rise from her chair, screaming at the man to let go, when he kicked her in the stomach. She collapsed in a heap onto the floor, hitting her head on the edge of the table as she fell. Her father began to cry, begging the men to give him time. He would get them the money; he just needed some time.

The man gripping Rosa's hair twisted her around. Rosa said he was looking at her body like one would pick out a steak from the butcher. Then he grabbed one of her breasts and squeezed, letting go only to reach between her legs, grabbing the uppermost part of her inner thigh and groin.

Michael watched as Rosa's eyes moved up and to the left. Although not foolproof, it was common for people to look up and to one side or the other when trying to visually recall a memory. It was known as voluntary saccadic eye movements, which consisted of oculomotor mechanisms wherein a person would look up to one side to recall a memory or to the opposite side to create or imagine something. Most people looked up and to their left when recalling something. Conversely, they would look up and to their right when telling a lie or imagining something.

Rosa had started to tear up again. She told Michael the man holding her said she could help. Since her father couldn't make a payment, she could make it for him. He never let go of her hair, keeping her head pulled back. She could see her father climbing to his feet. The man who had knocked him down pulled him the rest of the way up and pushed him against the wall with such force it caused the crucifix they had hanging on the wall to fall. He told her father he had two options: pay the money now, or they would kill him, and his wife would have to pay the money later.

Rosa strained to see if her mother was okay. She was still on the floor and didn't seem to be getting up. Rosa called to her mother, but there was no response. The man holding her finally let go of her groin; he slapped her ass and pushed her toward her mother. Rosa immediately checked on her mother, discovering that she was breathing. She had been knocked unconscious when she hit her head.

Her father begged for time. The man let him go, and he went to Martha's side to help his wife of thirty years. The men began to speak, but Rosa couldn't hear them over her father. He was in tears, talking to her mother, pleading with her as if she could hear him, telling her she had to be okay; it wasn't supposed to be like this.

The men stopped talking. The one who had been holding Rosa said they had decided to work with her father. They would spare his life on one condition. Rosa would be leaving with them, and she would work for them until his debt was paid in full. Her father objected, but Rosa agreed. She told Michael she couldn't bear the thought of watching her father killed, and she knew that if these men would kill her father, they would kill her mother and her as well.

She said she got up and simply walked to the door, remembering all the years before when her father had taught her how important it was to always help family. Once she reached the door, she looked back and said, "Are we going or not?" The men took her, leaving her father on the floor tending to her mother. Nothing more was said. She was put in the back of an old Chevy van that only had one small round window on each side and split square windows in the back. She remembered the windows looking as if they had limo tint on them, but once she was inside, she realized they were blacked out completely. She couldn't see into or out of the vehicle.

She was taken to a house somewhere in Calexico. She knew it was near the border as she could see the glow of the lights that came from the giant city to the south. She didn't know what was going to happen, but she had a pretty good idea. She was taken into the house and shown hospitality she didn't expect. She was introduced to a man she knew only as Carlos. The other two told Carlos what had happened and then explained to him that she would be helping her father work off his debt.

Rosa couldn't be sure, but she got the impression that whatever these men were, there was a hierarchy to their organization. They had mentioned Carnale Fernando, whom she had figured was the man her father borrowed money from. He must have been their boss, and these two were clearly some kind of collectors. It seemed as if Carlos was not their boss, nor were they his.

She explained that as much as she tried to figure out what was going on, she couldn't. The men talked briefly, and then Carlos took her to the back of the house and then down into a basement. She hadn't been in such a large home before or one with a basement. Basements were not typical in the area. Rosa remembered her fear creeping up again as she descended the stairs. When

Rosa had first arrived, she believed the men were going to rape her; but when they showed her the slightest hospitality at the house, she started to wonder. Now she thought it was going to happen again, but Carlos merely walked her down into the basement and told her he would be back. He closed the door as he exited the room. She heard what she believed was him locking the door. She went to check and discovered it had been locked.

She looked around the room. It was lit with fluorescent lights, like those you would find in a kitchen. It was sparsely furnished, with nothing more than a brown cloth sofa and a matching chair and ottoman. There was a second door that was closed and locked with a deadbolt. Only the keyed side of the lock was on the inside of the room.

Rosa explained that she had no illusions of escape. She checked out the room and wondered what was going on upstairs. She said it seemed like hours, when Carlos finally returned. He told her they had to go and then lead her to the garage. He walked her to the rear of an older black Oldsmobile Cutlass. He opened the trunk and told her to get in. Rosa knew she didn't have a choice, so she did as she was told, thinking only that it was necessary to keep her father alive. It was that thought that kept her calm.

She heard the car start, and they began to move. She had no idea where she was going, only that it took several hours to get there. When the trunk lid opened again, Carlos had to help her out. She remembered being so stiff and cramped from lying in the trunk she couldn't get out on her own. She was in another garage.

Carlos took her inside. This time, the house wasn't nearly as nice and had several other women in it. Rosa thought they were all relatively close in age. None of them seemed happy to see her. She wasn't exactly happy to see them either, just glad to be out of the trunk. She still had a horrible feeling, not knowing exactly what she was doing or what was going to happen to her. Carlos led her through the home. She remembered passing three small bedrooms as he led her down the hall and into what must have been the master bedroom. It wasn't much bigger but was the largest of the rooms she had noticed. He told her to get on the bed.

Rosa told Michael that Carlos began to undress. She couldn't believe what she had gone through only to get to this point. Although she didn't know for sure, it seemed as if she had been taken from her parents at least eight hours ago. She thought she may have been saved from rape when Carlos had taken her but now realized that he had only been saving her for himself. She said that was when Carlos explained to her what was going to happen.

He told her he had spoken with his cohorts, and they explained to him how she had volunteered to help her father repay his debt. Carlos told her it was very noble of her. He then explained that he had brought her to Los

Angeles. They were near Hollywood, and she would begin working tomorrow. Confused, Rosa said she asked Carlos what exactly she would be doing. He said he would show her.

Rosa said he stripped naked and walked up to her as she sat on the bed. He stood directly in front of her, his penis dangling in her face. She tried to lean back uncomfortably when he grabbed her by the back of her head and stopped her. He told her if she was going to make any money, she was going to have to be willing. People weren't going to pay her only to have to force her to have sex.

Rosa couldn't believe what had just happened. She went from fearing she was going to be raped to the realization she was being forced into prostitution. She took Carlos in her mouth; he never let go of her head. She was disgusted by what was happening. He forced her to move back and forth until he finished. He pulled her head back when he was done and told her to take off her clothes. Rosa said she was so shocked by the ordeal she froze. Carlos pushed her back on the bed and tore her shirt off. She lay there crying when she felt him ripping her pants away. She didn't fight, fearing she would be killed. He told her she better get it together, or they would just go back and kill her parents.

Rosa tried to calm herself down. She finished removing her pants and took off her panties. Carlos lay down on his back and told her to fuck him. He said if she couldn't get him ready on her own, she was worthless to them, and he would just send the others back to kill her parents.

With the constant reminder of her parents' lives riding on her performance, Rosa did what she was told. She said that when Carlos was done, he told her that would be acceptable for a streetwalker, but nothing more. He told her if that was all she had, she could expect to be doing this for a long time because she wouldn't make much money. If she wanted to pay off her father's debt and get on with her life, she was going to need to step it up. He told her that her looks would fetch a lot more money than the average hooker, but she had to be able to perform; she had to be able to convince someone she wanted him. She had to do the work for them, making it fun, exciting; and most importantly, she had to do things without being told.

Carlos was all business. She couldn't believe how matter-of-fact he was about it all. She realized she needed to be the same and did her best to come to terms with what was happening, but it was easier said than done. Carlos told her he would teach her the basics and then get her on the street so she could start earning some money. She was terrified of the prospect but knew it was not an option. He spent the next day telling her what was expected of her, how much she needed to earn each night, reminding her that if she failed, her family would pay the consequences. He also told her that he would always be watching.

She had worked the streets in Hollywood for a couple of weeks, mostly Sunset Boulevard and North Western Avenue between Sunset and Hollywood Boulevard. She got picked up one night by a young white man, who turned out to be an LAPD Vice officer. She was booked, and before she could even rationalize what was going on, Carlos posted her bail. It seemed he was always watching; there was no other way he would have known she'd been arrested.

The arrest was her turning point. She told Carlos she was worth more than some run-of-the-mill hooker and wanted to work inside. She had heard other women on the street talking about where the real money was, and it wasn't walking the street. It was in the clubs. Carlos had her working the Whitehorse Inn Cocktail Lounge the next day. It was a dive bar in the same area she had been working the streets, located on North Western, but at least she was inside. He had given her new expectations, but it was nothing she didn't expect at this time. Rosa said one thing led to another, and she was moving up in the world of prostitution, so to speak. Rosa became Carlos's top earner, and then one day, he told her the two of them were going to be moving to South Lake Tahoe to work the casinos. He said "the enterprise was expanding," and she was going to be part of it. It had been three months since then.

Now, sitting in front of Michael, with all of the memories flooding back fresh into her mind, she broke down again. She had tried so hard never to think about all of the details. It had been nearly eighteen months since it all began, and she had come so far emotionally. She had been able to get beyond the horror and accepted the realization of what had happened and what she had become. Recounting the story to tell this man she never really knew, other than from passing in the halls at the same high school, had an effect on her she hadn't considered. As the memories came pouring back in vivid detail, she couldn't help but weep.

Michael, sitting quietly, trying not to look as surprised and shocked as he was with the story, realized she was falling apart. He tried to bring her back to the task at hand. "Rosa, I am so sorry for what happened to you. I want to help. I really do, but we have to get through what happened tonight first, okay?"

It was almost as if she had forgotten about what had just happened. Rosa had been so consumed recalling everything that had happened she had actually stopped thinking about the fact that she had nearly been killed a little more than an hour ago, and that she had killed a man who would have done the same to her.

* * *

Cook was sitting in the observation room adjacent to the interview room. It wasn't quite like they depicted them on television, he thought to himself.

There was no one-way mirror he could watch his suspect through, but there was a video camera that was recording everything that went on and a monitor in an adjacent room. He had been watching the entire conversation between Michael and Rosa. He couldn't believe what he had just heard, yet everything she did indicated she was being truthful. Her body movement, the physical gestures, crying, the runny nose—everything pointed to the truth. He heard Michael tell her they needed to talk about tonight and recognized that as his cue to get in there with the coffee. He quickly poured three cups of coffee and stirred in a couple of creamers and one packet of sugar into the cup for Rosa. He grabbed two cups with one in each hand and then pinched the third between the other two, forming a small triangle. He walked next door to the interview room and gently tapped on the door with his left foot.

"That must be Detective Cook with the coffee," Michael said, standing to open the door for Cook.

"Sorry for the delay, I had to roast the beans." Detective Cook set the three cups down on the table with the cup with cream closest to Rosa. "Hope it's the right color for you." Referring to the latte appearance of the cup for Rosa.

"It's fine," Rosa replied as she grabbed the cup with both hands, lifting it to her mouth. She held it under her nose, breathing in the aroma, hoping it would help replace the horrid smell of death that still lingered there.

"So now that you two have had a chance to get caught up, can we get down to closing this case?"

Michael looked at Cook and said, "I think we're all ready to wrap this up, especially Rosa."

"All righty then, Rosa, can you tell us what happened tonight?"

Rosa was exhausted, both physically and emotionally. Telling Michael what had transpired over the past eighteen months drained her even more, and it showed in her face. She took a sip from the coffee. "I don't really know where to start."

"Well, why don't you pick up with how you got to the Harrah's parking lot?" Cook asked.

She looked at Michael and began, "Well, Carlos called me around eight thirty tonight and told me I was going to be working at Vex. He said he was going to pick me up around nine o'clock at my apartment."

"Where is that?" Michael asked.

"On Fern near Pioneer Trail in South Lake. I don't know the numbers," she said, realizing she really didn't. Carlos set everything up, and he paid the bills. He never let her know exactly what things cost, always using her expenses as an excuse for what was taking her so long to repay her father's debt. The reality was Rosa had made more than enough in her first year to settle things, but Carlos wasn't about to let her go when she was earning so much.

"Okay, then what?" Cook said.

"Well, Carlos dropped me off at the main entrance, but I figured it was a little too early, and I wanted to eat. So I went into the casino and walked over to the side exit. I walked over to little shops by the Embassy, looking for a restaurant. I found this place called Fire & Ice. It looked good, and I was really getting hungry, so I went in. I made up a bowl of chicken and vegetables. It was really good. I had a frozen raspberry lemonade with my dinner. I left some cash on the table and left."

As long as he had been a cop, Detective Cook still couldn't believe how much superfluous bullshit people would include in a statement. Sometimes it was humorous, but most of the time, it just took up more time on the recorder and added reams of paper to the transcription. He wouldn't have cared as much if he didn't have to transcribe the interviews himself, but since he did, he tried to speed things along.

"Okay, so where were you when you first came across the man we found in the parking lot?"

"I was getting to that," Rosa said. "When I left Fire and Ice, I was headed back to Harrah's. I was walking across Stateline when I heard someone. I couldn't tell what was said, but it was getting louder. I turned to look and saw this guy kind of jogging toward me. He was holding up some money and said I dropped it. I knew it wasn't mine because I always put my money in my wallet in a certain way and zip it shut."

Rosa took another sip from her coffee and held the cup under her nose again for a while. It did seem to help.

"So what did you do?" Michael asked.

"I just kept walking. I needed to get to Vex and wasn't going to let this guy try some lame pickup line he probably saw on TV or something. He was persistent though. He caught up to me and then actually admitted he was just trying to get my attention. The son of a bitch all but called me a prostitute and told me he had a room at Harvey's."

Cook noticed Rosa's irritation. "So what was the issue? You are a prostitute, aren't you?"

Rosa couldn't believe it. She couldn't believe the audacity of this asshole sitting across from her. She reached for her coffee, knocking the cup over and spilling the hot liquid all over Cook's lap. He was seated directly across from her, between the table and wall. He reflexively tried to scoot back out of the way, his chair hitting wall, preventing him from avoiding the drink. The coffee quickly soaked through his pants and began to burn his thigh and groin. He leapt to his feet, hitting his legs on the solid table.

"Motherfucker!" he shouted, frantically trying to pull his pants away from his flesh, glaring at Rosa.

"I am so sorry," she said insincerely. "I am just nervous and still a little shaky, I guess."

Cook just looked at her; he knew there was nothing he could do. "No problem, accidents happen. If you'll excuse me for a moment, I need to take care of this."

"I am sorry, the coffee was really good. Would you mind bringing me another cup?" Rosa asked with a smile on her face while Cook stepped out to check his manhood.

The door automatically closed. Michael looked at Rosa, realizing exactly what happened. "He's a little rough around the edges, but it would be best if you didn't do that again," he cautioned her. "You are the one being investigated for murder, Rosa, and not to be cruel, but you were . . . working tonight. Right?"

Rosa looked at Michael. She realized he was right, but it just pissed her off. "I know, I know, it's just been a rough night, to say the least, and it's not like I asked for this."

Detective Cook returned. He had another cup of coffee, except this time it had twice as much cream in it, leaving it a little cooler from the get-go. "Here you go."

"Thanks, I really am sorry. I hope your little guy wasn't burnt too badly."

Cook looked at Rosa. *Is she fucking kidding me with this?* he thought. "I'm fine, thanks. Let's get back to the night's events, shall we?"

Michael could see the tension in Cook's face. He held back a grin. "So he told you he had a room at Harvey's. Did he give you the room number?"

"No number. He said something about winning big at the slots and wanting to celebrate. He said he didn't want to spend the night alone. He offered me two grand." Rosa looked directly at Cook. "And you know, since I am a prostitute, I told him for $2,500 he had a deal."

Cook subconsciously grabbed his groin again. Michael noticed and couldn't let it pass. "You okay, partner?"

"I'm fine, thanks." He looked to Rosa. "Please continue."

"Well, he grabbed my hand and started walking around to the back of Harrah's," she continued, telling the two detectives how she thought it was odd since he had told her his room was at Harvey's. "I challenged him, but he had an answer, telling me we would just take the tunnel. I remember trying to pull away, but the man tightened his grip, pulling me along.

"It was when we got to the back of the hotel that I realized something was wrong." They weren't headed toward an entrance. He started pulling her away from the hotel into the parking lot between two rows of vehicles. Rosa tried to pull free from his grasp, but he was too strong. The man yanked her toward him, placing his other hand over her mouth and forcefully pulling her head to his chest. He let go of her hand and placed his other arm around her neck, driving his elbow down into her chest, holding her firmly against his body. He was dragging her deeper into the parking lot, using the vehicles to conceal them.

She struggled to get away, but the man was too strong. She was able to bite down on his hand that was covering her mouth. She bit him as hard as she could. He pulled his hand away but didn't let her go. He punched her in the small of the back and pulled her to the ground between two cars. Rosa had pulled the karambit from its scabbard in her purse while she was being dragged across the lot. When the man forced her to the ground, he let go of her. He stepped over her and began to kneel as if he was going to mount her.

Rosa described how he began to reach for her throat as he lowered himself on top of her. Holding the knife tightly in her right hand, she slashed at his inner right thigh with all of her might. She said she thought she missed at first; she never even felt the resistance of his flesh, but then she noticed the look on his face. It reminded her of the man who had raped her, the look on his face after Carlos was finished with him.

Rosa didn't stop; she grabbed the man's hand that was reaching toward her neck. She pulled his arm away from his body, just as Carlos had instructed her, and jammed the blade into the upper part of his chest, just under the collarbone, and then raked it in a downward motion toward the joint, severing muscles, tendons, and his subclavian artery if she was lucky.

The man fell backward onto his ass. Rosa pushed herself away from him. She rose to her feet and quickly ran. She ran back toward the casino to the first people she could find. She came across a couple crossing the street where she had been just moments ago. She told them a man had attacked her. They called the police and had her sit on the curb, which is where the police found her when they arrived.

Cook was trying to think if there was anything else he needed to know. Rosa had covered the event very well, really leaving him with nothing further to ask.

"I know this has been tough on you, Rosa. Thank you for talking to us. I just have one question," Michael said. "Were you afraid for your life?"

"Of course," Rosa said. "I thought he was going to rape me, but when I bit him and he pulled me to the ground, he had this look on his face . . . It was different, it was evil . . . That's when he reached for my throat, that's when I knew he was going to kill me."

"Okay, that should do it. You have anything, Detective Cook?"

"Not at the moment."

"Rosa, if you'll excuse us for few minutes, I need to talk to Detective Cook privately." Michael stood up and motioned for Cook to follow him. He grabbed his digital recorder, looked at his watch, stated the time, and concluded the interview.

SEVEN

The crime scene investigators were wrapping things up. Ben and Rick were taking the last of the measurements so they could recreate the scene at a later date if necessary. The bottom line was that regardless of prosecution, they had to diagram the scene. It was a redundant process. They had taken close to six hundred photographs all total, 587 to be exact. The likes of which covered every inch of the victim's and suspect's body. Additionally, they had a photographic overview of the scene, multiple photographs in all directions from the location of the body, as well as pictures depicting the approach to the body from each point of the compass. Ben had even taken pictures of every vehicle and its corresponding license plate within sight so detectives could follow up with the registered owners when looking for potential witnesses.

Other than the body itself, there was really no physical evidence to collect. The suspect was still clutching the knife when the first deputy arrived on scene. He collected the knife; thus, there was nothing more to gather other than the requisite information necessary to complete the crime scene diagram.

When they had completed all they could before moving the victim's body, they contacted the on-call coroner to have the decedent removed. Ryan Jones was the on-call coroner; he had been notified of the incident and was just waiting for the call; once received, he was there within fifteen minutes.

"What do you have for me tonight?" he asked as he approached the inner crime scene pushing a gurney in front of him.

"A Jack the Ripper reversal," Rick said. "Wait until you see this guy. This chic did number on him."

"Lead the way."

Rick walked Ryan over to the body. "His name is Nicklaus Walkley. Dicks think this is their guy who strangled those two women earlier this year."

"Wouldn't that be nice? A little street justice and we save the taxpayers a few hundred thousand dollars in court costs."

"Watch your step, you don't want to slip. I don't think this guy has an ounce of blood left in him. The suspect either got really lucky or knew exactly what she was doing. I think she cut a couple of arteries on this guy, the femoral for sure."

As they neared the vehicles Nicklaus's body was between, Ryan caught his first glimpse of the blood puddle. It was at least twelve feet across. He decided that was close enough for the gurney and locked the wheels. He hated getting blood on the wheels. It was just one more thing he had to clean later.

"Holy shit, you weren't kidding!"

"I told you, man. This lady fucked him up proper."

Ben was standing by the back of one of the vehicles with his Nikon digital SLR when they walked up. "Evening, Ryan."

Ryan walked up to the vehicles where he could finally see Nicklaus's body. The first thing he noticed was that his face looked almost ashen gray. He was leaning up against the front tire of a Nissan Altima. His right arm hung loosely by his side, with his left arm draped across his lap. His right leg was bent awkwardly underneath him, as if he had tried to sit down cross-legged, and something went terribly wrong.

"Well, how do you want to do this?" Ryan asked.

"If you guys can start by just lifting the right arm, I'll take some pictures of the wound," Ben said.

Rick and Ryan stepped in. Ryan looked at Nicklaus as he sat slumped, lifeless against the vehicle. "Poor fucker," he said. "I don't care who you are, that's a shitty way to go. Sitting there with one good arm trying to figure out which wound to apply pressure to."

"Screw him," Ben said. "He wanted to play rough. He got what he asked for. I feel sorry for the lady who did it. She's gonna be fucked up for life. You should have seen her, man. It looked like she bathed in his blood."

Rick grabbed Nicklaus's right arm and began to pull it up. "At least we don't have to worry about rigor or lividity," he said with a chuckle. As he pulled the arm up, he was amazed how easily it moved. It became instantly apparent why, as the flesh pulled away as well. The knife wound had severed the major and minor pectoral muscles and the tendons that attached them to the bone as well as the tendons that anchored one of the biceps' muscles at its origin.

Ben took several photographs of the gaping wound. "Okay, let's get to the leg. If you two can reposition the body so we can spread his right leg out, I'll get photos of it as well. The rest I'll handle at the morgue."

"No problem, he should be several pints lighter than usual," Ryan joked, referring to the massive loss of blood.

Rick pulled on the right arm a little more, dragging the body slightly away from the Altima. He reached down to grab the other arm while Ryan stood and watched. "A little help would be nice," he protested.

"What? Do you want me to try and lift him by one leg?" Ryan asked. "Just drag him back a little farther to get his other leg straightened out. Then I'll spread it out so Ben can try and meat gaze."

"You're an asshole!" Ben replied.

Rick laughed while he tugged on the body, dragging it back a couple of feet in an effort to get the legs to straighten out. "Is that good enough, your highness?"

"It'll have to do," Ryan proclaimed while he bent over to grab the right ankle to open the wound for Ben to photo.

Ben took several more photographs, zooming in a little more with each picture. He was just about done when he saw something in the photo he hadn't been able to see before because of the dark. He grabbed a small flashlight and shined it on the cut clothing. "Is he wearing another pair of pants or shorts under the outer layer?"

Ryan leaned in for a closer look. "Sure as hell looks like it. Just lends that much more credence to the theory this is the guy. Why else would he be layered unless he planned on changing his appearance? It's definitely not to stay warm."

"He's all yours, Ryan," Ben said.

"Okay, Rich, you ready?" Ryan asked.

"As I'll ever be."

The two lifted the body and began walking it out from between the two vehicles toward the gurney when suddenly, the body swung out of control, hitting the side of the Altima before Rick dropped it.

"You have got to be shitting me!" he proclaimed.

Ryan stopped, still holding the legs up, and began laughing. He dropped the legs and backed away, trying to regain his composure. Ben instantly started taking a series of pictures, capturing the scene. Rick just stood there with a dumbfounded look on his face, still holding Nicklaus's right arm despite the fact that it had been completely off the body. With all the major tendons having been severed, there just wasn't enough tissue left to hold the body to the arm.

"I'd offer to give you a hand," Ryan said between laughs, "but . . ."

"Fuck off!" was all Rick could come back with. He finally dropped the arm and walked away. "Fuck off!" they heard him say again.

Ryan was laughing so hard he had tears in his eyes. Rick made a lap around a couple of cars. When he came back around, he said, "Can we just get this over with?"

He grabbed the body by the shirt collar and lifted his end. Ryan gripped the legs again, and the two muscled the corpse onto the gurney. Ben grabbed the right arm and slapped it down on the chest. Ryan ran a belt over the body and arm, cinching it down. He placed a second belt over the legs and secured them for transport as well. He grabbed the edges of a plastic sheet he had laid over the gurney and finished wrapping the body, concealing from view and keeping any fluids from dripping on to the floor of his van once he got it loaded up.

"I think we have had enough fun for the night, gentlemen," he said as he pushed the gurney back toward his van. "You know where to go if you need anything."

EIGHT

Michael waited for Cook to step out of the interrogation room and closed the door, securing Rosa in the room so they could talk privately. "So what do you think?" he asked as soon as the door latched behind them.

"I think that's one hell of a story, Michael, and I think it's true, but it doesn't matter what we think. She's still just a hooker, who's currently looking at getting booked for murder. She may have rehearsed that story one hundred times, just waiting for the day she'd need it."

"You saw her, Cook. That was not just some story she concocted on the offhand chance she killed some John someday. That was genuine in there, man. This is a lot more than a simple homicide, justifiable homicide, Cook. I want to talk to her more about the slavery issues and this Carlos guy she mentioned. You know she can't be the only one this has happened to. We've got to follow this up. Carlos has to be in the area, and she knows how to get a hold of him." Michael could feel a rage begin to build inside him. He knew these kinds of things occurred but never imagined it happening in the United States, let alone right under his nose.

Cook recognized the anger in Michael's face as his eyes seemed to ignite from deep within. "Look, man, I've got a dead guy behind one of the biggest casinos in the city. My boss is never gonna let me put that on hold and go chase down some pimp because my suspect, who, I might remind you, just admitted to it, said she was forced to be a hooker. Besides, what are you gonna do, arrest this guy based on her story? You don't have any evidence."

"Are you fucking kidding me, Cook!" Michael was amazed at the relative indifference of his counterpart. "You have got to be kidding me. I don't have any evidence?" His pulse quickened as he began to raise his voice. "That's why we call it an investigation. I'll find the evidence, and to be honest, since this all originated in California anyway, I don't think I'll be needing your assistance or your approval for that matter."

"Look, man, you need to calm down. I called you in on this because you always see things a little differently. You pick up on things I miss, and to be honest, I like working with you, but this case is pretty much open and closed as I see it. I never imagined our suspect was going to cop to all of this. So if you think I'm gonna drop everything and take off chasing down leads on the Mexican Mafia, you're in for a surprise." Cook realized it was already too late to talk him out of it, but he had hoped to at least get Michael to refocus on the matters at hand.

Cook had a point, and Michael knew there wasn't any evidence other than Rosa's story. He couldn't exactly hold Carlos on her story alone. Furthermore, if he contacted Carlos, he would be placing Rosa and her family in more danger than they were already in. He needed time, and he knew how to get it. It wouldn't be much, but it was the best he could do.

"You're right, I'm sorry I snapped," Michael began. "I just hate the thought of this shit happening right here under our noses, and in the city where I grew up."

"No worries, brother, I understand. There's only so much we can do."

"Not exactly," Michael said. "I need a favor. You do still plan on booking Rosa, right?"

"Yeah," Cook said somewhat hesitantly. He could tell Michael was calculating; it was why he liked having him around; everything was like a game of chess with Michael, and he was always at least two moves ahead. "You know the drill. We'll still forward the case to the DA's office for review on something like this and let them decide if they want to prosecute."

It was exactly what Michael expected to hear. "Good, that's where the favor comes in. I need you to slow things down. You can hold her for twenty-four hours before you have to book her. So don't book her till the end of business today. It's Friday, so the DA won't even get the report until Monday, and they'll have forty-eight hours before she has to be arraigned, and if you can get them to stretch it until late Tuesday, it would be perfect. That gives me four full days to find the evidence I need."

Cook looked at Michael, pondering the request for several seconds. "I'll do it, but you better hit the ground running. You have a long way to go and lot to dig up to make a case on something that big over a weekend."

"I know. I'll owe you for this one. Now come on, let's get back in there and tell our suspect what's going on. I've got to get this show on the road."

Cook and Michael went back into the interrogation room. Cook took a seat across the table from Rosa again. Michael remained standing. Rosa noticed he looked tenser than he had before. She didn't know why, but she was pretty sure she was about to find out.

Michael started, "Rosa, I need to explain a few things. The next few days are going to be less than pleasant, but you have to trust me. I really need you to cooperate with us on this to make things work. Detective Cook is going to take you to the Douglas County Jail. He's going to charge with murder. However, he's not going to book you until later today."

"But my family—" Rosa began to protest, but Michael cut her off.

"Hear me out," Michael said, speaking over Rosa. "He's going to book you at the end of business today. You're going to have to hang out at the station until then. I'm sure he'll have some more questions for you anyway. Once you're in the jail, you'll just have to hang until Tuesday."

"You don't understand!" Rosa interjected. "Carlos will never let that happen. He'll bail me out. He's going to want to know what I told you."

"Don't worry about that. You're not going to have bail. Detective Cook will see to it that your bail is denied. You're a flight risk and likely to flee the country. In the meantime, I'm going to be heading to Holtville. I'm going to get your parents taken cared of and get you out from under La Eme." The Mexican Mafia was commonly referred to as La Eme, the Spanish enunciation for the letter *M*, by police and those familiar with the organization.

"You can't interfere. These aren't just some street thugs. They'll kill us all!" Rosa proclaimed.

"I know you are worried, and I know it's hard, but you have to trust me. You have to realize that there is no other way out. You belong to La Eme, and if you're making them as much money as I suspect you are, they're never going to let you go. They'll keep holding your family over your head until you are of no use to them, and then they'll kill you anyway. I know what I'm doing, and I know I can get you and your parents out of this safely," Michael assured her. *I just haven't got all the details worked out yet,* he thought to himself. "I'm going to need some information. I need to know how to get in touch with your parents and your brothers."

Rosa was hesitant, but she knew Michael was right. She had done the math, and she knew she had earned more than enough to have repaid her father's debt with interest. She proceeded to give Michael her parents' telephone number and told him where they and her brothers lived. She hadn't called them in so long she couldn't remember each of their numbers. She only called her father to let him know that she was still alive and to make sure that he was as well. She had told herself long ago that if anything ever happened to him, she would run. Maybe this really would be her chance. She said a prayer to herself as she watched the man in front write down the information she had given him. Hoping he was as smart as he was confident.

Michael finished jotting down the information. "Is there anything you left out, anything else you can remember? Maybe something distinctive about the house in Calexico or Los Angeles."

"I wish there was," Rosa said, "but I was never allowed to see where they were taking me in the beginning, and Carlos always drove me wherever I was going to be working and back to the house in LA. I had so many other things on my mind I never paid attention. I don't think I could find it again if I had to."

"Okay, but if you think of anything else, tell Detective Cook. He'll relay it to me. And if you need anything at all, Detective Cook will take care of it." Michael knew he was short on time, and he had a lot of traveling to do. He looked at Rosa and then to Cook. "I gotta run. I'll be in touch," he said as he walked out of the room.

"Well, all righty then," Cook said. "You and I are going to have some time to get to know each other. It's going to be long night. So why don't we take this back to the main office and go from there?"

"You know Carlos is going to be looking for me. He was expecting me to text him once I hooked up. He would have gone to check on me by now. When he sees all of what happened, he'll start trying to find out if I was involved."

"Well, we'll cross that bridge when we come to it. As long as you're in custody, you'll be safe. Detective Garrett is good, in fact he's the best I've seen. If anyone can get this sorted out, it's him."

NINE

Michael picked up his go bag as he left the interrogation room. He pulled his cell phone out and telephoned his supervisor, Sergeant Frank Eyrich. He had to let him know what was going on. He held his cell phone to his ear, waiting for an answer. It was on the fourth ring when Sergeant Eyrich finally picked up. Michael could tell he woke him up by the groggy sound of his voice.

"Hello."

"Hey, boss, it's Garrett," Michael said. "You aren't going to believe this, but I'm headed to Southern California on follow-up."

"What? What are you talking about? Dispatch called me a couple hours ago and said Douglas County requested you for a homicide. What's going on?"

"They did and there was. I'm working the case with Cook from Douglas County. But the suspect unloaded a story on us that requires immediate attention." Michael didn't want to get into too many details with his half-awake supervisor. He just needed to feed him enough information to get his approval for travel. Regardless of the job, there was always red tape involved when it came to the use of the department credit card. It wouldn't have been the first time Michael had found himself miles from home when he swiped the card to pay for gas, and it was declined because some bean counter in accounting just happened to zero the available balance when she discovered he hadn't gotten preapproval to travel. "I just wanted to keep you posted. I'll fill you in on the details tomorrow. You need to get your beauty sleep anyway."

"Okay, you driving or flying?"

"I'm pressed for time. I've gotta check the flights. If I can get out tonight, I'll fly, otherwise, I'll be on the road in less than twenty." Michael knew he was going to be hard-pressed to find a flight out of Reno or Sacramento at this hour. Most commercial airlines didn't operate after midnight anymore, and he couldn't wait until morning. He did know a couple of people who might be able to help him out though.

Ten

Detective Cook had what he needed. There wasn't any more that had to be done to wrap up his investigation. Rosa had confessed to what would inevitably be viewed as justifiable homicide. If it weren't for protocol, he wouldn't even book her. Cook was a firm believer in the people's right to defend themselves, and he was certain that Rosa had done nothing more than what was absolutely necessary to survive.

The truth be told, he was more interested in getting the results from the crime scene investigators and pathology on the victim. Cook was certain this was the guy who had killed two other women in the past year. The crime scenes had been scoured, and there was just never enough to get a lead on a suspect, which is what troubled Cook the most. Unless he got a lucky break, it was clear the guy had no intentions of stopping. If he had known the whole truth, that his cold cases were only couple among a string of twelve, he would have been far more disturbed.

Hoping that he would be able to close the other cases with the information he would receive from the crime scene investigators and the pathologist wasn't doing him any good at the moment. He needed to get Rosa out of the substation and over to main office. The Douglas County Sheriff's Department headquarters was located in Minden, about twenty miles from the substation at Stateline.

Cook asked Rosa if she needed anything before they left. He knew nothing could make a short drive feel like an eternity quicker than a full bladder. Sure enough, Rosa took him up on the offer. She went into the restroom and did what she had to do. She splashed cool water over her face one last time, hoping to rid herself of the menacing stench. The water was refreshing, but it didn't relieve the aroma that currently plagued her.

When she was finished, she stepped out of the restroom, finding Detective Cook waiting patiently. His demeanor had changed dramatically since they first met. She thought he seemed much more understanding and compassionate now.

Cook decided to make a head call one last time before taking off as well. "Do I need to handcuff you to the table, or can I trust you'll be here when I get out?" he asked.

"I'll be here," Rosa replied. "I have far too much riding on this to try and get away now."

Cook went in and took a leak. As soon as he was finished, he stepped out into the hall where he left Rosa, imaging she would be gone, but she wasn't.

"You really expect this guy Carlos to be looking for you?"

"Absolutely. The last time I was arrested, he was bailing me out before the paperwork was done. I think he was afraid I would tell the police what happened."

"Why didn't you? I mean you were in custody, and they could have protected you. A case like this is huge. Witness protection programs are in place for people just like you."

"I know, I've seen all the movies, but what kind of life is that? Besides, if I disappear, so will my parents. Carlos never misses an opportunity to remind me that they are only alive because I am cooperating."

"Then why this time? Why did you tell Detective Garrett?"

"I don't know to be honest with you. When I saw him walk into that little room, my emotions just came flooding back. I don't want to keep living like this. I guess I knew they would never let me go, and I just hope that he can get me out and save my parents."

"That's a lot of trust to put in a guy you haven't seen since high school."

"I know, I know." Rosa dropped her head, and her shoulders slumped as the reality of what she had done truly set in. She realized that the stress of the life she had been living finally outweighed the constant threat looming over her. She just had to tell someone. "I guess it was just the fact that he was the first familiar face I'd seen in so long. I just couldn't take it anymore."

Cook recognized the concern creeping back into Rosa's voice. He needed—no, he wanted to keep her calm. "Look, Rosa, I haven't known Michael a long time, but I have worked with him on some big cases. This is going to work out, and you'll be back with your family before you know it. Look at it this way. It'll all be over by Tuesday one way or another." As soon as the words left his mouth, he realized his mistake. He knew if Michael failed to find enough evidence to prove Rosa's story was true, there was no way any agency would protect her. No judge would hold her for killing someone in self-defense. She would be released following the arraignment, and Carlos would be there waiting for her. If Michael ruffled some feathers over the weekend, she would disappear, and Cook knew it.

Rosa looked at Cook with painful resolve. Tears began to well up in her eyes again. She could tell Cook regretted his last words. She also knew he was right. She wiped the tears from her eyes and took a deep breath and laughed uncomfortably. "You're right. So I guess I'll just have to make the most of my weekend and just see what happens."

Not wanting to make things worse than he already had, Cook said, "We better get going. It's already after midnight, and I've got to get you to the main office." Cook gently grabbed Rosa by the upper arm and escorted her out of the office to his Tahoe parked out front. He withdrew his keys from his pocket and depressed the auto unlock button. He was getting ready to open the rear passenger when he felt the muscles in Rosa's upper arm begin to tense. It was the same way he had felt hundreds of suspects react right before the fight began.

Cook tightened his grip and pulled Rosa closer to him. It was an unnatural response for many as most people desire to separate themselves from potential danger, but for Cook and thousands of other law enforcement officers, it was a way to ensure they maintained control. If Rosa tried to pull away, he would push her against the side of the Tahoe, pinning her body with the weight of his. He would drive his elbow and forearm into her upper back and slide his other hand down her arm, grabbing her wrist, pulling her wrist back, and energetically driving it up between her shoulder blades. It would happen in one fluid motion, causing Rosa great pain, but he hoped it didn't come to that.

"Don't do it, Rosa!" Cook cautioned her. "It's not worth it." Rosa remained tense and didn't respond. Cook quickly opened the door and directed her into the vehicle. She climbed into the backseat, her eyes directed straightforward. "Hey!" Cook said sharply. "What in the hell is going on?"

Rosa shook her head, breaking her daze. "He's here," was all she could manage.

Uncomfortable with her response, Cook shut the door and went to depress the lock button on his key fob. He hadn't realized it at the time, but he had dropped the fob when he felt Rosa begin to tense up. He didn't want to have something in his hands if the fight began.

The natural tendency for people when they tighten their grip with one hand is to do the same with the other. It is a phenomenon commonly referred to as sympathetic grip. Whether done intentionally or as the result of a fall or being startled, it's a natural reaction. Experienced officers worked to train their bodies to break these natural reactions. A must if you want to survive a thirty-year career in a profession wrought with violence and those who would do you harm, even women.

Cook pressed his left arm against Rosa's door as he began to pick up his keys. He wanted to feel the door start to move if she tried to open it. He knelt down on his right knee rather than bending at the waist, everything a result of years of training and experience. He kept his head up and felt for the keys where he'd seen them. He found them quickly and then immediately depressed the lock button, securing Rosa in the vehicle. The back locks in the Tahoe had been removed so suspects couldn't unlock the door manually, and the child safety system had been secured in the lock position so they couldn't just open the door with the handles.

Most large agencies actually removed the door panel completely and replaced it with a retrofitted solid panel that neither had locks nor handles, but small agencies took a less expensive approach. Simply removing the locking mechanism and driving a short sheet metal screw above the child safety lock that was located on the inner edge of the door accomplished the same thing.

With Rosa secured in the vehicle, Cook relaxed slightly. He rose to his feet and began to walk around the back of his SUV when he observed a Hispanic male approaching him from across the driveway. "Can I help you?" he said with authority. He wasn't certain, but he suspected this was the cause of Rosa's sudden tension.

The man continued approaching Cook with a certain determination in his stride. "I am trying to get to Sam's Place, but think I'm lost. I was supposed to meet some friends there. Can you tell me how to get there?"

Cook recognized the determination in the man's gait. He positioned his body with his right leg slightly behind his left, blading his stance toward the man. It was a position he used when talking to people on the streets as well as when standing on the range. It did a multitude of things and, most importantly, gave him a strong base and shooting platform while all placing his sidearm on the side of his body, not visible to the man in front of him. He placed his hand on his gun.

He couldn't be certain, but he assumed this was Carlos. "Yeah, no problem. You're on the right path. You just need to keep going a little farther. Take a right out of the parking lot and follow your nose a couple more miles, and you'll see it on the right."

The man slowed his approach, finally stopping within ten feet of Cook and the vehicle. "Thanks a lot, boss," he said. He began walking toward the road as if to take a look for himself. "So I just hang a right, and it's a couple miles up the road?"

Cook moved to the driver's side of the SUV, keeping his hand on his pistol. "It's that easy."

The man stopped again and looked back at him. He stared at him as if he was looking right through him. "Thanks a lot. So what do you guys got going on? I saw all the police at the casino when I drove by."

"There was a murder, but nothing to worry about. We have the suspect in custody."

"Wow, that's crazy shit. Was that her?"

"I'm not at liberty to discuss that right now. If there's nothing else, I've got a lot to do."

"Yeah, all right. Thanks for the directions." The man headed back to his vehicle.

Cook waited until the man reached his vehicle before relaxing. He continued to watch as the supposedly lost man got in and drove out of the parking lot. Cook made a mental note of the vehicle, a late-model silver Buick. He unlocked his door and climbed into the Tahoe.

"That was him, that was Carlos," Rosa said excitedly.

"I figured as much. That's okay though. It's exactly what we needed. Now he thinks you've been arrested for murder, and I know what he looks like and what he drives."

Cook started his vehicle, and they were on their way to Minden. He watched his rearview mirror, expecting to see the Buick every time he looked back. It never happened.

He explained to Rosa that the sheriff's headquarters was both the sheriff's office and county jail. It was where she would be staying for next several days. The drive was uneventful. When they arrived, Cook parked on the street amid a sea of marked black-and-white patrol vehicles. He hadn't seen the Buick but didn't want to take any chances. He climbed out of the SUV and looked around. There were no vehicles approaching. He got Rosa out of the vehicle and walked her quickly to a single nondescript back door on the back of the building. When they reached the door, he held his keys in front of a small black box located on the wall adjacent to the door handle. A small red light on the box changed to green, and there was a sharp click as the electronic lock was released. He yanked the door open, and they were in.

He could finally relax and get Rosa settled in. He would have to put her in a holding cell until he booked her later in the day. In the meantime, he needed to get something to eat. He asked if Rosa wanted anything; she didn't. He explained that he was going to take her to the jail and have the correctional officers place her in holding. He had some things he needed to do, but he'd be in the building.

He walked Rosa down the hall toward the middle of the building. They came to a heavy steel door Rosa figured was the entrance to the jail. There was a small cache of metal lockers built into the wall across from the large steel door. Several of the lockers had keys hanging from their locks. Cook opened one of the lockers and withdrew his Glock pistol from its holster. He placed the pistol into the locker, closed the door, and removed the key.

He stood in front of the steel door with Rosa at his side. He depressed a small green button located on the wall next to the door. Rosa could hear a buzzing sound coming from the other side, followed by a louder buzzing sound coming from the door. Cook pushed the heavy door open and led Rosa into the next room, where there was another door identical to the first. The same buzzing noise came from the second door after the first swung close behind them. It was a standard security measure in jails that prevented people from escaping. Both doors could not be opened simultaneously, keeping those who might try to escape or aid others in the attempt from disengaging both locks.

Cook pushed the second door open and led Rosa to another small room that somewhat resembled the interrogation room at the substation. It was a little larger, and instead of a table and bench, it had a metal platform that was roughly the size of a twin bed. There was a short pony wall made out of cinder blocks that was no more than four feet high. It stuck out just far enough to allow Rosa enough privacy to use the small metal toilet if she needed to, without exposing herself, yet keeping her visible through the small glass window in the door.

Rosa observed correctional officers moving about, obviously fast at work. Cook called for one of them and asked for a female officer and holding cell number 3 to be opened. Shortly thereafter, a female officer arrived and opened the holding cell door. Cook explained to the woman, whose name tag on her uniform read *Cruz*, that Rosa was involved in the homicide at Harrah's. He impressed upon the female correctional officer the importance of treating Rosa with the utmost respect, explaining how cooperative she had been and also that it was very likely a case of self-defense.

Rosa listened as Cook talked to Cruz.

"I've got some things to tend to, but I'm not finished with her yet," Cook said, motioning toward Rosa with his head. "Can you put her in one of the holding cells until I get back?"

"No problem," answered Cruz. "We've got a few open cells right now."

"Perfect, but don't double her up with anyone if the others fill up. I can't stress that enough, and no one, I mean no one, talks to her without my approval," Cook stressed.

"You got it. Anything else?"

"Yeah, if anyone comes in asking questions, call me. I'll deal with it."

Cruz acknowledged and opened the door for Rosa. As Rosa stepped in, she heard what truly mattered.

"Hey, Cruz, she could really use a shower and a change of clothes. Any chance you could hook her up before I finish the booking?" It wasn't customary for inmates to get jail clothing until after the booking process, nor was it normal for Detective Cook to make such a request.

"I think we can take care of that," Cruz said as she gave Rosa an understanding nod.

ELEVEN

Carlos had been sitting in his car, prepared to stay as long as it took to gain the information he needed. It had only been a couple of hours when he saw someone exit the sheriff's substation. He watched as the man stepped from the building and walked directly to the white Explorer Carlos had seen pull into the parking lot earlier. Whoever he was, he was in a hurry. No sooner had he reached the vehicle, he was in it and backing out.

Carlos was just getting settled back in when he finally got what he was waiting for. The door opened again, and he watched as another man led his best earner out of the building. He noticed she wasn't in handcuffs, but she didn't seem to be free to leave either. He had to figure out what was going on. He had to know if Rosa was in trouble or merely a witness; the question was how.

Carlos didn't have time to figure it out in advance. He had to move, or he may lose his only chance. He got out of the Buick and quickly headed toward Rosa and the detective. He had to hurry; if this guy moved half as fast as the last guy, he may still miss the opportunity. As Carlos approached, he could tell something was happening. He watched as the detective aggressively pulled Rosa toward him.

Carlos was incensed. Ironically, he hated it when men mistreated women. Despite the fact that he was in the business of human trafficking and forcing women into prostitution, he had deluded himself into believing it was just business, and part of the business was for him to protect his women from men who would do them harm. Carlos placed his hands in his pockets, casually gripping the handle of his karambit in his right front pants pocket. All that remained was to get close enough to employ the weapon.

Carlos continued his advance with determination. His actions betrayed him; he forgot he was not walking up on some everyday Joe. The man had moved quickly. No sooner had he yanked Rosa into him, he had opened the door and shoved her into the backseat of the vehicle. As soon as he had secured her in the SUV, the detective was on to him.

"Can I help you?" queried the detective.

There was an intensity in his voice that could not be mistaken. In addition to the detective's seriousness, Carlos also watched him as he took a fighting stance. He realized this was not the time nor the prey he would be taking advantage of in the dark, lonely parking lot. Rosa would have to wait. "I am trying to get to Sam's Place, but think I'm lost. I was supposed to meet some friends there. Can you tell me how to get there?"

"Yeah, no problem. You're on the right path. You just need to keep going a little farther. Take a right out of the parking lot and follow your nose a couple more miles, and you'll see it on the right."

The man's voice had relaxed somewhat compared to its previous intensity. Carlos thought he may still have a chance to gain some insight into what was going on; he just had to play his cards right. He slowed down, trying to look more lost than determined. He continued to tighten the gap between himself and the vehicle in hopes of getting a better look at Rosa. He got to within ten feet and decided he better not push it as the detective continued to watch him ardently. "Thanks a lot, boss," he said.

Carlos watched as the detective began to move around the vehicle to the driver's side. Not wanting to risk further investigation, he began walking toward the road as if to confirm the directions he had just been given. "So I just hang a right and it's a couple miles up the road?"

"It's that easy."

The detective never took his eyes off of him. Carlos knew he had made the right decision avoiding this confrontation. Contrary to cliché, the last thing Carlos wanted to do was take a knife to gunfight. He knew the odds in such cases and only chose to chance them when he had the element of surprise or knew his opponent was inept. He did hope to elicit just a little information regarding the night's events, at least enough to start working on his next moves. "Thanks a lot. So what do you guys got going on? I saw all the police at the casino when I drove by."

"There was a murder, but nothing to worry about. We have the suspect in custody."

"Wow, that's crazy shit. Was that her?"

"I'm not at liberty to discuss that right now. If there's nothing else, I've got a lot to do."

"Yeah, all right. Thanks for the directions." Carlos hadn't gotten exactly the answers he had hoped for, but he got enough. He was certain Rosa was involved somehow; he just wasn't sure to what extent. He hated not having more details, but either way, he was going to have to call Fernando and let him know what was going on. If Rosa came clean, there would be work to do. Certain people would have to be dealt with before the authorities could speak with them.

Carlos weighed the odds. Rosa had been loyal to this point; he had made sure of it with constant reminders that her family's lives hinged on her continued cooperation. He wasn't overly concerned, but it didn't matter; there was protocol for matters such as this. The Mexican Mafia hadn't risen to such power being an unorganized bunch of thugs like some LA street gang with a two-block turf. They ruled the prison system, half of California, and were expanding farther all the time.

It would weigh on him for the rest of the night. If they had to kill Rosa's family, they would have to kill her too. He knew the only reason she didn't run was because of them. He would have to try and find out a little more before the morning. Rosa had made them a lot of money, and she was worth the effort. He would have to see what he could find out; hopefully it would be enough to spare her family.

TWELVE

No sooner had he received the authorization to travel, Michael pulled up the contacts in his Samsung. He had contemplated looking for commercial flights but quickly ruled out the idea once he had thought it through. First, there would be the line to check in, which would take longer than usual because he would have to notify them he was armed. Then some overzealous clerk would undoubtedly call the supervisor and security to verify all of his identification and credentials. All of which would do nothing more than delay the inevitable, going through the process again at security. Then he would either have missed the flight, if there even was one, or have to wait until morning to catch the next one out. Such a delay was a luxury he did not have.

Having already decided he was not going to fly commercial, he was left with two options. Either of which required he be headed west. He was on Highway 50, crossing from Nevada into California. He glanced over at the crime scene as he passed Harrah's and could see the CSI guys had already wrapped up their end of the investigation. The only people left were patrolmen, and they were pulling down the bright yellow crime scene tape.

Michael quickly came to Pioneer Trail and turned left onto the road. It was a great shortcut for a couple of reasons—one, he could avoid the myriad of traffic lights along the highway going through the city. Not that he wouldn't have just treated them like stop signs and rolled through anyway, but also because it took a good ten minutes off the drive and would drop him into Myers, where he could get back on the highway headed west over the summit of the Sierras.

No sooner had he turned onto Pioneer Trail, he saw the sign for a little cross street not more than fifty feet up, Fern Road. He remembered Rosa telling him about the apartment she lived in right near there. Michael saw a small little fourplex and figured that must have been where she lived. He wondered for a brief moment which one was hers. He passed the intersection quickly, accelerating down the road. He kept scrolling through his contacts, looking for a friend he hoped could do him a favor.

He finally found the name he was looking for—Tim Picone. Tim was a captain in the Army National Guard. Michael had some dealings with him in the past during a major marijuana case he was working. He had received a tip about a marijuana garden that a couple of hikers had stumbled upon in the national forest. Michael took the lead on the case instead of passing it to the Narcotics Unit because he was familiar with the area, and he knew they were swamped chasing leads and working cases of their own.

Captain Picone had started his career in the National Guard copiloting a UH-60 Blackhawk as a first lieutenant stationed in San Diego. He had been part of Team Shadow, a drug interdiction unit tasked with assisting the United States Border Patrol along the U.S.-Mexican border in San Diego and Imperial counties. As a result of his tremendous success, he had been promoted to the rank of captain in record time and was reassigned to Air Wolf, a similar unit located at Mather Field near Sacramento where he continued to fly drug interdiction and eradication operations. Part of the function of his current unit was to assist local federal, state, or county agencies with their operations as well.

Michael hit the Call button in hopes that Tim would be able to help. In his typical fashion, Tim picked up the phone on the second ring. He didn't even sound as if he had been asleep when he answered, "Air Wolf, Captain Picone speaking."

"Captain Picone, this is Detective Garrett with El Dorado County."

"What can I do for you, Detective?"

"I need a favor. I know you guys primarily only work dope, but I have a major case and time is critical. I need to get to LA post haste, and I was hoping you could swing it."

Tim could sense the sincerity in Michael's voice, and he remembered Michael from their previous dealings. He had been impressed with Michael's sense of duty and knew that he wouldn't have called him if it wasn't critical. "Where are you now?"

"I'm in coming into Myers, outside of South Lake."

"Okay, I'll get my crew up and the bird prepped. We'll be ready long before you get here, so I can either stand by for you, or we can come and get you. Your call." Tim knew his guys; he had a dedicated copilot of his own now, a crew chief, and a specialist. All of whom he could reach and have on base ready to go in thirty minutes. It would take them another twenty-five to get the Blackhawk checked out and ready to go. By his calculations, that should put Michael around Placerville if he was hustling. Mather was another forty-five minutes from there. Time that could be cut way down if they just picked Michael up.

"Roger that, Captain. I'm in a hurry, so call when you're ready and we'll go from there. I'll meet you at the Placerville or Cameron Park Airport, depending on my location at the time." Both Placerville and Cameron Park were small cities along Highway 50 in El Dorado County, and each had a small private airport used by local businessmen for air taxi operations and hobbyists. Neither airport was very large, but both could accommodate multiengine prop planes and small jets. The Black Hawk would have no issues getting in or out as they were used too far less.

"You got it," was all Michael heard, and the line went dead. Relieved that he had been able to make arrangements to get down south, he could now concentrate on driving. He was sixty miles from the Placerville Airport, and the road was anything but straight. It was normally about an hour and fifteen minutes to an hour and half drive, but he needed to make it in no more than an hour; forty-five minutes would be better. He looked at the clock on the dashboard; it was nearing one o'clock in the morning. Michael hoped to be in Placerville by 1:30 AM but thought 1:45 was more realistic. He dropped his phone into a cup holder in the center console, turned up the radio with a Toby Keith CD playing, and focused on driving.

THIRTEEN

Tim hung up and immediately dialed his copilot, Kate Stevens. She was slightly older than Tim because she hadn't joined the Guard until later in life. Kate had gone into law enforcement right out of high school. She had started working in corrections and, upon turning twenty-one, was sent to the academy and began as a patrol deputy for Sacramento County. She worked the road for several years until she married and had her first child. She was currently the mother of two but missed the adrenaline rush she once got from the excitement of her job. She would have never considered going back to work, but her mother had retired and was more than willing to help with the kids. That was all the incentive Kate needed, so she went back to school and joined the Guard under the warrant officer program. She had every intent of flying Apache helicopters, but when she had graduated from flight school, she was specifically recruited for Air Wolf. She had been with the unit for just shy of six months, and her work ethic rivaled that of Captain Picone.

As expected, she picked up before the third ring. She saw it was Captain Picone on her caller ID as she answered, "Good morning, Captain. To what do I owe the pleasure?"

Tim was a no-nonsense leader when it came to his job and his people. He was consistent and fair and respected because of it. "We have a mission. I need you at Mather most ricky-tick," a phrase used by the military for *as soon as possible*. "I'll fill you in when you get there."

"Roger that, Captain, I'm as good as out the door. Do you want me to call the crew?"

"Negative, I'm on it. You just get here." Tim hung up and called his crew chief next.

Kate hung up, kissed her husband gently, and rolled out of bed. She went into the bathroom and closed the door before turning on the light. She brushed her teeth just to rid herself of that morning breath sensation and grabbed her flight suit. She kept one pressed and ready, hung on the back of the bathroom door for occasions such as this. She refused to be the last one to arrive on a short notice callout because being a woman in the military already made her subject to criticism. The last thing she wanted to do was give the guys a reason to make comments about how she must have had to do her hair or her makeup, and thus far, she never had.

She got dressed and quickly pulled her shoulder-length hair into a ponytail that came together at the back of her neck, which kept it from interfering with her flight helmet. She killed the light and walked out of the bathroom and into a small walk-in closet. She had to turn the light on before closing the door because the home builder placed the light switch on the outside wall. It never made sense, but that's just the way it was. She tried to keep the door as closed as possible so as not to disturb her husband. It wouldn't be the first time he woke up, and she was gone. She walked into the closet and shut the door. She quickly put on her boots and was ready to head out. She opened the door just enough to hit the light switch before exiting. She hurried out to the kitchen and placed a prewritten note she kept clipped to the side of the refrigerator onto the counter.

Got called in. I'll call you when we land. Kiss the kids for me. Love you all!

With that, she grabbed her keys and was out the door. From phone call to starting the Cummings diesel in her Dodge Ram 2500, it only took her six minutes.

While Kate was getting ready, Tim had also called his crew chief, Sergeant First Class Jack Taylor, and his specialist, Kelly Morton. They were also quick to answer and ready to roll in a matter of minutes.

Many people often think of the National Guard as nothing more than a bunch of weekend warriors, but units such as Captain Picone's were actual full-time, active-duty military personnel. This was their job. It was referred to as Active Duty Special Work by the National Guard. Each soldier worked under a six-year enlistment contract for the National Guard as well as with an additional contract for active duty that was currently being renewed annually. Responding to callouts such as this was part of Air Wolf's agreement, and each member of the unit knew it. So if they wanted to keep being able to renew their contracts, they would always be available. Nothing got a guardsman kicked out of a specialty unit like this faster than saying he couldn't make it when his CO (or Company Commander) called.

As commanding officer, Tim wanted to be the first one on site for every mission. He had purchased a home just outside Mather Field to ensure this would be the case. It took him longer to get ready than it took to get on base. Once he arrived, he pulled up to the hangar where his office was located. He went in and grabbed the paperwork to start the checkout for his Black Hawk.

The UH-60 Black Hawk was the army's replacement for the Huey. It was first introduced in the late '70s, when it competed for the military's bid. It beat out all the competitors and was set into production by Sikorsky Aircraft. It was first deployed in 1980 and has been in use since. Although it has undergone some modifications over the years, for the most part, it has remained relatively unchanged. The helicopter can fly at speeds up to 182 miles per hour and has a 19,150-foot service ceiling, making it suitable for just about every mission the military has.

While Tim awaited the arrival of crew, he quickly plotted his course. It was thirty-five miles from Mather Field to the Placerville Airport and another 415 miles from Placerville to Los Angeles. The Black Hawk only had a 373-mile range with its standard fuel tank, a distance that could be more than doubled with the addition of an auxiliary fuel bladder, giving it a total possible range of 882 miles. With a total distance of 450 miles air travel, Tim was going to need to have his crew chief hook up the auxiliary fuel bladder. It would not take much longer to get set up and would be worth the extra time to avoid the need to refuel. He then calculated how much fuel he was going to need. He gave himself an extra 10 percent and was ready.

Once he completed his flight plan and fuel calculations, he headed out to the helicopter. Kate was just pulling up, as was Specialist Morton. They parked their vehicles alongside the hangar next to Tim's. Kate met Captain Picone at the helicopter while Morton went to the hangar to ready his gear. Sergeant Taylor showed up a couple of minutes later, riding his Harley-Davidson Road Glide. Everyone always teased him about the riding the bike to the base because military regulations required he wear an obnoxiously bright blaze orange safety vest. A combination that just didn't fit on a Harley.

"Where do we stand, Captain?" Kate asked as she approached the helo.

"We're headed to Los Angeles with a local cop in a big hurry. I've already plotted our flight plan and have our fuel calculations. Get these to Sergeant Taylor and get back here so we can get the bird checked out. Double time." Double time was how the military referred to running. He handed his chief warrant officer the fuel calculations, and she immediately set off at a near sprint toward the hangar and the crew.

Kate was back in less than a minute. Captain Picone was already in his seat with his flight helmet on and his com unit plugged in. The com unit was short for communications unit, which was currently a noise-cancellation, voice-activated Motorola headset built in to the flight helmet with a boom mic that projected from the left side to just in front of the mouth.

Kate boarded the Black Hawk and took her seat to the right of Picone's. She grabbed her helmet and slipped it on. She plugged her com unit into the overhead jack plug and began to run through her checklist.

In the meantime, Taylor and Morton reviewed the flight plan, retrieved the auxiliary fuel bladder, and hurried to install it. They went to work in the cargo hold of the helicopter. They had everything complete in under ten minutes. The Black Hawk was always left fully fueled for rapid deployment; however, they were going to need to add fuel to the empty auxiliary bladder. Morton went for the fuel truck while Taylor remained to go over the checklist with the pilots. They went through the list like the experts they were. They had just begun to power up the two T700-GE turbo shafts when Morton returned with the fuel truck. He and Taylor added the requisite amount of fuel to make the journey.

The logic behind keeping the fuel level at 10 percent more than was required when adding the auxiliary bladder was simple. The extra fuel was extra weight and also took up a major portion of the cargo area. Picone didn't want to cramp his crew any more than was necessary, and the added weight would only slow the Black Hawk. If there was no need for the bladder, the tanks were filled to capacity.

With the fuel brought to capacity, Morton parked the fuel truck and returned, ready to go. He boarded the helo and took his place in the cargo door. He loved his job, and as far as he was concerned, he had the best seat in the house. To the casual observer, it appeared that he hung precariously from the open door on the side of the Black Hawk; however, for long flights, he only remained there for takeoff and landing as a lookout. In operational mode, he had a safety harness that he clipped to a rappel-style harness that prevented him from falling in the event the pilot had to initiate evasive maneuvers. In reality, he seldom used the safety strap and simply relied on the laws of physics and a firm grasp on the steel cable above the door to keep him in place.

Picone had the twin turbo shafts up to full power. He glanced over his shoulder and gave his crew the thumbs-up, indicating they were good to go. His copilot verbally acknowledged, "We are checked out and good to go." While his two crew members simply gave a quick nod and returned the thumbs-up sign. Picone then spoke into his boom mic, "Stevens, why don't you take us up and bear east toward Placerville. I have a phone call to make."

Kate acknowledged, "Roger that, Captain." As she eased the Black Hawk off the tarmac and into flight.

Picone connected his mil spec (or military specification) cell phone to the communication unit with an adaptive plug. He placed the call to Detective Garrett to let him know they were off the ground and inbound to his location.

Fourteen

Michael had made good time. He had been fortunate that there was very little traffic coming over the summit. Highway 50 was a two-lane road for most of the way with only a few passing lanes every so often that he would be able to use to get past slower vehicles. He would brave the odds passing over the double yellow lines in some areas, but more often than not, you couldn't see around the next bend regardless of the direction because of the forest or the mountain. Emergency lights didn't help much as most people didn't stop anyway. They only had narrow shoulder to pull over on.

Since it was one in the morning, Michael hadn't expected much traffic, but it only took a few cars to really hinder progress on such a highway. As luck would have it, he only encountered a few; and every time, it was close to a passing lane. As a result of this, he was able to make great time; and once he reached Ice House Road, which was a major roadway for the area that led back into the Cleveland National Forest and several local reservoirs, the highway opened up to two lanes in each direction, and he was able to speed up.

It had only been forty minutes since they had last talked. Michael thought he had at least fifty-five minutes based on Captain Picone's own assessment of how long it would take Air Wolf to get off the ground. He heard his phone begin to ring and looked at the screen. He saw it was Picone calling and then looked at the clock. It was 1:35.

Michael was just dropping into Placerville. He picked up his phone. "That was quick."

"We are inbound to your location. Where do you want to meet?" asked Picone.

Michael had hoped to make it to Cameron Park simply out of pride and competition, but he knew it would be faster at this point to make the LZ (or landing zone) at the Placerville Airport. "I'm coming into Placerville now. I'll meet you at the local airport."

"Roger that. We'll be there in ten or less."

Michael set his phone back down and took account of his location. He was approaching the Point View off-ramp, the easternmost off-ramp for the city and his exit if he was going to the Placerville Airport. He was going nearly one hundred miles per hour. He began to brake and exited on the fairly steep downgraded off-ramp. He instantly remembered why he liked to keep it around ninety mph as the off-ramp veered to the right and then curved back to the left following the highway. The Explorer leaned uncomfortably to the left as he initially exited the highway and then to the right as he negotiated the sweeping arc that was tighter than he recalled. Then there was the small issue of the rapidly approaching Stop sign.

Michael jabbed the brakes hard, instantly engaging the antilock system. The vehicle shifted its weight forward, and Michael struggled to keep from losing control. The suspension settled; the vehicle stopped swaying, and he all but ran the Stop sign, finally coming to a halt halfway into the first lane of cross traffic. Again, he counted his blessings. Due to the time of day, there were no other vehicles coming, and he simply made a left turn onto Point View Drive, passing under Highway 50.

As soon as he was on the other side of the highway, Point View came to an end. He turned left at the T intersection onto Broadway and followed the signs to the airport. He had only been there a few times throughout his career and was grateful for the signs because he wasn't sure he remembered exactly how to get there. Once he arrived at the airport, he came to the locked perimeter gate. He quickly unlocked the gate with his Knox key. It was special lock system that all private landowners who wished to secure their property used. The Knox key was a master key to the security system that allowed law enforcement, fire, and emergency medical personnel access during emergencies. Once he had the gate open, he pulled through and relocked it. Nothing irritated a property owner more than when the gates were left unsecure by the very people who were supposed to respect their right to privacy and only use the keys in the course of their duties.

Michael found a place to park where his vehicle would be out of the way and grabbed his cell phone and go bag. As soon as he was out of the vehicle, he could smell the brakes. He knew he had pushed it, but that last little incident on the ramp was closer than he cared for. He took another breath, more to relax than to smell the smoldering brake pads, and then realized he could hear the thumping sound of the four-blade rotor on the inbound Black Hawk.

FIFTEEN

Michael knew he only had a couple of minutes tops, so he took a quick personal inventory to make sure he wasn't forgetting anything. He placed his right hand on his right hip and ran it from front to back. He had his badge, gun, and not his wallet. He checked his go bag; it wasn't there. He opened the Explorer back up and reached into the small cubbyhole located in the center of the dash below the stereo. He found his wallet right where he had left it. He hated sitting on it; it always made his ass hurt, so out of habit, he would take it out and stow it in the small cubby. He seldom forgot but had done so a time or two in the past. Thus, he started going through his own little checklist when going anywhere.

Now that he had his wallet, he checked his left side. He had his extra magazines and his keys. He opened his go bag again and took inventory of it as well. He had his small tactical light, extra magazines, handcuffs, his folding knife, and note-taking essentials, along with a small digital camera and recorder. His cell phone was in his pocket.

Now for his list of things to do. He thought about the job that lay before him. He knew what was at stake, and he had to stay sharp. He hated to think about the consequences of failure, so he didn't. He knew failure was not an option. Once he was in the air and on his way to Los Angeles, he would call his former academy classmate David Ross. David had been one of his closest friends in Los Angeles. Michael had moved to the city to attend the academy. He hadn't known anyone and didn't really even have a place to stay. For the first couple of weeks in the academy, he stayed with a man who was the brother of a family friend. They had never met, but the guy was gracious enough to allow Michael to stay there long enough to find a place of his own as a favor to his sister, who had been a longtime friend of Michael's mother.

David still lived at home when they started the academy. They met on the first day, nothing extraordinary, but they also became friends instantly. David and Michael formed an alliance and would help each other from that point on. Running on weekends and studying for tests, simply providing overall moral support to ensure they were successful. It worked as Michael graduated at the top of the class and David not far behind.

Since then, David had gone on to work a variety of assignments and was currently working Hollywood Vice. He had been fortunate to get the assignment as it was a coveted position. It was no doubt due to his continued hard work and perseverance, a trait he shared with Michael and probably the reason they got along so well. In any case, Michael knew David had a handle on the prostitution rings working the area, and if La Eme was running prostitutes in the area, David would know how to find them.

Michael realized this was a gamble, but it was all he had. He hoped that David would be able to help him locate the house Rosa was held in. If they could find it, they were likely to find more girls in the same situation. Even if they couldn't, Michael knew he was going to need some help, and there was no one he trusted more.

*   *   *

Kate knew the coordinates and began her visual search for the airport. This was an unscheduled arrival, so she wasn't expecting any runway lights, and she was right. The only indication she had that she had arrived was the larger area of darkness that was the short runway surrounded by porch lamps from all the homes around the tiny rural airport.

She checked her gauges and her altitude. The altimeter registered just under three thousand feet and dropping. She was right on, confirming her GPS coordinates as she came over the dark runway. She continued her descent and began to slow as she dipped to 2,650 feet. The airport was at 2,585 feet elevation, so even though the instrument said she was at 2,650 feet, she knew she was only sixty-five feet off the earth. This was an important element to flying by instrument. Kate liked to practice her instrument skills because she never knew when the time would come that she wouldn't be able to see due to weather, smoke, or just the dust stirred up by the intense rotor wash of the powerful helicopter. Kate had been aware of the tragedy that struck the very first Delta Force operation in Iran when a naval helicopter pilot became disoriented during takeoff due to dust. The pilot drifted into a nearby C-130, and the disaster that ensued nearly cost the entire force their lives. It is not to blame the pilot but rather the training. The military learned from past mistakes, and modifications had been made; thus, Kate was focused on her instruments tonight. There was no better time to master the craft of instrument flying than when stress was low and conditions were good.

SIXTEEN

Hurricane force winds whipped up every loose particle within a fifty-yard radius under the Blackhawk as it approached for its landing. Michael had been on helicopters in the past but never grew tired of the ride. He could feel his heart rate start to climb as he watched the approach. Squinting his eyes, he finally had to look away due to the intensity of the gale force winds created by the rotor wash. He couldn't help but marvel at the sheer power of the Blackhawk.

Kate set the big bird down with all the precision one would expect of a military pilot. As soon as they were on the ground, she let off the collective control stick, reducing the rotor wash while keeping the turbine engines powered up so they could lift off as soon as their passenger was on board.

Michael felt the wind begin to fade against his body and quickly looked up and headed toward the cargo door of the Blackhawk. Morton had already slid the door open and was waving at him. As soon as Michael reached the doorway, the young specialist introduced himself.

"Good evening, sir, I'm Specialist Morton. May I take your bags?" he shouted with a smile.

Michael tossed his go bag to Morton who promptly tossed it to his crew chief. "Detective Garrett," he shouted as he climbed in.

Morton reached out and grabbed Michael by the arm, both helping him in and directing him to his seat for the flight. As he steered him toward an open space next to Sergeant Taylor, he advised the pilots they were good to go. The helicopter began to lift off before Michael had completely sat down. Once he was situated, Sergeant Taylor handed Michael a helmet of his own and plugged the communications link into the overhead.

"Passenger is on comm," Taylor advised the Blackhawk crew. "Nice to meet you, Detective. I'm Sergeant Taylor. I'll be your flight attendant this morning. If there is anything you require, please don't hesitate to ask."

Michael appreciated the humor. He was somewhat surprised at how chipper everyone was considering the time. "Thank you. Can you tell me what the in-flight movie will be?"

Stevens was already headed toward Los Angeles when Picone came over the headset. "Detective, I know you need to get to Los Angeles, but it's a big city. Can you be a little more specific?"

"I need to make a call. I have a contact in LA who will set the location if that works for you, Captain."

"Roger that, Detective. We'll use my phone to make the connection. It'll work a little better than yours." With that, Picone handed Taylor his cell phone and instructed the sergeant to connect it to the passenger comm unit.

Taylor quickly connected the phone to Michael's communications link and asked him what number he needed to dial. Michael pulled his cell phone from his pocket and scrolled through his contacts until he found the name he was looking for. He called out the number, and Taylor punched it in to the captain's phone. Once he had finished dialing, Taylor looked at Michael and gave him a thumbs-up.

Michael heard the ringing over his headphones. He continued to be amazed by the little things that he had never really considered, such as making a cell phone call from within a military helicopter and actually being able to hear the conversation. Even though it was 1:50 in the morning, Michael knew it was still Thursday night in Los Angeles, and David would no doubt be working. That's when he realized he hadn't even touched bases with David yet. Michael's heart sank with every ring that David didn't answer. What if he was tied up on a major case of his own and couldn't get cleared to help? "Fuck," Michael whispered.

"Just FYI, we can still hear everything you say, Detective," came Picone's voice over the headset. "Is there a problem?"

"Is there a problem? Who is this?" demanded a confused and somewhat unfriendly voice. David Ross had just answered his phone.

"David, it's Michael . . . kind of." As he scanned the helicopter at all who were listening. "I'm headed to LA courtesy of the Army National Guard."

"Michael?" David said sleepily. He was trying to wake up. "What's up, brother?" he said after a moment's silence. "Sorry about that, I was sleeping. What did you get yourself into now?"

"I'm on a case, a big one, and I need your help. We're going to be there in . . ." Stevens's voice broke into the conversation, "About two and half hours."

"I don't have anything pressing, so I'm good to go. Where do you want to meet?"

"That's the sixty-four-thousand-dollar question, my friend. These guys will land just about anywhere, so pick some place close, and I'll be there."

"Okay, make it the Redondo Beach Pier. My townhouse is only about ten minutes from there. You can fill me in when you get here. I'm gonna sack out and try to get a little more sleep. I'll see you when you get here."

"Sounds good. Thanks, David." Michael ran his thumb across his throat to indicate he was done with the call. Sergeant Taylor disconnected the line and handed Picone his cell phone.

Captain Picone quickly entered the coordinates into the Blackhawk's navigation system while Stevens continued on her flight. The helicopter was at full speed, and the weather was cooperating. "If everything stays as it is, we should be there slightly ahead of schedule," said Picone.

Michael settled back and closed his eyes. It had already been a long day, and he knew it wasn't anywhere close to being over. He hoped to get a little rest while he had the chance, but all he found himself doing was running through a mental list of things that had yet to be done. He had a sinking feeling that he was forgetting something; he just couldn't put his finger on it. It didn't help that he couldn't get the thought of Rosa and her entire family being executed if he failed out of his mind.

*   *   *

David hung up his phone and looked at the clock next to his bed again. It was almost 2:00 AM. He lay back in bed and began to wonder what exactly was going on. What had Michael said, he was on a big case and headed to Los Angeles, at two o'clock in the morning, courtesy of the National Guard. David sat up and turned the lamp on next to his bed. He was going to go back to sleep but figured it would only make it that much harder having to wake up in a measly two hours. He rubbed the sleep from his eyes, got up, and walked into the kitchen to get some coffee going.

He was a year older than Michael, had been married once, and had two children, Casey and Noah. His wife, Stephanie, had left him shortly after the birth of their second child. She blamed him, accusing him of loving his job more than his family. David tried to defend himself, explaining he didn't love his job, but he did have to do it. It was the same old argument every time he got called out, which inevitably occurred in the middle of the night or on weekends and holidays.

Shortly after his wife moved out, David found out she had moved in with her new boyfriend, some dipshit she met at the grocery store. It pissed him off more because he never saw it coming. He was supposed to be a detective and find the clues others missed. It hit him like a ton of bricks, but not having his children was even worse. The divorce had been ugly, but he was able to keep the townhouse. He figured the only reason his ex relented on that issue was because she was already living comfortably with her boyfriend. Otherwise, they split everything evenly except the custody of their children.

Stephanie was awarded custody of the children and, thus, was also granted child support. She made it clear all along that she didn't care about alimony, which her attorney had explained wouldn't be much as she made decent money already, and they had only been married for three years, but the child support she knew she could get until each child turned eighteen.

David didn't mind providing for his children. He made his payments willingly and stayed as involved with his kids as much as possible. He was supposed to pick them up later today for the weekend. He wondered if that was going to happen now or not. He would have to call Stephanie at a reasonable hour to let her know what was going on.

He had the coffee brewing and jumped in the shower. He was in no hurry, so he enjoyed the hot water and just watched the steam in his bathroom get thicker and thicker until it was like a foggy coastal morning in the fall. When he finally got out, he was wide awake and ready for whatever lay ahead. He dried off and wiped some of the fog off of the mirror. He was getting ready to shave but decided not to. He threw on a pair Levi's, a light grey T-shirt, and a short-sleeved dark blue button-down. He grabbed his socks and shoes and headed back to the kitchen for some coffee.

He looked at the clock on the stove. It was 2:37 in the morning. *Great*, he thought to himself, *only two hours to go*. Nothing was worse than anticipation, and at the moment, he didn't even know what to anticipate.

SEVENTEEN

Unable to relax, let alone sleep, Michael had covered every conceivable option he could think of during the flight, yet there was still one thing bothering him. *What am I forgetting?* he thought to himself. He had developed plans and contingencies depending on how things panned out with every step of his investigation while, at the same time, remembering what his grandfather always used to say when something didn't work out. "The best-laid plans of mice and men often go awry," referencing the poem by Robert Burns, of course made infinitely more famous by Steinbeck. He found himself wondering which his grandfather was referencing—the poem or the novel. The thought only lasted a moment as Picone's voice came over his headset, "We're five out."

Michael hoped that David would already be there, and he was. As Kate Stevens began to descend and slow the Blackhawk in preparation for landing, she could see someone standing in the sand at the entrance to the pier, waving a flashlight back and forth. She brought the giant helicopter down and touched the sand softly; this time, she cut the power completely. Everyone disembarked this time to stretch their legs while they could.

Michael and the crew of the Blackhawk made their way over to the pier where David was waiting with a thermos full of coffee and a stack of Styrofoam cups.

"I didn't know who all would be here, but I figured you might like a cup of joe." Everyone graciously accepted, and while David handed out cups and began to pour, the crew introduced themselves. Once everyone had a cup, Michael cut to the chase.

"So here's the deal. I got called out to assist Douglas County on a homicide last night. They've had a few homicides fairly recently with enough similarity that everyone was starting to get concerned. Nobody wanted to say it, but we figured we had a serial killer on our hands working the state line vicinity." Michael could see he was not just talking to David as he had the attention of the National Guardsmen as well. "Here's the twist. When I meet up with the

DCSO detective handling the case, he tells me that he thinks it *was* our guy. The suspect they had in custody was the intended victim."

"Wait, wait, wait," said David, "you have a homicide, and the victim turned into the suspect . . . so the victim killed the would-be attacker."

"Bingo for the kid with the coffee, but if you'll let me continue, I'll get to the good part."

"Okay, okay, please proceed."

"So during the interview, I recognize the suspect. We had gone to high school together only a few years apart . . ."

As Michael relayed the story to his audience, he could see everyone taking it all in. He could also see the wrath and compassion well up in each of them as they listened intently. Ultimately, it took him about fifteen minutes to summarize the nightmare that Rosa had been living for the past couple of years and what he needed to get done before the end of business Tuesday. When he finished, Captain Picone was the first to speak.

"You need anything else while you're working this case, you call me. I'm going to make arrangements right now to refuel, and we're going to stand by at El Toro for the day. If you need anything, let us know, and I'll make it happen."

"Thanks, Captain, I just may take you up on that," Michael replied.

David swallowed his last drink of coffee and said, "That is some crazy shit, Mike. If I didn't know better, I'd say you were full of it, but I know you aren't creative enough to make up a story like that. One problem I see on this end."

"Not exactly what I was hoping you were going to say, David."

"Look, man, I'm in for the long haul, you know that, but we're going to be hard-pressed to find that house. It sounds like we have a general location, but I can't tell you how many holes there are between Hollywood and East Los Angeles that are nothing more than crash pads for illegals and hookers, and any one of them could be owned by Eme. They aren't amateur and know how to cover themselves. Besides, we have everyone from Mexico to Guatemala hiding in this city. I don't know if you've heard, but the Mexican president wants to build a new residence in LA so he can be closer to his people."

David's joke couldn't have been timed better. Albeit brief, the moment of levity got the group to take a step back for just a moment as they had all been so drawn into the horrific tale.

"Saddle up, everyone, we're going to get the bird refueled and make arrangements to get some rack time. Detective, you have my number. Let me know if we can be of any further assistance," said Picone. With that, the Air Wolf crew headed back to the Blackhawk with the waves crashing in the background.

David slapped his friend on the shoulder. "Follow me, I'm parked over here, and we best get rolling if we're gonna meet your deadline."

EIGHTEEN

Carlos had followed the directions Detective Cook had given him, although they were unnecessary. He had some things to sort out and time to kill, so he figured he might as well go to Sam's Place and work things out. He had to find out what Rosa had already said to the police. As far as Carlos was concerned, she was finished either way, but her family still had a chance.

The last thing Eme wanted was to draw unnecessary attention to themselves. The drug cartels in Mexico were already making things more difficult. The more media attention they drew as a result of their extreme ways, the more money and resources the United States government allocated to help the Mexican government battle them. This had resulted in increased difficulty getting back and forth across the border undetected. The tunnels they used were good for the small shipments of the past; however, they were incapable of handling the sheer volume of traffic Eme was dealing with now.

It was time to let Rosa go. If Carlos could bail her out, he would simply kill her himself. If she was going to go to trial, he would have to make arrangements to have it done while she was in custody. What he wanted now was to talk to her face-to-face and see what she said. He knew he could get her to admit anything; Rosa was too emotional when it came to her family. If he thought she was lying, he merely had to bring up how he would enjoy torturing her father, and she would crack. Carlos smiled at the prospects; he loved his job. It gave him a sense of power that one could never realize until he watched and listened as another human being pled for her life and, later, simply begged to be killed and put out of her misery.

He looked at his watch and figured enough time had passed for the detective to have booked Rosa into the jail. He left some money on the table to cover his tab and headed out to his car. Once in his vehicle, he fished an old business card out his wallet he had received from a Douglas County deputy who had spoken to him about a fight in a bar that Carlos had witnessed. Carlos had said he didn't see anything, hoping the deputy would not ask him anything further. It had worked, but before the deputy moved on, Carlos asked him for a business card. Told him if he remembered anything, he would give him a call. In reality, he merely wanted the card to use if he ever got pulled over. It was one more way he tried to avoid tickets, dropping the name of a law enforcement officer, saying he was good friend. Sometimes it worked; sometimes it didn't.

Carlos dialed the number on the card and waited for someone to answer.

"Douglas County Sheriff's Department, how may I help you?" said a man on the other end.

"Hello, I'm with KTRA news in Reno. I understand you have the homicide suspect in custody from the Harrah's incident. I was wondering if there was a press release yet?"

"I am sorry, sir, there is no press release. You will need to contact our press information officer with any further questions," came the response.

"Well, can you at least confirm that someone is in custody?" Carlos asked.

"Yes, sir, a woman was booked earlier this morning, that's all I can say. If you have any—"

Carlos hung up. He had what he needed. He started his car, headed to the jail. It didn't take long, and Carlos was there. He pulled in around back, which was actually the front entrance, and parked the Buick. He went to the main entrance and pulled on the glass door. It was locked. A few seconds after tugging on the door, a voice came over a small speaker box in the cinder wall to the right of the door.

"Can I help you?"

"Yes, I'm here to post bail for someone."

"I'll buzz you in. Follow the green line," said the voice flatly.

Carlos waited until he heard the electronic clicking come from the door. He pulled the door open and stepped inside. He couldn't believe how easy it was to get into a secure facility. He looked around and found the green line they must have been referring to. He followed the line painted on the floor to another door. As he approached the door, he could see a small camera above it. He reached out to open the door, but it was also locked. At that moment, the lock buzzed, and he walked through. He stopped and waited for the door to close behind him this time. He wanted to see if he would need to be let out in the same fashion he was let in. The door clicked shut, and he attempted to push it back open. As he had suspected, he could not get out on his own. He continued to follow the line until he came to a counter with bulletproof glass protecting the person sitting on the other side.

"Hello, Officer . . ." Carlos looked at the name tag of the person sitting behind the glass. "Simmons. I'm here to post bail for an inmate."

"And who might that be? We have 402 in the facility at the moment," Simmons replied sarcastically.

"I'm sorry," said Carlos. "How foolish. She was just brought in. Rosa Jimenez."

"Just a moment while I'll pull up her information." Simmons entered the name into the jail's network system. "I'm sorry, sir, there is no one here by that name."

"There must be a mistake. I called earlier and spoke to someone who said she was in fact here. She was booked for the homicide at Harrah's."

"Sir, if that was the case, she would not have bail." Simmons was already growing impatient. He was only half through his shift, hated his current assignment, and, to make matters worse, was in the midst of winning a game of computer solitaire.

"There must be some mistake. Can you please check again to see if she is in custody? I understand the bail issue, but maybe I could speak with her. Rosa Jimenez, she must be here."

Just as Carlos was suggesting that there was a mistake, Officer Cruz happened to walk by. She overheard the man at the window asking for Rosa and remembered what Detective Cook had said. She stepped up to the window and whispered something in Simmons's ear Carlos couldn't hear.

"Sir, my partner said she would double-check our holding cells. Sometimes people are housed in a cell prior to being processed. That may be the error. I'll let you know as soon as I hear from her."

Carlos didn't like the whispering; something about it bothered him. There was no need for it. "No problem. Thank you for your time. By the way, is there a restroom I can use while I wait?"

"Sure, just go back out to the main lobby. I'll buzz you through. It'll be on the left."

Carlos gave a small nod, acknowledging the directions, and turned to walk out. Simmons grabbed his portable radio and advised Officer Cruz that the man asking to see Rosa might be leaving. Upon receipt of the message, Cruz hastened her pace. She wasn't heading to check on Rosa at all; she was going to a phone, one that was out of sight from the window so the man wouldn't know what she was doing. With the information that he had left, she went to the closest phone and called Detective Cook.

"This is Cook."

"Hey, this is Cruz from the jail. We just had a guy come in asking for your suspect. We tried to stall him, but I think he might be leaving."

"Okay, I'm on my way."

Cook was in his office, going over his notes from the interview when Cruz called. He pushed the paperwork away and grabbed a small flashlight he kept in his desk. If this guy was leaving, he wanted to get a look at him before he left. He wanted to know if it was the same guy although he already knew the answer.

Cook hurried to the main lobby where the unwelcomed visitor would have to exit the public entrance to the jail. His office was at the other end of the building, so he had to hurry. When he reached the lobby, he heard the main door closing.

Carlos had reached the door to the lobby. He knew that if Rosa had told the police anything, they were likely to just keep him locked in. He reached the door and tried to open it. It was secure; he could not get out. He looked for a box similar to the one he saw outside next to the main entrance. He found it and pushed the small silver button under the speaker. A voice crackled, "Can I help you?"

"Yeah, I'm trying to get to the bathroom, but the door is locked." Carlos figured it was the moment of truth. For just a moment, he couldn't believe Rosa had said something; but as he began to get angry at himself for getting locked in, the lock on the door released, and he was able to push the door open. At that, he reassessed the situation and assumed she had been quiet. He veered to the left and headed to the restroom, assuming the man at the counter was now watching him in the camera.

Cook reached the lobby just as Carlos entered the bathroom. He walked over to the bathroom and went inside. He pushed the door all the way open to ensure no one was behind it and made his way to the last urinal. The man he had hoped to get a look at had gone into one of the stalls. Cook was pissed. He stood there for a moment and then flushed so it wouldn't seem strange. He walked over to the sink to wash his hands, just trying to kill some time.

"Hey, Eric, is that you? These double shifts have got to be wearing on you by now." Cook waited for a response. He figured he would at least be able to place the voice, but there was no response. "You okay in there? You fall asleep or get stuck?"

Carlos didn't want to answer, but he could tell this guy wasn't going to go away. "Sorry, not Eric. Just got a bad case of the shits. I'd get out as fast as I could if I were you, it's gonna get ugly in a couple seconds."

Cook had what he needed. He recognized the voice. It also just dawned on him that this guy may have done the same. He shut off the water and walked out of the bathroom. He had to decide what to do and quickly. Let him go or stick around and say hi. He realized he hadn't really thought it through. He hadn't expected to get a call like this in the first place. If he made contact, it may jeopardize Garrett's investigation and Rosa's family, but he may have done that already. "Shit," he swore to himself as he stood in the lobby.

Carlos walked out of the bathroom at that very moment. He saw Cook instantly, and the recognition was clear on both of their faces.

"I thought you were going to Sam's," Cook asked as nonchalantly as he could.

"I did, until a friend of mine called to tell me she had been arrested. I came down to see if I could bail her out."

"You're a good friend. Well, I don't mean to be rude, but I have a ton work to do. Good luck to your friend."

"Thanks."

The two went their ways, both wondering what just happened. Cook was praying Carlos would simply consider it a coincidence and nothing more. Carlos was suspicious but uncertain. He headed back down to the counter to see what would happen next.

Cook got back to his office and called Cruz back. "Hey, when that guy comes back, just tell him that Rosa hasn't been processed yet, but that she will be held without bail until she can see a judge, which may not be until Tuesday."

"You got it . . . He just walked back up to the window." Cruz hung up and went back to the window where Simmons was just telling Carlos he hadn't heard anything yet. "Hi again. Your friend is here, and as I suspected, she has not been processed yet. Unfortunately, she is being held without bail due to the seriousness of her charges."

Carlos looked at the two officers on the other side of the glass for a moment, feigning disappointment. "Thank you anyway. Do you know if she can have visitors?"

Simmons responded this time. "I'm sorry, sir. Inmates are only allowed visitation by attorneys outside of regular visiting hours. You'll have to come back later."

With that, Carlos thanked the two for their time and left. As he drove back to his apartment, he couldn't help but wonder what was really going on. He thought it was quite the coincidence that he ran into the same detective in the bathroom. At the same time, the detective didn't seem to have any issues with his story. Maybe it was nothing. Either way, he couldn't stop thinking about it. He hated coincidences.

*　　*　　*

As soon as he got back to his office, Cook picked up the phone. He was going to call Michael and let him know what happened, just in case Carlos called someone and warned him. Cook didn't want him walking into a trap. He started to dial but hung up. The more he thought about it, he figured he was just overanalyzing the whole situation. It made perfect sense for him to be at the office. He worked there, and Carlos knew he was on the homicide case. He saw him earlier at the substation, and furthermore, Carlos's story was sound. There were phones in the holding cells; arrestees used them all the time to call lawyers and bail bondsmen. Cook hung up and went back to reviewing his notes. He would talk to Michael later.

* * *

As soon as he got back to his apartment, Carlos called Calexico.

Nineteen

Michael followed David to his vehicle parked along the sidewalk on Redondo Drive. It was approaching five in the morning, and people were already starting to show up at the beach for their morning exercise. Michael watched as runners and walkers alike were making their way down to the beach until they saw the large military helicopter. They all stopped and stared, undoubtedly wondering what was going on. The spectacle didn't last long as the flight crew was already on board, and the turbines started to whine. Shortly thereafter, it was lifting off and banking out over the sea. As the large helicopter departed, Michael could hear the people muttering among themselves as they began to go about their business.

David clicked the key fob, unlocking the doors of his LAPD detective car. It was a no surprise to Michael to see him driving a grey Ford Crown Victoria, the same car the city used for patrol since the early nineties when they went away from the Chevy Caprice. He opened the door and tossed his bag into the backseat and climbed in.

"Nice car, real incognito," Michael joked.

"Yeah, I know, but the price is right and the gas is free." David started the car, and they pulled away from the curb as Michael took one last look at the beach.

"So you think locating the house I was telling you about is a dead end at this point?" Michael asked.

"Unfortunately, yes. I've been working Vice for a couple years now, and we just don't come across stuff like that. The closest thing to that I've worked was an Asian massage parlor. The place had nothing to do with massages. We got a tip when some local tried to make an appointment and couldn't find the number on the Internet or in the phone book. So he walked in one day to see if he could get a massage and was told all business was by referral only. He said he saw a couple of girls that barely looked old enough to be in high school, let alone there, so he called it in."

"And . . ."

"And it turned out to be the biggest cases the department has had in some time. All the girls were smuggled in on a ship and forced to work there to pay off the debt for being brought to the land of opportunity. They were all given asylum, of course, and we were able to arrest a half-dozen people who were at the business, but we never caught the financers, the bigwigs. Pretty sure it was run by Chinese mafia, and just like Eme, they cover their tracks."

"If that's the case, then I need to get to Holtville. The next step is to make contact with Rosa's family . . ." Michael stopped in midsentence. It had just dawned on him what he was forgetting. He needed to call Rosa's parents to tell her father not to go to work. He hoped it wasn't too late as he recalled Rosa saying the man worked for a farmer. Having grown up in the area, Michael knew he would start his days before the sun rose. "I've got to get ahold of them before he leaves. I have to tell them we have his daughter. I don't have time for these kinds of mistakes. How could I have been so stupid?" Michael hadn't realized it, but he was still talking.

"You all right?" David asked, but there was no response. "Hey, bud! You forget this is supposed to be a two-way conversation."

Michael snapped back to reality. "Yeah, yeah, I just remembered what I had been forgetting."

"I gathered that. So fix the problem. There's still plenty of time. We have about 240 miles to go."

"I know. I will, we have to get them to safety and try to find out exactly how her dad contacted the guy who gave him the loan. You're sure your boss isn't going to have a problem with your involvement?"

"Absolutely not. I called in and told him I was going to hook up with you to assist on a case you had with local follow-up. As soon as I let him know it's another sex slavery case, I'll have carte blanche."

"If that's the case, then let's get this show on the road. We need to get to Holtville. We should be able to make it by eight o'clock if you put your foot in it. We'll contact the family first, and see where it leads."

David accelerated and steered the vehicle toward the Harbor Freeway, enjoying the fact that the major rush of traffic had not yet started. With any luck, they would miss it completely.

Michael fished his phone out and looked through his notepad for the phone number Rosa had given him. As soon as he found the number, he began to dial. He held the phone to his ear and raptly waited for someone to answer. It was on the second ring that he heard the gruff, raspy voice reflective of a man who'd worked outdoors in the dust under intense sun his whole life.

"Bueno."

"Mr. Jimenez, Enrique Jimenez?"

"Yes, this is Enrique."

Michael sighed in relief, hearing the strongly accented English. "Mr. Jimenez, my name is Detective Michael Garrett. I went to school with your daughter, Rosa. I just finished talking with her."

Enrique Jimenez could not believe what he was hearing. He had talked to his daughter not that long ago, and it seemed nothing had changed; nothing was getting better. He hoped with all his heart he would one day see her again; he had to just get by. He suffered a little more every day he went without seeing or hugging his Rosa, knowing it was all his fault. She had urged him not to do it, but he was too proud to simply keep working for somebody else. He wanted something to leave his family. He never imagined this is how his children would remember him. The man who let his daughter be taken right out from under him and forced to do God knows what. He stood silently in the kitchen with the phone pressed to his head, his wife working around him, fixing his breakfast.

The line was silent for some time. "Mr. Jimenez, are you still there? Did you hear me?" Michael asked.

"Yes, yes, I heard you," the accented voice said. "How can this be?"

"Sir, it's a long story, and I can't tell you over the phone. What I need you to know is that she is okay for now, and I am on my way to your house. You have to stay home today! Do you understand?"

"I have work, I work every day to try and get her back."

"Not today. You have to stay home. Your safety and the safety of your family depend on it. Please, you have to stay home. We have to talk." Michael could hear Enrique sniffle on the other end. He could only imagine the horror that the man lived with wondering where his daughter might be and what was happening to her, not knowing exactly what was going on now, and having some relative stranger call him and tell him he had just talked to his Rosa. Michael wondered when the last time Enrique had the chance to speak with her.

"Okay, I stay home. Where are you?"

"I am in Los Angeles now, but I'm headed to Holtville now. I'll be there as fast as I can."

"Okay, thank you. Thank you very much."

Michael hung up, took a deep breath, and looked at David. "Thank God. That could have been a showstopper."

"So why don't you fill me in on the rest of the details while we drive? I have a feeling the version you gave me earlier is rather like Cliff Notes. Great for a high school book report, but not gonna cut it in the real world."

"You got it," Michael said as he reached into the backseat to grab his bag. He pulled his digital recorder out and hit Play. He and David then listened to the interview and Rosa's incredible story in full. This time, Michael took notes of key elements while he listened. David just kept driving. They were making great time, and by the time the recorder stopped, they had reached Interstate 10 East and were well on their way to the small border town of Holtville.

*   *   *

Enrique placed the telephone down on the counter. He was so taken aback by what had just been told he didn't even hang it up. He was awash with emotion. His wife, Martha, had stopped preparing breakfast and stood next to her husband. She had heard his half of the conversation and seen his expression become so solemn. She knew who ever it was on the phone was talking about Rosa.

"Enrique, what is it? Is it about Rosa?"

His eyes became glossy as the tears began to well up in the corners. He gazed at his wife as a tear began to trickle down his cheek. "The man said he talked to our Rosa. He is on his way here now from Los Angeles to talk with us."

"What did he say about Rosa? Is she okay? Is she with him? What is going on?" Martha couldn't believe what she was hearing; she didn't understand what was going on. She began to cry.

Enrique went to his wife and grabbed her in his arms. He held her tight. "I don't know what is going on, but I think it is good. This man, Detective Michael Garrett, he said he went to school with Rosa. He didn't say much else. I don't think she is with him, but I think he is helping her. It was his voice, it wasn't bad. I think the Lord is finally answering our prayers."

Enrique squeezed his wife, and she hugged him back. They had been so devastated in the days and weeks after Rosa had been taken that they completely abandoned any plans they had made to try and go to Mexico. All they wanted was to get their daughter back. They went into their bedroom and knelt down in front of a humble statue of the Virgin Mary they had on a small table they used as a nightstand and began to pray that their little girl was finally coming home.

Then they waited.

TWENTY

It was 6:45 AM, and they were racing down Highway 86; it was a four-lane road now with two lanes in each direction and a large dirt median separating them. Michael remembered the last time he had been home, the highway was still nothing more than one lane in each direction. The road followed the Salton Sea for quite some time. It was the largest body of water in California, and its surface was 226 feet below sea level.

"In all the years we've known each other, I never realized just exactly where you grew up," marveled David.

"We're not there yet, but we should be in about an hour."

"You ever come out and ski or fish here?"

"Not a chance, my friend. Although the water looks tempting, it's fed by the filthiest, nastiest rivers on the planet. The New River comes into the U.S. from Mexicali, and it is basically an open-water sewer, nothing but floaters and other sorts of excrement filling up the Salton Sea."

"Nice," David replied, disgusted.

"Yeah, tell me about. One more reason to build a dam on this side of the border and just let the river back up. My mom and grandparents used to use the sea as a source of recreation, both fishing and skiing, but that ended almost forty years ago now."

As they approached Brawley, Michael told David of a little taco stand he remembered on the west end of town. "We should stop and grab a bite to eat and some coffee. I don't know about you, but your coffee was good but didn't quite stick to my ribs like a good breakfast burrito will."

"Sounds good. I need to stretch my legs anyway," responded David.

As they pulled into town, David couldn't believe how sun washed all the buildings looked. The faded paint only added to the dilapidated appearance of the buildings; many of which were tagged with graffiti or had construction-style, pop-up chain-link fences around them.

"What the hell happened to this place? It looks like an atomic test site," David proclaimed.

"I know, it's not exactly the jewel of Imperial County, but wait until you have one of the local breakfast burritos," Michael responded. He kept looking for the little taco shop until, the next thing he knew, the little city was coming to an end, and there were nothing but agricultural fields on either side of the highway.

"Wow, that was good. Glad you got my hopes up for nothing. Of course now I'm really hungry. At least before I wasn't thinking about it."

"Yeah, yeah. Well, after your comment, I figured you wouldn't want to stop anyway. Just put the hammer down. We'll be in Holtville in twenty minutes if you'd quit driving like my grampa."

David took the bait, and predictably, fifteen minutes later, they could see the small iconic Holtville water tower and what looked like a grove of palm trees on the horizon. The water tower had been there for over a century and stood nearly 150 feet. Although it had been empty for nearly forty years, the city council never bothered to have it taken down. As a result, it had become the symbol of the town. The palm trees reached nearly seventy-five feet into the sky and swayed so dramatically in the wind they were referred to as the dancing ladies by many of the town's residents.

Michael loved the sight; to him it meant one thing—he was almost home. He had always been fond of returning to his roots and visiting with old friends. The city only had around five thousand people in it and was little more than a mile in any direction. Michael used to joke when explaining to others where he had grown up that if they blinked, they'd miss it. David was starting to realize it wasn't really that much of joke.

"Where to from here?" David asked.

"Just take this to the end and hang a left. That'll be Evan Hewes Highway, and it'll drop us off on Main Street in downtown. Then we can get that breakfast that is slightly overdue. I know a spot that is still open and will have been worth the wait."

*   *   *

It was just after 8:00 AM as they passed a wooden sign on the outskirts of town that read, Welcome to Holtville. David followed the old highway into town and noticed it was much different than he had expected. It was definitely not a booming metropolis, but it did have much more of a small-town feel. They came to a lone Stop sign on the corner of Fifth Street, which everyone referred to as Main Street, and Holt Road. There was a large park on the left side of the road, with green grass and at least twenty of the dancing ladies they had seen from afar.

"This is just about the middle, my friend. We are now on our way out of town."

"You have got to be shitting me!" said David.

"Nope, but don't worry, the Taco Shop is just ahead, and I know it's still open. My mom eats there every once in a while and always rubs it in because she knows how much I like the food."

Three and half blocks later, they were parking in front of the Taco Shop. Business was good for the little restaurant. Although there were parking spaces to spare, it was largely because it shared the lot with the local grocery store. Michael and David each untucked their shirts, covering up their guns. It was more instinct than anything, but neither wanted to be immediately identified as a cop. Even though most everyone knew Michael was a police officer, there was no need to broadcast the fact to those not really paying attention.

Shirt out and weapon covered, David opened the door of his car when the heat rushed in. It was only a little more than three hours ago that he was standing on the coast in the early morning, enjoying the sixty-degree weather. He hadn't thought about it as he had the air-conditioning on in his car for the entire ride down. The cool interior helped keep him awake on long drives. Nor had it registered when they passed the bank across from the big park that had the digital sign that blinked between the time and the temperature. David recalled seeing one hundred pop-ups in round yellowish lights, but it wasn't until now that he realized it was the temperature.

"Holy Hades, man, it's only eight o'clock in the morning."

"What are you complaining about? Wait until it warms up this afternoon. This is nice." Michael chuckled to himself. Even he thought it was warm, having acclimated more than he may have realized to the wonderful Sierra temperatures.

"This is bullshit. I'm already starting to sweat, and I didn't bring a change of clothes."

"Can we just go inside and eat? We have work to do."

Twenty minutes later, they were leaving the small family-run restaurant. David pushed the heavily tinted glass door open and was instantly reminded of just how hot it was. He paused momentarily in the doorway, only to be pushed from behind by Michael.

"Don't be a chicken, it's just little sunshine."

"Yeah, yeah, yeah . . . ," David grumbled. "So I take it we're headed to Rosa's parents' house to try to get a lead on this guy Fernando, the carnale Rosa mentioned."

"Unless you have a better idea, that's the next step. We have to do two things—find out what the parents can tell us, and find a way to get them and their family out of the area undetected for safety. There's no way of knowing what this guy Carlos has done thus far, but if La Eme are as organized as I think they are, he will be reporting the night's events to someone." Truth be told, that was what worried Michael the most. He was trying to stay ahead of the curve and hoped that making the trek overnight had worked. He had until Tuesday to make his case, but he had no illusions that it would take that long before Rosa's handler started making phone calls.

The two men climbed into the vehicle, both feeling less than invigorated following the giant breakfast burritos they had just devoured. Folding themselves into the front seat sent a message to each that they had better not need to chase anyone in the near future, or they'd be getting a second look at their meal. Michael looked over at David, recognizing the look on his face, and imagined he must look the same, but it was worth every bite, he thought to himself. "Okay, how do we get there?" asked David.

Michael guided David to Alvarado Avenue. They headed back in the direction they came and turned right at the city park. David couldn't believe just how small the town really was. He remembered the stories his friend had shared with him, but much like the Grand Canyon, photos and tales just didn't do it justice. You had to see it for yourself to truly appreciate the reality of it, not that the little town rivaled the canyon. The reality of it was that the city could fit within the canyon walls.

"So this is it, huh? The hometown you used to tell me so many stories about. How could you have done half the shit you talked about in this little city?" David mused.

"Easy, the city limits only hold the city back, not the residents. If we get things taken cared of in time, I'll give you the grand tour. In the meantime, hang a left. We'll be there in a couple of minutes."

There were vehicles headed through the city in all directions. Mostly trucks, some of which were towing tractors. David expected as much based on the great expanse of agriculture he observed on the way into town; what he didn't expect was the immense size of some of the tractors. Having never seen anything but a backhoe or bulldozer working construction sites, the agricultural tractors were new to him. When one rig went by with a windrower, a farm machine nearly twenty feet wide used for cutting hay and alfalfa locally, he instantly realized why the roads were twice as wide as those in most areas.

"You're gonna have to tell me about that thing on my tour," he said as the behemoth tractor went by.

It wasn't but a few more blocks, and it appeared as if they were already headed out of town. The city blocks seemed to come to an end rather quickly.

David was starting to think he might have missed something, when Michael pointed to what appeared to be a small housing development up on the left.

"We always called it Tortilla Flats as a kid. I don't know exactly where the name came from, presumably because the residents were predominantly Hispanic." It didn't even make sense to Michael as the city itself was largely the same. Regardless of reasoning, everyone knew where you were headed if you told them Tortilla Flats. "Anyway, Alvarado is the middle street. It should be the second to last house on the right."

David turned onto the road, thinking he had a little farther to go, when he immediately realized Alvarado was no more than a couple hundred yards, if that. The homes were small. Most didn't have garages; thus, everyone was parked on the street. The homes varied in color from off-white to light earth tones, with a couple that stood out more so than the rest. One was pink and the other a light yet bright green. More than half of the houses had short chain-link fences stretching from the edge of the sidewalks that ran the length of the street on both sides, all the way around the property. The front yards were a mix between overgrown grass in need of attention to well-manicured lawns that would make anyone proud, with others that had more dirt and weeds than anything else.

The end of the small development opened up to a large gulch created by erosion over the years from the Alamo River. The river itself, no more than fifty feet wide, ran through the center of the gulch. It was completely hidden by the mass of gnarly old mesquite trees growing along its banks.

Nearly halfway down, David began looking for a place to park. He was surprised how many vehicles were still there despite it being eight thirty on a Friday. "What's with all the cars? Don't these people work?"

"Yeah, they work, some for twelve to sixteen hours a day. They also believe in the extended family concept. Something many Americans seemed to have forgotten. Take you and I for instance, we both live by ourselves, when we could have stayed home, helped our families with bills, and everyone would be better off."

"It does make sense when you put it that way, but it would be weird to be our age and still live with your parents."

"That's because that's what our culture has taught us. Kind of screwed up, when you consider how much better off many of us would be if we didn't think like that."

David found a place two houses down from the Jimenez address and parked his car. He and Michael gave each other a look indicating they were ready, or at least as ready as one could be for something like this, and got out. Michael grabbed his bag, and the two headed for the house.

"David, I don't know if the parents will cooperate or not. Eme may have been hounding them just like that fuckstick Carlos did Rosa. If they think cooperating with us will get her killed, we may be at another dead end."

"Well, that's why you brought me. I can sell ice to Eskimos . . . But on a serious note, that's where we offer to take the whole family and move them for protection. One call and my captain will have a team of guys and truck ready to relocate the Jimenez family to an unknown location if they'll agree."

"You guys have way too many resources. I thought that was only the U.S. Marshals that did stuff like that."

"We don't provide a new identity or anything, we just help get them moved. Get them out of harm's way, so to speak."

They had reached the house. There was a small gate in the three-foot chain-link fence, allowing access to the yard. Through the gate was a small cement walkway leading to the front door. Before Michael could even open the gate, Enrique opened the door and walked out to meet him. Michael and David met the man halfway.

"Mr. Jimenez," Michael said as he offered his hand. "I am Detective Garrett, this is partner Detective Ross."

"Please come in, Detectives. My wife has made coffee if you would like." He grabbed Michael's hand, giving it a gentle shake while placing his other hand on Michael's shoulder, directing him toward the open door. "Please, come in."

TWENTY-ONE

Martha Jimenez was anxiously waiting inside. She had made a fresh pot of coffee for their guests and had already poured two cups and placed them on the kitchen table. She was a nervous wreck; the anticipation of finding out what was going on was driving her crazy. She had tried to stay busy while they waited; both she and Enrique tried to stay busy for that matter. It didn't matter; the anticipation of what was to come was the worst.

Now that the man was coming in, she couldn't contain herself any longer.

Michael stepped through the doorway first. He was immediately greeted by Martha. She was a short woman with short greying hair. She had extremely expressive eyes and olive skin. Michael could instantly see that Rosa took after her mother. She walked toward the men as they entered and then stopped short of reaching them. "Please come with me." And she led them into the kitchen and pulled out the two seats at the table with coffee in front of them.

Michael introduced himself as did David. Enrique was right behind them and introduced his wife. They took their seats at the small square table. Enrique sat across from them. Martha was getting cream out of the refrigerator just in case either man would like some. She had already placed sugar on the table. She set the cream in the middle of the table and sat next to her husband.

Michael took out his notepad and the digital recorder. He placed both on the table but didn't open the book nor start recording. He looked at both Enrique and Martha for a moment. They each took a deep breath and leaned forward. Michael knew the only way to get to the end was to start at the beginning, and he believed the parents had a right to know everything that was going on. With that, he began.

Michael began with how he came to meet Rosa. He explained that he was a detective working for the El Dorado County Sheriff's Department in South Lake Tahoe. The Jimenezes looked slightly confused at first as they had assumed he worked for the Los Angeles Police Department. Michael explained that he had started in LA and then moved to Northern California and taken a job there. He told Rosa's parents that she had been attacked by a man he believed to be a serial killer and how she had defended herself and killed the man, which resulted in her being arrested.

Michael was working on the homicide with Detective Cook from Douglas County, Nevada, since the actual attack occurred just outside Harrah's Casino, literally across the street from the state line. As Michael was relaying the story, Enrique and Martha had sat back in their chairs. They sat quietly, holding each other's hand. Martha began to cry at the thought of her daughter going through such an ordeal while Enrique simply couldn't believe what he was hearing.

Michael told them it was when he arrived to interview Rosa that he realized he recognized her from high school. When he asked her what had happened, she proceeded to tell him the most astonishing chain of events that led her to where she was today.

"Rosa told me all about the money you had borrowed to use as a down payment for your land in Cuernavaca, and how some men showed up at your house one day and demanded you make a $30,000 payment immediately. She explained how they beat the two of you and then kidnapped her."

Upon hearing the story out loud, Enrique hung his head in shame. Not a day had passed that he did not think about what had happened that fateful evening, but hearing it out loud seemed to make it even worse. He felt embarrassed and ashamed as he sat in front of these two men and next to his wife.

Michael could see how deeply the memories cut into Enrique. He stopped for a moment, looking at the father before him. He couldn't help but feel for him, but not being a father, he could not fathom the depths of sorrow and guilt that Enrique truly felt.

David reached forward toward Enrique. He placed his hand gently down on the small table in front of the ashamed father. "Mr. Jimenez, I know how you must feel. I have a daughter too, sir, but I want you to know there was absolutely nothing else you could have done. If you had tried, you would all be dead, as it stands right now, you are going to get your daughter and your life back."

Enrique looked up at the detectives in front of him. His eyes were read with anger yet filled with tears of sadness. "You say you know, but how can you? This did not happen to your family, your daughter. You know nothing about how I feel. I wish I was dead, I would have traded my life in an instant to keep my daughter from these men."

His wife leaned in to him, gently releasing his hand only to wrap her arms around his body and hug him tightly. She had only seen him like this a few times in all the years they had been married. He was normally the most patient and kind man she had ever known. When they had lost Rosa to these men, she had not only lost her daughter, but much of the man next to her as well. He had not been the same since.

"I understand your anger, and I am sorry. I do not mean to offend you. I just want you to know there was nothing else you could do," said David. "We are going to get her back."

Michael didn't want to lose his momentum by having the parents become too emotional. He knew if he gave them too much time to think about everything, it would only prolong the process as he would have to allow them time to grieve all over again. He grabbed his cup of coffee and quickly added sugar to it. He began stirring rapidly, clanking the spoon onto the sides of the coffee mug loudly. He could see that everyone was somewhat distracted by it and quickly broke back into the critical events that led them to this moment.

"The man that loaned you the money, the men that were sent to collect it, and the man that had Rosa yesterday, are all part of the Mexican Mafia," Michael said.

"We know that now, Detective, but had I known that at the time, I would have never even considered meeting with that man in Mexicali." Enrique took a deep breath and let it out slowly. "So Rosa is okay, but where is she right now? How do you know she is safe?"

"After I talked with her and she told me what had happened to all of you, she was taken to the Douglas County Jail. I know it may sound strange, but it's the only place I know she'll be safe until I get this taken cared of. That's why I am here now. I was hoping you could tell me more about this Fernando and how you contacted him."

Enrique looked at Martha and back at the detectives. "They told me if I ever talked to the police, they would kill all of my children. They said they would make us watch as they cut their throats, and then they would make me watch as they raped and killed my wife. I am willing to die for my daughter, but I cannot be responsible for the death of my entire family."

"I understand, Mr. Jimenez. It is a terrifying prospect to think that talking to me would cause such atrocity to be brought onto your family. Rosa has been living with just that for the past year and half, sir. She has done the unconscionable in hopes of getting you out from under these men, but she finally realized neither of you will ever be free. That's why she told me. She trusted me enough to let me help. Now you need to trust your daughter. She has sacrificed enough. If you will help me, you will be helping her." Michael pleaded with Enrique. He knew that not only was it going to be nearly impossible to succeed without more information, La Eme would likely kill them anyway. He was holding on to that information, hoping not to have to mention it. The family had been through enough; they were already terrified as it was. It would serve no purpose at this moment to scare them even more.

Martha let go of her husband and stood up from her chair. Pushing the chair back, she turned to him and placed a hand on his face. "Talk to them, my love. We have all suffered enough. If Rosa trusted this man to help, it is the least we can do to honor her. Tell him what you can. Answer his questions. We will deal with what happens like we have dealt with everything else this life has brought us, together." With that, she leaned down and kissed his forehead.

Looking at his wife, Enrique nodded as if to say, *As you wish, my love.* He then looked back at Michael. "I will tell you what I can. What would you like to know?"

"The man you met in Mexicali. How did you contact him? What can you tell me about the meeting?"

"I was told I could find him at the Café Nueva Asia in Mexicali. All I had to do was call the café and ask for Fernando, so I did. They took a message, and he called me back. We set a time to meet, and that's when I secured the loan so we could buy our property."

"Can you tell me his last name?"

"Ortiz, his name was Fernando Ortiz. I will never forget it, although he never told me his last name. It was the men that came to my home that called him that. They referred to him as Señor Ortiz."

Michael was taking notes now. He finished talking with Enrique, gathering as much information as he could about Fernando Ortiz. When they were done, Michael had what he had come for, the next piece to the puzzle. He knew he was far from finished, but his case was getting stronger. Enrique would be able to identify Señor Ortiz, which was as good as evidence in a trial. Every facet of the investigation he could use as evidence put him one step closer to closing his case and getting Rosa and her family out from under the constant fear of death.

"There is one last thing. Mr. Jimenez, we are prepared to move you and your family to a safe location. Detective Ross need only make a phone call, and a team from the Los Angeles Police will relocate you."

"We are not leaving until we can all leave together. If what you say is true, and you are going to help us, then there is no need to go anywhere. Correct?"

"Mr. Jimenez, it's not that I am not going to finish this, but until I do, you may be in danger. The man I told you about, Carlos, he may call Fernando and tell him what has happened. I am concerned that they will then try to get to you as a way to send a message to Rosa, reminding her not to say anything. If I could tell her that you have been moved to a safe location, she would feel better. Do they know where your sons live? Can you stay with one of them for a few days?"

"I don't think they know where my boys live. But I cannot be sure, and I will not place them in danger. We will stay at our home, and I will go to work as usual. We still have bills to pay, and if I don't work, they don't get paid."

"I understand," said Michael, "but if you change your mind, please call me. Day or night, I'll answer." With that, David and Michael excused themselves and bid the Jimenezes farewell. As they made their way back to car, they began to talk about the next step. They needed a place to sit down and make some phone calls and try and gather some more information on Fernando Ortiz.

"David, I think it's time I showed you where I lived. We can use my mom's place to make our calls, and besides, I'd never hear the end of it if I didn't stop by while I was in town."

"Sounds good to me. I need a place to go to the bathroom anyway," said David as he tossed his keys to Michael. "This way I can take in the vast scenery."

Catching the keys, Michael cracked a wry smile. "Just don't bag on the city in front of my mother. She's very active in the community." Which was an understatement. Louise Garrett was a retired local business owner, the president of the Chamber of Commerce, a commissioner on the board of Housing Authority, a member of the Soroptimist Club, and sang soprano in the church choir, and, in her youth, had once reigned as the queen of the Carrot Festival, the annual celebration recognizing the city as the carrot capital of the world.

They pulled away in the Crown Vic and headed the short distance to Michael's old home. They had been at the Jimenez residence longer than they realized. It was a little after ten thirty now. The day was rushing by, and the temperature was rising. What they didn't know, what they couldn't know, was that as they rounded the corner at the end of the block, circling around the neighborhood, another vehicle heading out the other way would be following them.

Twenty-Two

It was not much more than a mile to the home where Michael had spent his youth. He pulled into the driveway, parking next to the little white Ford Ranger his mother drove. Despite the house having a three-car garage, there was scarcely room for one vehicle, and it was occupied by a 1972 Jeep CJ5. It had been Michael's first vehicle. He spent an entire summer with his father restoring it from the ground up, and he never could bring himself to part with it. He left it with his parents, and his father used to drive it on weekends just to keep it going. It hadn't been driven near as much since his father had died a few years earlier.

"Well, the good news is my mom is home. Not that I expected she'd be gone, but since I don't have my key, it is best we didn't have to break in," said Michael.

"It amazes me just how small this town is. You could see the fields just down the road. Let me guess, that's the school you went to?" David asked quirkily, pointing south to the end of the block.

"Yep, kindergarten through fifth grade, then I went to junior high, which is only a couple blocks that way," Michael responded, pointing east. "And we already passed the high school on the way over here. I'll give you the nickel tour later," he added.

As they walked up to the front door, David couldn't help but notice the front garden. Amazingly, Louise Garrett had managed to maintain a beautiful flower garden despite the intensity of the summer sun. There was no other like it on the block. When they reached the door, Michael gave the handle a try; it was still locked. He rang the doorbell and stepped to the side of the small window that ran down the center of the door. Although it wasn't a social visit, he did want to surprise his mother a little.

A few seconds later, the bolt could be heard being drawn back into the door as his mother turned the latch on the other side. She opened the door to great her guests and, for a moment, was speechless.

"Surprise! Thought we'd drop in for a champagne brunch," Michael said as he stepped in and gave his mother a hug. "You remember David? We went to the academy together."

His mother squeezed him tightly and kissed his cheek. It had been too long since he had been home as far as she was concerned. She let go and looked at David. "Of course I remember him, I am not that forgetful in my old age," she joked. "It's nice to see you again, David." And she gave him a hug as well.

They stepped in, and she closed the door behind them. Michael walked into the kitchen; it had always been the place where everyone congregated.

"I wish you would have called, I would have put my face on," Louise said, referring to her makeup. She always felt as if she had to have a little makeup on to be presentable. Nothing could have been further from the truth. She was a fair-skinned woman who had taken care of her skin for the better part of life, except for a few years when she spent weekends on a boat and water skiing. That being the case, she looked ten (if not fifteen) years younger than she was. At sixty-five, she could easily pass for fifty. It didn't hurt that she also had a beautiful red hair with only a hint of grey.

"What fun would that be? There's absolutely no thrill in telling someone you're going to surprise them. Besides, we're actually working a case, Mom. I didn't know I was coming until earlier this morning. It's a long story. In any case, we need a place to do a little homework, and I knew you wouldn't mind."

"Make yourself at home. You know where everything is."

The statement couldn't have been truer. Michael had moved out nearly ten years ago, and the house looked exactly the same. His mother was never much for major changes; whether it was because she was always busy with her business or simply happy with what she had, things were still where they had been when he left.

"Can I get you boys anything to drink?" she asked.

"I could go for anything cold, Mrs. Garrett," replied David.

"I'm good for now, Mom, thanks," said Michael. He was already spreading his notes out on the kitchen counter.

She poured a glass of iced tea for David and asked, "So what exactly brings you boys my way?"

David responded while Michael poured over his notes, making a list of things to do. "Michael caught a homicide last night where the intended victim actually took out the bad guy. Then during the interview, this victim tells a story about being kidnapped and forced into prostitution to help her family pay off a dirty loan."

"That's horrible, but how does that get you involved, and why are you here now?"

"Well, it turned out she was first forced to work the streets in LA, so Mikey there thought I might be of some assistance. Unfortunately, the big city was a bust for leads on this ring of human sex traffickers, so Holtville was the next stop. They went to school together, and her family still lives here."

"You have got to be kidding me!" Louise was aghast that such a thing could have originated in what she still considered the quaint and quiet little town of Holtville. "Who was it?"

Although Michael wasn't talking, he was paying attention. "I think it would be best to leave that part out for the time being, Mom. The family is in danger as it is, and I don't know just how bad this will get. We only have a few days to make a case against these guys, which is why I've been working all night, otherwise, I'm afraid Rosa and her family will be killed. I'll tell you the rest when I know everyone is safe. Okay, Mom . . ."

Louise didn't understand why it was an issue. Her son had always shared things with her throughout his career in law enforcement. Although, truth be told, he only told her a fraction of the things that he had done, enough to satisfy her curiosity and make for a good conversation, yet never anything too hairy that would make her worry more than she already did.

"Fair enough, but you two better be careful. You better call for backup before you go charging in somewhere."

"Yeah, yeah, Mom. We will, right now we just have to do our homework. I need to use the computer, if you don't mind."

Louise grabbed her laptop off of her dining room table. She handed it to Michael and told him she had finally gotten a wireless modem, so he could access the Internet anywhere in the house. He placed the computer on the counter, opening it up, and hit the power button.

"I can't believe you finally broke down and bought a laptop. You had that old IBM for . . . I don't know how long. It must have been hard to move into the twenty-first century."

"Keep it up, you little twit. I'll unplug the damn thing if you're not careful," Louise threatened, referring to the modem.

Michael laughed. "I haven't heard that one in a while," referring to being a called a twit. It was what his mother always called him when she was feigning anger when he was a child. It wasn't until she used his full name that he knew he was really in trouble.

The computer was up and running. Michael double clicked on the icon to open the Internet and began his query. He was looking for phone numbers.

*   *   *

Jose Calderon and Miguel Rios had followed Michael and David from the little home on Alvarado Street. They knew the house well; they had been there many times before checking up on the people who lived there. They had only been inside the house once, about eighteen months ago. Although both men recalled the incident, it wasn't because it was particularly different from what they did from one day to the next. It was because of Rosa. They had both talked about her and how they were pissed that Carlos took her to Los Angeles before they could have at her.

It was far more common for them to all take a turn with a new piece of ass. They never looked at their victims as women (or girls in some cases); they merely considered them to be merchandise. A commodity to be sold. As such, they considered what they did necessary to break them in, break their spirit and prepare them for what was to come. More often than not, they would gang-rape their prey, taking turns for half the day or night. It was different for some reason when it came to Rosa, and they never really knew why. They both figured that Carlos stole her away because she was so attractive. He wanted her, the same way they did, but he wanted her first and to himself.

Today, their reason for being back in the neighborhood was different. They had received a phone call from Carlos in the middle of the night. He had told them that Rosa had been arrested for murder, and that she may have talked. He wasn't sure, but he wanted the family watched to see if they altered their routine or had any visitors. They all had hoped that she hadn't, for if it were true, they would simply kill the family, which was of no great loss, but they would also have to kill Rosa too.

Killing Rosa would result in great financial loss. She earned more money than any ten other girls combined. Where most of these sex slaves were locked up in rooms or brothels, drugged, terrorized, and basically raped, the price was never very high. $50 to $100 dollars was all they were worth, the younger girls fetching the higher price. Then after they were broken completely, addicted to the drugs and so terrified of getting beaten again, they wouldn't run; they were pushed out onto the street where they turned tricks until they overdosed, got killed, or simply quit earning. In which case, Jose and Miguel would simply make them disappear. This is why everyone hoped Rosa had kept her mouth shut, but if she hadn't, she would die like the rest, for it would be much harder to prove anything if there was no one to talk.

Jose and Miguel had parked on the opposite side of the street in the middle of the block and watched as the obviously unmarked police car drove past them and parked a couple houses away. They knew they would not be seen as they sat in the back of their tan 1977 GMC Gypsy van. Although similar to the one they had transported Rosa in, this one had dark tint on the side and rear windows so they could see out while others could not see in. Thus, they sat in the back of the van and watched as the two men walked to the house. Obviously law enforcement of some sort, with their button-down shirts untucked to conceal their sidearm. It worked for anyone who didn't know what to look for, but Jose and Miguel weren't just anyone. They both recognized the slight bulge on the right side as the shirts didn't fall naturally to the side. Then there was the haircut. Although short hair was in style, it was the military taper that only added to the look. The only thing these two lacked was the motor cop mustache, but that would come with time. They were young; it wasn't until cops hit their forties that they seemed to grow the mustache if they were going to.

They watched everything unfold, as Rosa's father met them outside, and her mother waited inside. Although they couldn't see or hear what transpired inside, the two detectives were there way too long for the visit to be anything but what they had feared. Jose and Miguel knew what was to come, but for now, they needed to try and find out just how much these two knew. The family was easy; they could be controlled, until they were dealt with for the last time. Depending on just how much the officers knew would determine whether or not they would be killed as well.

Jose slid into the driver's seat and waited for the unmarked car to get out of sight. As soon as it was, he pulled away and slowly eased up to the corner. When he saw them pull out the next block down, he pulled out and began to follow them. He drove slowly, allowing them to get about three blocks ahead. He didn't know where they were going, but if they stayed in the city, the car would stick out no matter where it was; and if they headed for the highway, he would need the distance and more to remain undetected.

Miguel sat in the back with a silenced TEC-9 resting on his lap. Although it was classified as a semiautomatic pistol by the Bureau of Alcohol, Tobacco, Firearms and Explosives, it was anything but. Miguel had converted his to a fully automatic 9mm machine pistol. He had it loaded with a fifty-round magazine and had another wedged in the seat next to him just in case the first fifty wasn't enough. The gun was inherently inaccurate, but what it lacked in accuracy was made up for by the volume of lead it could send downrange.

He kept the pistol ready in the event they needed to shoot first and ask questions later. However, if during the course of their own investigation they determined they would have to kill these two newcomers, they also had a much more effective arsenal in the back. In the meantime, they continued to follow the grey car ahead of them.

Jose watched as the car turned left a few blocks up. He negotiated a left turn at the next block and speed to the other end. He waited long enough for the other car to emerge at the other end. When it didn't, he turned right and went to the same street the other car had turned down. He slowed down as he went past the street; Miguel looked for the vehicle. Just as they suspected, it stood out like a sore thumb.

"Middle of the block, right side," Miguel said.

"Okay, I'm going to go around the block. I'll come through the other way, and we can get the numbers on the house."

"Take your time. They didn't seem to be in a hurry. I wanna give them plenty of time to get inside."

"I know what I'm doing, *pinche pendejo*. This ain't the first time we followed the cops."

"Whatever, dude. Just slow the fuck down, *puto*."

Jose drove around the block. By the time they came back around, Michael and David were inside. Miguel wrote down the address as they passed the single-story residence. They drove down to the end of the block and went straight. The road did not continue through but rather made a big loop with vehicles parked all the way around it. It was the primary parking area for a small government housing unit. The small complex was composed of a series of single-story triplex homes, none of which had individual parking, so Jose's van would not stand out or seem like anything other than a renter or visitor. He parked in the first opening he came to. The entire loop gave them a good view of the road, so they could see when the officers left.

As soon as he parked, the two men settled back into the back of the van and waited. They weren't sure what this house had to do with. The fact that this is where they ended up gave them cause to wonder if maybe they were wrong, and Rosa hadn't said anything.

"You know who lives there?" asked Jose.

"No, I've never seen this place before. The old man never came here when we followed him in the past. Maybe it's nothing, maybe we're good," Miguel said optimistically.

"That would be nice, but I'm not so sure. Let's stick around and see what happens, but we won't call Fernando until we know more. No need to get him fired up just yet."

Both men knew that if they told Fernando what was going on, he would likely tell them to simply kill the cops, kill the Jimenez family, and then he would tell Carlos to kill Rosa. It was always easier for him to have people killed, but he wasn't the one doing it. Not that either Jose or Miguel had a problem with the killing, but this wasn't Mexico, and when it came to killing American cops, it was a whole different ball game. They had killed several policemen in Mexico, and there was no concern whatsoever that they'd ever get caught. American authorities, on the other hand, were entirely different. When one of their own was killed, they pulled all the stops. The investigation that followed would involve not only local law enforcement, but also the FBI, and in this area, the Border Patrol and ICE (Immigration and Customs Enforcement) might get involved as well. Jose and Miguel both realized that if it came to that, they would have to go back to Mexico, maybe indefinitely, and that was the last thing they wanted to do.

"Yeah, good idea," said Miguel. "Besides, we don't even know what they are yet. Local cops, feds, who knows, maybe they were just IRS or Social Service or some shit like that. You know they give everyone a badge nowadays."

"Exactly, we'll wait until we know enough to be able to answer Fernando's questions. Then if we have to kill them, so be it."

With that, the two men settled into the back of the van and watched.

TWENTY-THREE

It didn't take long, and Michael had found the numbers he was searching for. He had written down the telephone number for the El Centro FBI office, the Border Patrol headquarters in El Centro, and the regional customs office as well. His mother popped in and looked over his shoulder to see what he was up to. David was sitting at the counter next to him, reviewing the information they had gotten from Enrique.

"What are you doing? It looks like you are just writing down phone numbers."

"I am, I have some calls to make to see if these guys have any background information they'll share, but I had to get the numbers first."

"You ever think of just grabbing the phone book? It's faster, you know." Louise couldn't believe just how dependent people had become on the Internet; she had only subscribed to it after Michael had hounded her for months so he could send her e-mail and pictures. She always told him to just drop them in the mail; how difficult could it be? He tried to explain the benefits of going digital, but it was lost on Louise. She seldom used the Internet, and more often than not, he would have to remind her to check his e-mail, and she still took all of her pictures with disposable thirty-five-mm cameras. They suited her needs, and the pictures always came out.

"Poor mom, you will never catch on. First, this was easier and probably faster. I would have had to look in the blue pages, then the black pages, or the red pages only to find out that the number I was looking for wasn't listed in the first place. Not to mention, if you have looked at the government section lately, you'll find two of everything, like the Department of Education and the Education Department, and they'll both have different numbers because they are different offices with the same job. Go figure right."

"I think you're just getting lazy," retorted Louise.

"It's not that, I just prefer to go with a sure thing."

"A sure thing you say. Is that why I'm not a grandmother yet? You can't bring a sure thing home to your mother, so you can't get my approval. I'm not getting any younger, you know."

David erupted in laughter; he was laughing so hard his eyes began to water. "She's gotcha there, buddy," he said to Michael as he wiped a tear from the corner of his eye. "Are you telling me he doesn't send you any pictures of his girlfriend, Mrs. Garrett? I'll forward you the few he has sent my way."

"Real nice," Michael said to both of them. "First off, *Mom*, you are the one who beat into me that I shouldn't get married before thirty-five. Second, he's full of shit. I have never sent him any pictures." Turning his attention to David, who was wiping tears from both eyes now. "Thanks a lot, partner. Glad to see you've got my back," he said cynically.

With that, Louise left them to their work. She had gotten a good chuckle from the banter as well. It reminded her of how much fun they used to have when Michael was growing up. Although he had friends and spent countless hours with his grandfather, the two of them always had a very good relationship. As an only child, Michael never had siblings to talk to or fight with for that matter; so as he got older, he would always share his adventures and disappointments with her. She had always wondered if he wouldn't have preferred to do so with his father, but he worked a lot and was seldom home. Whatever the reason, she was grateful for it and missed it.

Michael pushed his notes toward David and tapped on the Border Patrol number. "Why don't you give them a call and see if they have any information on Eme and their sex slave ring? See if they have anything on this guy Fernando Ortiz as well. I'll do the same with the FBI and will go from there."

"You got it. Whoever is done first can follow up with the customs office."

* * *

Michael telephoned the FBI's El Centro field office. He dialed the twenty-four-hour hotline number, hoping to get a real person who could direct him appropriately once he told them who he was and what he was working on.

"Federal Bureau of Investigations, El Centro, how may I help you?" came the receptionist.

"Hello, this is Detective Michael Garrett with the El Dorado County Sheriff's Department. I am working on a case involving the Mexican Mafia and need to speak with an agent."

"Sir, what specifically are you looking for? We have several agents in the office, and each has a particular field they are responsible for."

"I need to speak with whoever would handle human trafficking, specifically sex trafficking, and I have cause to believe that La Eme is the organization behind it."

"Okay, sir. I'll have you speak with Special Agent Savage. I'll transfer you to his desk now."

"Thank you." Michael waited momentarily while he was being transferred. He wondered if this guy was going to be of any use, or if he would simply blow him off. It only took a second for Agent Savage to answer, so he didn't have to wait long to find out.

"FBI Organized Crime Unit, Agent Savage," said the man on the other end of the line.

"Good morning. My name is Michael Garrett. I'm a detective with the El Dorado County Sheriff's Department."

"What can I do for you, Detective?"

"I'm working on a homicide, and during the investigation, it was brought to my attention that the intended victim had been kidnapped and forced into prostitution by the Mexican Mafia. She has been working off her father's debt for the past eighteen months. I am trying to get her and her family out from under these thugs by making a case strong enough to put them away, but I'm running low on leads and was hoping you guys might have some information you could share."

"It sounds like a great story, Detective, but I am still not sure how the FBI can be of any assistance. What do you have so far?"

"That's the rub, Agent Savage. I have a reliable victim, whose family corroborated the story 100 percent. Beyond that, I only have a name. Fernando Ortiz with La Eme."

"Fernando Ortiz!" Agent Savage said rather excitedly. "How did you get that name?"

"It's a long story. The short version is that my victim's father borrowed money from him. What can you tell me about him?"

"Let me get this straight. You have a guy who said he borrowed money from Fernando Ortiz?"

"Yeah, that pretty much sums it up, oh yeah, and the fact that his daughter was later kidnapped by a couple of his thugs, was raped, and forced into a life of sexual servitude for the past year and half." Michael was getting the impression that Agent Savage found his story a little too good to be true.

"Detective . . . Garrett, was it? I don't mean to be crass, but it seems a bit improbable that you have a criminal link to Fernando Ortiz. He is our only link between La Eme and Los Zetas. He is the only member of La Eme we have ever identified that does not have any criminal record. Every other member we have validated with that organization has a criminal history. For years we thought that Ortiz was nothing more than a myth until I confirmed his identity, but his exploits had never been known to reach outside the security of Mexico and the protection of the Zetas. Now you come calling with a story linking him to human trafficking case."

"Good to know you were listening. Look, I have the information, not enough to build a solid case. That's why I called. I'm more than happy to show you what I've got, but the one thing I don't have is a lot of time. Do you have anything to offer or not?"

"Look, if what you say is legit, then yeah, I have information. However, none of it is going to be shared over the phone. I want you to come to the office here in El Centro. I'll need to see some credentials and what you have in its entirety. Then I'll run it up my chain, and we'll see if we can be of assistance."

"Fair enough, where's your office?"

"310 South Fourth Street, at the corner of Fourth and Olive."

"Done, my partner and I will be there within the hour." Michael never really expected anyone to give him much over the phone, so he wasn't disappointed to have to meet with Agent Savage. He had just hoped that it wouldn't be a waste of time.

*   *   *

David tore a few sheets of paper off of Michael's notebook and headed for the dining room table. He figured if they were both on the phone at the same time, it would get a little difficult to listen, not to mention be irritating for someone on the other end. He pulled out his cell phone and punched in the number for the Border Patrol Office.

"United States Border Patrol, how can I help you?"

"Hello, this is Detective David Ross, LAPD. Can you please direct me to someone working in your Human Trafficking Unit?"

"They're all out in the field right now, sir. I'll patch you through to their—"

"Wait, wait, wait," David interrupted sharply, knowing what was coming. The inevitable transfer to voicemail that so many receptionists were notorious for before you could even finish talking. Half the time they would transfer you to some automated recording. It was almost worse than starting off with the automated systems; at least with them you could usually get a human on the other end, even though you may not be able to understand them.

"What is it, sir?" came the receptionist, slightly annoyed at being cut off.

"Look, the call is urgent. I can't stress that enough. It is truly a matter of life and death. Please, let me give you my number, contact one of the agents in the field, and have them call me back as soon as possible."

"Sir, if it's a matter of life and death, you need to hang up and dial 911," came the acerbic response.

"This is not that kind of emergency. I need to speak with someone in the Human Trafficking Unit. Tell them I am working a sex slave case linked to the Mexican Mafia and a man named Fernando Ortiz."

"Okay, sir. I'll pass the message along," responded the receptionist, knowing appeasing her caller was the only way to get him to shut up so she could go back to reading the latest release of her favorite *Harlequin* novel.

David pressed the End button on his cell phone. "Stupid bitch," he muttered.

"Excuse me?" asked Louise as she was walking by.

"I'm sorry, Mrs. Garrett. That was not intended for you," David said apologetically as he started to blush.

"You know, you'll catch more flies with honey than you will with vinegar."

"Yes, ma'am."

David looked at his phone for a second; realizing she was right, he punched the Send button, bringing up the last number dialed. He pressed the button a second time, dialing the number.

"United States Border Patrol, how can I help you?"

He recognized the voice of the receptionist as she answered the phone. It's not that he expected someone else, but he had hoped she would answer so he didn't have to explain things over again.

"Hello, this is Detective Ross again."

"Yes, sir, I know it's important. I'll pass the message along."

David could tell she was obviously irritated and was glad he had called back; otherwise, it was not likely the message would be forwarded anytime too soon. "Look, I called back to apologize. I didn't mean to be impolite, it's just that this case really is time sensitive, and my partner and I have reached a point where we need to do some intelligence gathering. We can't proceed safely without more information, thus, I am calling the experts."

"Okay, sir. Apology accepted, and I will notify our dispatch now. They will have Agent Robert Porter contact you."

"Thank you very much." David hung up. He was thankful he had called; there was no way of knowing how long it was going to be, but one thing was for certain—it wouldn't be as long a wait had he not apologized.

He walked over to see how it is, if Michael was faring any better. Michael was in the process of scribbling down what looked like an address. David figured he would hold off on calling the customs office to see what Michael had going. It wasn't long, and Michael was hanging up.

"Well, what have you got?" asked David.

"I am not sure yet. I talked to an agent, who seemed a little incredulous, but he wants to meet and see what we have. Basically, it sounded like he wants to make sure we're legit before he shares anything."

"Yeah, either that or he just wants to know what we know because he doesn't have shit. Then he'll write some special bulletin and put his name on it, trying to make it look like he's actually done something other than warm the cushion in his chair."

"Anything is possible, but it's all we have for now. How about you?"

"Well, I managed to piss off the receptionist, but I think I smoothed things over enough for her to at least relay a message. She is going to have dispatch pass on my number to an Agent Porter. Hopefully he calls back sooner than later. I told them it was urgent."

"Well, it is what it is. You call customs?" asked Michael.

"No, I wanted to see if you had better luck than I did."

"Well, let's go meet with this guy Savage and see how it pans out. If we need more, we'll see if he can't point us in the right direction."

"Sounds good to me. Maybe we can avoid some of the BS that way. Although with as much as federal agencies communicate among themselves, which isn't much at all, it'll probably be highly unlikely that he can help us out with any other agency."

"You're so pessimistic," said Michael. "You know they resolved all those interagency communication issues after 9/11," he jibed.

"That's what they keep telling us anyway."

The two began to load up their effects when Michael's mother came back into the kitchen to see what was going on. They explained that they had a possible source of information with the FBI, but they had to meet in person. They were waiting for a call back from the Border Patrol and would decide whether they needed to call customs after that.

"It's supposed to get up to 115 this afternoon, so you boys make sure you drink a lot of water. You're not used to this kind of heat."

"We're big boys, Mom. Besides, we deal with the extreme all the time."

"Thank you for the advice, Mrs. Garrett. I'll make sure Michael stops on the way out of town so that we can stock up on some water bottles," said David as he jabbed his friend in the ribs with his elbow.

"Here we go again with the whole Eddie Haskell thing," Michael said, mocking his friend about his sycophants.

"You two just be careful. I'll cook up some carne asada for dinner, say, around sixish, if you can make it. Otherwise, it'll be in the fridge." Carne asada was a pre-marinated, thin-cut flank steak that Michael's mother always doctored up even more before cooking. Ever since he had moved away from the border area, he couldn't find it anywhere.

"I don't know when, or even if we'll be back today, Mom. We really are on a deadline."

"Deadline or no deadline, you boys are going to need to sleep sooner or later. Your room is still made-up, and I'll clear the junk off the bed in the guest room." Louise Garrett had a lifetime of trinkets she referred to as treasures. So many that she had to decide which to display and which to place in storage, thus, the three-car garage that only had room for one car. On top of that, she had more that she had wrapped carefully and placed in her guest room.

Michael told his mother it would not be necessary. They did not mean to impose on her any more than they already had, but she would not hear it. She did not see her son near enough, and as far as she was concerned, David was like family. Although he had never been to the house before, Louise knew just how much he and Michael helped each other in the past and how close they had been. Ultimately, both men conceded and agreed to stay for the night; whether or not they were on time for dinner was yet to be seen. Now that they had resolved where they would be staying, the two grabbed their things and headed for the El Centro FBI office.

Twenty-Four

Jose and Miguel had watched and waited patiently from their van. When they finally saw the two detectives leaving the house, they had learned nothing other than an address. Jose climbed back into the driver's seat and fired up the old van. He pulled away from the curb and was on the way to continue their surveillance until they knew enough to take action. He continued straight, through the intersection, and continued past Louise's house again. As he reached the other end of the block, he slowed down at the Stop sign, fully intending to just roll through if no one was coming when he was caught off guard with the return of the grey Crown Victoria. He quickly jabbed the brakes, causing the van to pitch its weight forward.

"Motherfucker!" exclaimed Jose.

"What the shit," queried Miguel, not realizing exactly what was going on as he was still sitting in the back.

"They're coming back."

"So what? Just turn and go back to where we were. They aren't looking for us," Miguel said blatantly.

"Oh, it's just that easy, bitch?" Jose shot back. "Why don't you drive then? Now they've seen the van."

"You need to relax, man. The fucking pigs don't even know we're on to them."

Angry at the prospects of getting made, Jose completed the right turn and drove around the block in hopes the detectives wouldn't notice them, and he would have time to figure out what was going on.

*   *   *

Michael and David were driving by his old elementary school when it dawned on him that he still didn't have a way to get into his mother's house, and if they ran late into the night, he would have to wake her up to get inside.

"We have to go back and get a house key. If we run late, I don't want to have to wake her up to get in, and I definitely don't want her leaving the door open," Michael announced as he made quick U-turn.

"Good call. Would she really just leave the door open though?"

"Oh yeah, she thinks all is well in the little city. She used to go out to shop, or get groceries or whatever and leave the door unlocked. She figured because she had a little Australian sheepdog she'd leave indoors that no one would dare come in."

"That's putting a lot of faith in the dog."

"Not to take away from Indy, because she was a great little guard dog, but when my mom was gone, anyone with a meatball was her new best friend, but she died a couple years ago, and my mom just hasn't broke the habit."

Michael was getting ready to turn back onto his mother's road when another vehicle came to intersection a little faster than expected. The driver quickly jabbed the brakes, as if he had intended to run the Stop sign and was apparently startled by the approaching vehicle.

"Paint that thing black with a red stripe, and it would be a dead ringer for the old A-Team van," Michael mused.

"No doubt. I grew up watching that show. I think you just scared the crap outta the driver. He probably thinks you're an unmarked CHP unit and is waiting to see if you red-light him."

"Yeah, thanks for reminding me about how stealth we are in this bad dog," Michael scoffed as he recalled just how evident the Crown Victoria was as an unmarked police car. "Oh well, we've got bigger fish to fry, and they'll feel lucky for a little while."

Michael turned the corner and returned to his mother's home, parking on the wrong side of the road this time rather than using the driveway. He ran inside, frightening his mother who was sitting in an old-fashioned-looking chair with floral print while she read the latest release to her favorite novels about a plump female private detective.

"Sorry, I didn't mean to scare you. I just wanted to grab the spare house key so I can get in if you happen to be out later." Michael didn't want to tell her the real reason was because they might get back so late she'd be in bed. He figured it would be less of hassle this way, and he was right. Had he told Louise the real reason, she would have gone into a deluge of stories reminding him that he can't go without eating or he'd get cranky. None of which Michael needed to hear, nor that he really cared about at this moment.

"Okay, see you later. You boys be careful."

"We will, Mom. Thanks again!" he said as he grabbed the key off the key rack. The key was still right where he remembered; he then hurried back out the door. However, this time, he stopped and locked the door behind him. He jogged back to the car, where David sat waiting, and jumped in. He checked the mirror quickly to make sure no one was coming up behind him and then checked the road in front of him before pulling out. As he looked forward, he noticed a van that appeared to be slowing at the intersection at the other end of the street.

"Hey, isn't that the same van we just saw?" Michael asked.

"It sure looks like it. Windows are tinted and everything."

"That's kinda weird, don't you think?"

"Yeah, but then again, we're right back where we started too."

"Fair enough." Michael dismissed the van for the time being; he had bigger things on his mind at the moment. He dropped the car into drive and accelerated away from the curb.

Michael drove to the end of the block where Jose and Miguel had just gone by. Not realizing the potential danger he and David were in, he turned left and headed for El Centro to meet with Special Agent Savage. As Michael headed out of town toward Interstate 8, he took David by the old water tower they saw on their way into town.

"There she is, up close and personal," he said as they drove past the aging tower.

"It looks better from a distance," joked David. "Kind of like my ex-wife."

Both laughed as Michael hastened the pace as he exited the little town. They were speeding down Orchard Road headed to the freeway, rows of crops on both sides of the road zipping by, when suddenly, Michael came skidding to stop.

"Son of bitch!" He had been gone longer than he realized, and things had changed. There was a new Stop sign at that beginning of the small residential development they were getting ready to travel through that now had signs posted on both ends, for just that reason—to slow speeders and try to allow the residents a fair chance at backing out without getting creamed by some idiot not paying attention and driving too fast.

"Maybe I should be driving," David said rhetorically. He couldn't tell if Michael was ignoring him or simply didn't hear him. He was getting ready to mock the driving again when he noticed Michael was intent on something in the rearview mirror. He was about to ask what was going on when Michael accelerated through the stop. "You okay?"

"Yeah, I thought I saw something, but must have been a glare. That thing wasn't there last time I came through here. I wonder when they put it up." Michael had seen the second sign and was already slowing down for it.

"You need to visit your mom more often. Remember, you are her only child."

"I know, I know. What are you, my girlfriend now?" David hadn't realized just how sensitive the nerve was he'd just hit. Michael was keenly aware that he didn't get home nearly enough. His father had been ill, dying with cancer the last time he made the trip. His mother called and told him his father was getting weak and urged him to come. He headed out the next day at the end of his shift; his father died as Michael was on the way. He had never forgiven himself; he should have left immediately. He had to finish his shift; he was still the same today, wrapped up in his work. This weekend, the one he was now missing, was the first long weekend he had in some time, and he was going hiking. He justified it to himself; driving the twelve hours to Holtville was just too much for a short visit, and he hadn't taken a vacation in almost four years. Avoiding the topic completely, he pulled out his phone and began searching for a number. "I need to make a quick call."

*   *   *

Jose drove around the block. He didn't want to pull into the small parking loop where he had parked before until he knew whether or not the detectives were back at the residence. He was going to make the same loop he had the last time, verifying the location of the vehicle first. Just as he hadn't anticipated them coming back around the corner, he hadn't figured the vehicle being parked on the wrong side of the road, facing directly toward him as he drove through the intersection.

He slowed the van down, looking for the car. He hadn't recognized it at first; with the midday sun beating down, the reflection made it look a different color. It was Miguel who noticed it first; he also saw that someone was still sitting in it.

"Keep going, man, they're still in the car. We need a new place to watch from."

Jose couldn't believe they got caught twice. He was usually much better at watching people, but then, he wasn't used to this. He was used to watching the everyday average Joe come and go, someone who never expected to be under observation and who never looked over his shoulder. This was his first time tailing the police, and it was an art he had yet to master.

He drove to the end of the road. It came to a dead end a couple blocks farther down, cut off by the local junior high school. Jose pulled into the staff parking lot, a one-way parking area at the entrance of the school that doubled as the bus drop zone. He exited the other end and headed back the way he had come. He fully intended on using his old parking space in the government housing parking, when he noticed the grey sedan pull out ahead of him still a couple blocks ahead.

"There they are again," Jose said as he pulled over immediately on the side of the road. Miguel watched quietly from where he sat. Jose let the car get several more blocks ahead and then pulled out again when he was sure he was far enough away not to draw suspicion to himself. He mirrored the vehicle's turns, turning the same direction it did, only with several blocks in between. The tactic worked; it was easy in the small town where most every street ran parallel or perpendicular to the rest. It wasn't long before Jose knew where they were headed or at least what direction. He followed safely behind all the way out to Interstate 8 West.

Once on the freeway, Jose let the gap grow all the way to El Centro. It only took ten minutes to get there, when he watched the car exit on the Fourth Street off-ramp. A mile or so later, Jose watched as the sedan pulled into the parking lot behind the Federal Bureau of Investigation, and the two men walked inside.

TWENTY-FIVE

Michael had found the number he was looking for—Detective Cook's. He punched the Send button and waited for an answer. It took longer than expected, but Cook finally picked up.

"Hello," came a groggy voice.

"Cook, is that you? It's Garrett."

"Hey, what's up, man? Where are you?"

"I'm in Holtville. How'd the rest of the night go?"

The tired detective shook the cobwebs from his head and rubbed his eyes. He glanced over at the clock and realized it was already a little after 12:00 PM. It wasn't normal for him to sleep so late, but then, he didn't usually go to bed when the sun was coming up. "Holtville, I thought you were headed to Los Angeles?"

"I was. I went to LA, hooked up with an old friend who works Vice there, and then we headed to Holtville. Anything happen after I left?"

"Nothing of great consequence. Although Rosa was right about one thing. That guy Carlos always seems to be close by. He showed up at the substation and then again at the jail after I booked her."

"What?" Michael couldn't believe this was the first he was hearing this. "And you didn't call me. Does he know what's going on? Did he talk to her? How did—"

"Slow down, man," Cook interrupted. "He showed up at the substation when I was leaving. He approached me, acting like a lost tourist. I didn't know it was him until it was too late. Besides, what was I going to do? You're the one working that angle. Once he was gone, Rosa told me it was him. Then several hours later, he popped in at the jail and tried to talk to her."

"Please tell me he didn't get that far."

"Come on, man. We run a tighter ship than that over here."

"So what happened then?" Michael could feel his patience growing short; an entire family's safety hung precariously in the balance of his investigation.

"It was handled discreetly. I had given explicit instructions to the jail staff in the event anyone tried to contact Rosa. So when this guy showed up offering to post bail, they told him she was being held without bail due to the severity of the charges. He asked if he could speak with her after that, and was told only lawyers were allowed to see inmates outside of visiting hours."

"That was it. It could be worse, I guess." Michael didn't like it, but there was nothing he could do.

"There was one more thing." Cook didn't really know how Michael was going to take the next little piece of information, but he had to tell him. "I ran into him again in the bathroom at the sheriff's station."

"What do you mean you ran into him?"

"After I got the call that someone was there to see Rosa, I needed to find out who it was. I wanted to see if it was the same guy from the substation. Anyway, long story short, we sort of ran into each other in the lobby. It was pretty obvious he recognized me from the substation, so I asked him what was up. He said he got a call that a friend had been arrested, so he was going to bail her out. That was it."

"So you're telling me Rosa called him and told him she was arrested! You have got to be fucking kidding me. Did you check the call records to see what she might have told him?"

Cook hadn't thought to check the records last night. He had been tired and had other things on his mind, like dragging his feet on a homicide booking to help Garrett with his ghost chase. "No," he admitted, "it never crossed my mind. I'll call the jail now and get back to you in five to ten."

All Detective Cook heard on his end was Michael starting to shout something before the phone went dead. He felt bad, but it was an honest mistake. It wasn't really even a mistake, he thought; whatever was said was recorded and retrievable. He'll just call in and have someone pull the call log, play back the call, and then he can fill in Michael on the details. What he hadn't considered was that if Rosa was calling Carlos, just maybe her whole story was made up as a diversion to blur the eyes of those looking into the murder, and she was simply seeking another way out.

Michael hung up the phone and entered into a tirade of expletives that would have made a sailor proud. David sat next to him quietly, simply watching as his friend vented whatever was ailing him.

"So I guess that went well. Care to share?"

Michael let go of the steering wheel, throwing both arms up in disgust. "Yeah, my counterpart in Douglas County ran into Carlos last night, *twice*."

"The guy that's been pimping Rosa. The one who holds death over her family like it's nothing more than a phone call away?"

"One and the same, my friend."

"And he didn't think it prudent to call you. He didn't consider the ramifications on our end if this guy had called ahead to let someone know the gig was up and decided to whack the family just to be on the safe side . . ."

Now it was David's turn. He instantly realized the danger they could have been placed in, and the fact that this other detective hadn't bothered to call with such information was beyond belief. He looked at Michael, with his face reddening in anger. "You need to move back to LA. Those guys are gonna get you killed up there."

"He's pulling the recording now. He's going to call back and let us know what was said. Once we know a little more, we'll carry on. We may need to get a security detail to the Jimenez family sooner than later. At least we'll be in the right office to pass the buck on that one." Michael was referring to being at the FBI office, where someone would be able to officially request witness protection for the family if necessary. "Don't get me wrong, he screwed us on this. I'm pissed, but it was an honest mistake, and Cook is a good cop. He was probably just tired. We all know how the long days can creep us up."

"Bullshit! That's a bullshit excuse and you know it. The guy fucked up, and we're lucky nothing happened. They could have been waiting for us when we got there and fucking sniped us as soon as we turned onto the street!"

Michael knew David was right. He also knew that David needed to vent just as he had moments before. He just prayed that they were both making more out of this lapse in judgment than was necessary. Just then, his phone began to ring. He looked to see who it was; it was Cook.

"What's up?"

"There was no call. She never called anyone."

"Really?" Michael was perplexed. "He had to be watching. If he saw you at the substation, he had to see her too. So he knew she was in custody for something, and if he dropped her off at Harrah's, it wouldn't be too hard to put the pieces together. He waited for a while, probably figuring he'd give the booking process enough time, and then he just popped in like before to bail her out."

"Makes sense," responded a relieved Cook, reasoning that nothing was amiss at this point. His relief was short-lived.

"So if this guy is thorough enough, or paranoid enough to show up at the jail and try to get her out, I wouldn't be surprised if he reported to someone above him in the food chain to let them know what's up."

"Yet again, you bring up a valid point. Either way, you may be compromised. Are you sure you don't just want to dump this on the feds and let them run with it? They'll pick it up in a snap. They love shit like this. And they can relocate everyone if they want to."

"I know, I thought of that. The problem is they beat to a different drum, and nothing is done in snap. Everything is a big production to them, which doesn't help Rosa or her family right now. Besides, I need to see this through, I gave Rosa my word."

"Well, it's your call at this point. Just stay safe, and I'll be in touch if anything else comes up."

"Roger that."

The phone went dead again. Cook looked at the clock again. He'd only gotten a few hours of sleep but figured it was enough and, barring the conversation he just had, decided he better get back to the office and get back to work.

Michael explained the circumstances to David. Both men were relieved that Rosa hadn't actually placed the call but still found it disconcerting that Carlos had shown up at both the substation and then the jail so soon after the homicide.

"I don't know, Mikey, I'm starting to get a bad feeling about this," David said.

"I know. It's a little hinky. We are going to have to presume Carlos called ahead. Maybe we are just ahead of the curve right now. If Carlos went home and went to bed, just like Cook, it stands to reason Eme is just finding out as well. We'll have to plan accordingly from here on out."

Michael saw the Fourth Street off-ramp and got off. It was about a mile and half to the FBI's office.

Twenty-Six

Michael and David walked into the government building. It was nothing like the grand buildings depicted on television or even those that Michael and David were used to in their respective jurisdictions. The building was a simple, insipid two-story structure. The kind that made onlookers think the second floor may have even been an afterthought. It was definitely not designed to impress or intimidate those who entered it, much like most federal courthouses.

The main entrance was open, with seemingly no security or protective measures in place. Michael thought that this was odd for a federal building in this day and age. He was relieved to discover that beyond the main door was another, one that was secure, and the small foyer they were standing in was being monitored by surveillance. At least the interior was not as antiquated or dilapidated as the rest of the building appeared. Michael pressed the Call button next to the door. When the voice vibrated from the small speaker, Michael announced his name, and that Agent Savage was expecting him. Shortly thereafter, a man came to the door. "I'm Agent Savage. I'm going to need to see some identification."

Michael and David each produced their law enforcement IDs and held them out for the man to inspect. Once he was satisfied, Agent Savage pushed the door open for the men.

"Follow me," he said.

He was a shorter man with oval wire-rimmed glasses; Michael could easily see the thinning hair on the top of his head. He also had more of a spare tire than one would expect for someone in law enforcement. Then again, Michael thought to himself, *Is this guy really in law enforcement or merely intelligence gathering?* Either way, Michael was already turned off by the man's attitude. Although he really didn't know what to expect upon arrival, the one thing he had always been taught was that proper introductions were more than a simple matter of courtesy; they were also part of being professional.

Walking through the office complex, Michael noticed the majority of the interior seemed to be broken into half a dozen individual cubicles with free-standing half walls separating one from the other. The two of the perimeter walls of the building were made up of more private offices, and one wall had an impressive array of video monitors placed end to end, top to bottom. The mosaic of video screens was at least eight feet high, occupying the majority of the wall space, and twice as wide. Michael was curious about the wall, but it would have to wait. He had more pressing matters on his mind at the moment, proper introductions for starters.

"Agent Savage, I am Michael Garrett, and this is Detective David Ross. He is with the Los Angeles Police Department, and we have partnered up on this case." Michael made the introduction to the back of the man's head in a caddy tone, derived for the sole purpose of letting Agent Savage know how he felt.

"Nice to meet you both," responded Savage without slowing his pace or looking at either man. He then came to a small office, really more of a cubicle with a door, and walked in. He promptly sat down behind his desk and waved his hand at the two seats against the wall adjacent to the door. "Go ahead and close the door and have a seat."

"Don't mind if we do," said David, as he was the last one in, and made it a point to slam the door hard enough to make the plaques and certificates on the wall behind the desk shift on their hangers. It was obvious to both detectives that the agent had placed them there so those sitting in his office would notice his accolades; both also thought it was quite ostentatious as well.

"So which one of you was Garrett?"

"That'd be me," Michael said. "This is David Ross, in case you missed it earlier. Nice wall by the way. Those are all yours, I presume?" Michael asked, more in an effort to ensure Agent Savage would notice every ornament he had placed on his wall was now hanging crooked.

Agent Savage took the bait and looked over his shoulder proudly, noticing that his wall dressings were all askew. "Yes, they are," he said a little less proudly. Realizing he was being goaded, he quickly moved on. "So you think Fernando Ortiz is a player in this case of yours. Why don't you elaborate for me?"

Michael explained the events as they had unfolded over the course of the past day. He covered every aspect of the story as he had heard them from Rosa and her father, Enrique, piecing the information together until the saga was complete.

"That is what brings me to you. I have a complete story, however, it's nothing more than a story since everything I have is relatively circumstantial at this point. I have no other evidence of these events or proof of this loan other than the word of a known prostitute and her father."

"Well, it's a good story," responded Agent Savage. "I'm almost inclined to tell you you're on a wild goose chase and simply wasting your time, but you've got the first good lead on Fernando Ortiz we've ever had directly linking him to criminal activity in the United States. The man's squeaky clean."

"How can that be?" asked David. "La Eme is a prison gang, that's developed and grown beyond the walls of the prison. Everyone in La Eme has either been to prison or is a known gang member. Thus, they all have criminal ties."

"You can never deal in absolutes," rebuked Agent Savage. "Doing so will bite you in the ass someday. You are correct in that the Mexican Mafia originated in the prisons, and that they have expanded. What you are lacking is the fact that they have now expanded across the border as well. They are not just a prison gang inmates use as protection anymore, they are major players in the world of organized crime, and they have begun making profit on a monumental scale. Not something street gangs are known for."

"I think we are all aware it's not just a prison gang with street connections," said Michael. "And it's nothing new that they are in the business of making money. But since when did they go into human trafficking, and what do you mean they've expanded across the border?"

"First of all, human trafficking is a growing trend. More accurately, what we are talking about here is referred to as human sex trafficking because that is what it really is, which you are obviously aware of. Normally, they are bringing in younger females from out of the country. I don't know exactly how much you are aware of, but it is the fastest growing business in organized crime and the third largest criminal enterprise in the world, behind drugs and weapons of course. The victims are generally taken from Asia, the former Soviet Union, Central and South America. The less-developed or poverty-stricken areas are targeted, and the females and sometimes young boys are taken and shipped to the more developed areas of Asia, the Middle East, Western Europe, and, yes, North America. It is not nearly as common that women from the U.S. are targeted, but that is rapidly changing."

"I knew it was big, but I had no idea it was at that level," responded Michael.

"Well, it's not like we are out there telling the press all about it. Most of our investigations into these cases are classified as matters of national security. I can't go into all the details, but suffice it to say that part of the mafia's expansion into Mexico was aided by their joining forces with the Zeta Cartel."

"What is the Zeta Cartel?" asked David. "I know the Mexicans are having drug wars all along the borders, and Texas is really bearing the brunt of it in

El Paso with Juarez just across the border, but I've never heard mention of Zetas."

"Well, it's about time you learned because you're already knee-deep into it. Los Zetas used to be a group of Mexican Special Forces soldiers, who decided that they could do better for themselves in the criminal world than the measly eight hundred pesos they were making a month in the Mexican army.

"Led by one of their lieutenants, the group originally deserted the army and stole an unknown amount of military weaponry and explosives. We know they have small arms and machine guns, including .50 cal. weapons and even surface to air missiles. They made their start by being guns for hire, mercenaries if you will, and the Gulf Cartel picked them up fast to take care of their dirty work. They proved to be more violent than any of the other cartels to date, and with their specialized military training in guerrilla warfare, rapid deployment, aerial assaults, ambushes, intelligence, and countersurveillance, they have proven themselves to be worthy."

"How the hell did the Mexican army let so much shit get taken? Did they think these guys were just going to sell it off for an early retirement?"

"Your guess is as good as mine. More than likely, they didn't even know about it, and by the time they figured it out, well, it was too late. Regardless, the Zetas began to feel their oats and soon decided they didn't need to work for the Gulf Cartel, and they proceeded to take over their business and handle drug shipments of their own. Shortly thereafter, they engaged in an all-out turf war and annihilated the Gulf Cartel's command structure."

"So how did the Mexican Mafia hook up with them? What could they possibly have had to offer the Zetas?" asked Michael.

"That's where it gets interesting. As the Zetas gained power, they began to recruit some of the former cartel members they hadn't already savagely executed. People who were willing to give up all allegiance to the cartel and who the Zetas thought had something of value to bring to their organization. In doing so, they were turned onto Fernando Ortiz. He used to be a Mexican federale lieutenant, Mexico's version of a federal agent, and he had averted investigations on more than one occasion, allowing the cartel to conduct its business without the hassle of law enforcement intrusion.

"When the Zetas approached him, Ortiz gave them names and addresses of hundreds of the Federal Judicial Police and also kept an open communication link that we still haven't been able to identify within their federal police. The Zetas verified the information and then set out killing each of the federal agents and their families. This ingratiated Ortiz to the organization and sent a message to the rest of the community that this was the fate that awaits anyone who dare get in their way."

"That doesn't answer my question though?"

"Patience, I'm getting there. The Zetas are ambitious. They began to broaden their area of operations, and are currently battling the Juarez Cartel to the east, as well as the Sinaloa Cartel to the south. They continue to advance easily through Mexico, but the real golden goose was going north. They needed a way into the United States. Something or someone that would provide certainty and assurance they could readily cross the border with their shipments. This is where La Eme came in. With their known ties to correctional officers in the prison system, it was only a matter of time before they found a way to bribe officers on the outside. La Eme knew how to develop law enforcement contacts. They'd been doing it for years in prison. They knew what characteristics to look for, and thus, who was more likely to accept a bribe. We're not talking about getting out of a traffic ticket kind of money, we're talking early retirement to the tropics. That's where Ortiz really earned his keep. He made contacts with La Eme, and offered them the financial backing they had previously only dreamed of. He convinced them to partner with the Zetas for the sole purpose of using them to build assets in the U.S., and hence, the Zetas found the route they were looking for."

"What route? The case we're on is all within the U.S.," said David.

"All except for the money," responded Michael. "Enrique met Ortiz in Mexicali. The property was purchased in Cuernavaca. The money is all in Mexico, and some of it is illegally obtained drug money, am I right?"

"You catch on fast," said Agent Savage. Looking at David, he responded, "To answer your question, the route is through the Holtville border crossing. We've been watching a customs agent we suspect is on Eme's payroll, thus, he is also on the Zetas payroll. We just can't prove it yet, but we think he clears the route at the border for the Zetas shipments. As long as he is on the payroll, they have free passage. It's better than NAFTA."

"I can't fucking believe this shit! That does pretty much sum up our case though. How much of that can you testify to? Your testimony would seal the deal on these thugs that have been literally extorting Rosa into prostitution with the threat of death to her family."

"Look, I am a subject matter expert when it comes to the Zetas, but I have never been able to get enough to nail Ortiz. What I just told you is factual, but can't be proven beyond a reasonable doubt. We know where Ortiz came from, we know the Zetas and La Eme are playing nice, and we know the dirty customs agent is James Elmond . . . Oops, was that my outside voice . . . But we can't prove it. We are in the same boat you are in right now."

"All right then, we can work—"

"Hold on there," interrupted Agent Savage. "Have you been listening to me? I am telling you this for your own good, not so much for your case. You go digging too much, and you'll be the next ones on their hit list. The Zetas haven't killed an American law enforcement officer on American soil yet, but they will. We know they've killed agents in Mexico, but they operate with impunity down there. Sooner or later, however, they will take action on this side of the border. No one has really been brave enough to challenge them yet. Our government merely sends money to the Mexican government and supports their efforts, but we have not gone after the Zetas ourselves yet, and when we do, it will not be with law enforcement. It will be with our own little band of black ops soldiers, I assure you."

"So what, you think we should just drop the case? Tell Rosa and her family sorry, peace out, and good luck? I can't do that." Michael was growing angry at the thought.

David knew his friend well enough to see he was growing cross. He also recognized that Agent Savage might be right. What was this really worth? He didn't know Rosa or her family, and other than going to school with her for a year, it seemed that Michael didn't really know her either. "Michael, Agent Savage is right, and he's just giving us some friendly advice. I don't think he's saying we just give up, but I do think that maybe we should slow down. We could hand over all the information and let the feds handle it. Like he said, the money is in Mexico. It's an international issue, and we have no jurisdiction across the border. What are we going to do, walk up to Ortiz and ask him to come to America with us so we can question him? Not likely."

Michael looked at both men briefly. "Look, we have an active case involving kidnapping and slavery to put it mildly. That is occurring in our county and in our state, where we do have authority. I, for one, do not intend to just turn the other cheek this time. It's not a fucking speeding violation. So I'm going to follow up on my case, bearing in mind what you have told me. All I need is enough evidence to corroborate the story, and if I can't get it by Tuesday"—he looked directly at Agent Savage—"maybe you could have a contingency in place to relocate the family for their protection. I'll write it all up and turn everything I've got over to you in a tidy little package. Then you can continue to work your angle and, hopefully someday, use the Jimenez family as witnesses if you ever make the case."

"Listen, Detective," cautioned Savage, "I can see you're not going to walk away from this, and I counted on that. It's why I shared the information with you in the first place, but I would have been remiss if I hadn't warned you as well. In any event, I don't think you should be crossing any borders . . . Seriously, don't go there. Just do your follow-up. You don't even know who these other two guys are yet, right? So come Tuesday, you call me. I'll have the protective detail in order, and we'll move the Jimenez family to a safe location until they can permanently relocate. Just keep a watchful eye."

With that, Michael stood up, ready to leave. "Thanks for the information." David stood and opened the door; he headed out. Michael was right behind him when he stopped and turned back. "I have one last question. Do you know when this guy Elmond works?"

Agent Savage looked at him quizzically for a moment. "Rumor has it he may or may not be working swing shift, but I really can't say. I understand shift change at the border checkpoint is around 2200 hours. You might check and see."

"Rumor has it, huh? I don't like rumors much. I'll have to confirm that information."

"I figured you for that kind of guy. Talk to you later."

Michael gave the special agent a devious grin and an approving nod as he turned and caught up to David. He was quite the dipshit Michael had originally thought.

*   *   *

As Michael and David were walking back out to the car, David's phone chimed, indicating he had a new voicemail. He must have missed a call, but it didn't make sense; he had his phone on the whole time. He looked at his bars and saw that he had only one. He wasn't used to being without full bars everywhere he traveled, but it was not often he left Los Angeles. During the rare occasions that he did, he was usually on vacation and kept his phone off, unless he was expecting a call from his kids. Things were different in Imperial Valley; cell coverage was improving but anything but full proof. He called his voicemail to retrieve the message.

They reached the car and climbed inside while David listened to the message Robert Porter had left. He sounded a little put off, which David fully understood. He had expressed the urgency of the situation and then didn't even answer the phone. He knew Porter was probably wondering just how urgent it could be at this point. Fortunately, he had left his cell phone number, which David dialed immediately.

"Go for Porter."

"Porter, this is David Ross. Thanks for getting back to me. I was in a meeting with Agent Savage with the F—"

Porter cut him off, "I know Chris, we worked together on a JTTF operation once." JTTF was the Joint Terrorism Task Force; it was comprised of representatives of several agencies under direction from the Department of Homeland Security working to help follow up leads received on terrorist tip lines, not to mention things analysts picked up from Echelon, a signals intelligence software capable of interception and content inspection of phone calls, faxes, e-mails, and other data traffic through the interception of communication bearers including satellite transmission, public switched telephone networks, and microwave links.

"Excellent. He just brought us up to speed on Fernando Ortiz and the Zetas."

"Really, you are working on a case involving Ortiz? He doesn't ever venture into the U.S. Not to be rude, but how did a city cop catch a case involving Ortiz?"

"It's a long story, but it started with the Mexican Mafia and basically went south from there, no pun intended."

"I'd say. Well, hey, man, if you have already talked with Chris, I'm sure you can't learn anything from me. He's supposed to be the local expert on those guys. Just do me a favor, hang on to my number and call if things develop further. I can get the BORTAC guys together lickety-split if need be." BORTAC stands for the Border Patrol Tactical Unit. They are the equivalent of the FBI's SWAT team, just with less recognition, which they prefer. They respond to crises nationwide and have an extremely high success rate. Which also explains why they aren't leading the headlines; the press only wants to cover a tragedy or government screwup like Ruby Ridge or the Branch Davidians in Waco.

"Thank you. Hopefully we won't have to call, but either way, I'll keep you posted. It's good to have friends in a case like this."

"Amen to that, brother. You guys watch your six. Eme isn't the pooh butt prison gang they used to be. They went big time when they hooked up with the Zetas."

"I don't think they were ever pooh butt." David laughed.

"Compared to their new compadres, they were just that. Don't underestimate these guys. They'll go after you and your whole family. There is a reason we only have intelligence at this point. No one upstairs wants to pull the trigger and send people into harm's way. Personally, I think the bigwigs are just afraid any retaliation may lead all the way back to their doorsteps, if it doesn't start there."

"All righty then. I'll keep that in mind. Thanks again and we'll be in touch." David hung up and took a deep breath.

"Listen, Michael, that's the second guy that left us with a warning. You know me, man. I've never had issues with the dangers of the job, but this is different. You're talking about trying to break into a cartel and take down one of their key players. We don't have the resources to do that in the next couple days, buddy."

"I know. I'm working on that. For now, let's just do our homework. I realize this is turning into a bit of a monster. I just don't want to throw in the towel yet. If we can give the feds what they need to take action across the border, we'll have done our best. I would hate to have to tell Rosa and her family that I failed. They've been through so much already."

"Look, man, if you can make the arrangements to have them reunited and moved for protection, you've done what you said. So what if the bad man walks today? There's always tomorrow. You know that."

"You're right. No need to take unnecessary risks. There will always be another chance, especially with these guys."

More than just the case was heating up. It was mid-afternoon now, and the desert sun had heated the air to a sweltering 113 degrees. Things were speeding up, but Michael knew he needed to slow down. He had started the car and cranked up the air-conditioner while David talked. He knew better than grab the steering wheel right away; it was likely to be closer to 140 degrees. He figured he had waited long enough for the AC to do its job. "I have an idea," he said.

"Shoot."

"Let's take that tour. We'll go back to my mom's place. It'll make her happy we're there for dinner, and then we'll fire up my old Jeep and go for a ride in the desert. It should be bright until almost eight."

"Good call. We need to digest all this and plan accordingly. We are definitely swimming with the sharks on this one. Let's grab a sixer. You can't have Mexican food without a cold one."

"Dude, this isn't some vice detail. I don't know about you, but I'm on the clock and am zinging my department for the OT."

"Whatever, Killjoy. Let's go."

Michael pulled out and headed back to Holtville. He took the scenic route this time, heading back toward the interstate but turning east on Ross Avenue. This took slightly longer to get back but allowed him and David time to think.

TWENTY-SEVEN

Jose and Miguel kept watch while the two detectives visited the FBI. It was the boring part of their business; only rarely did spying on others result in anything entertaining—the occasional fight or a heated argument with their significant other, which, on a good day, resulted in makeup sex. Of course it only made it worthwhile to Jose and Miguel if the windows were unobstructed, but every once in a while, the couple would be in such a heated moment that they never bothered to close the blinds.

Jose and Miguel both favored moments such as that especially if they were looking for the right moment to break in, as they had with the Jimenez family, to collect on debts and make the proverbial offer that couldn't be refused. Unfortunately, this was not going to be one of those times; and regardless of what they thought about Rosa, they knew at this point it was just too risky not to inform Fernando. Miguel made the call while Jose continued to watch.

"Hello, Miguel, how are things with you today?" Fernando loved caller ID. It allowed him to get straight to the point.

"We got a call from Carlos late last night. Rosa had just been arrested and was in the process of being booked. He tried to bail her out, but was told she was being held without bail. She killed some white boy, and he thinks she may have told the cops a little more than necessary this time. He's not sure, but he wanted us to start watching the family."

"And?"

"Well, some detectives showed up at the Jimenezes' place this morning around eight thirty."

"That is interesting, yet I am curious as to how they would have gotten there so quickly. You say he called very late last night?"

"More like early this morning," Miguel recalled.

"Do you think they are following up on something else, or could they be looking into us?"

"It is hard to say. We thought they may be simply following up on something else at first because they went to a home we have never had any dealings with and never seen any of the Jimenezes at, but we are at the FBI office in El Centro right now. So we figured it was time to bring you up to speed."

"It is good that you called. I don't want you to do anything just yet. It could still be something benign, and I would hate to have to start killing police in the United States this soon. I would like to do some digging before we take any action. What was this address you saw them at?" Fernando knew Rosa was a big earner as far as Miguel and Jose were concerned, but her worth was insignificant to him. She was but a small speck of sand in the business he was developing with the Zetas. Nonetheless, he wanted to keep his men content; thus, a little extra effort would go a long way with them.

Miguel quickly grabbed his notes to verify the address. "It was 440 Olive Street. Why?"

"I'm going to find out a little about the owners. I'll be in touch. In the meantime, you stay on them. If anything changes, you let me know and we'll go from there."

"You got it, Jefe."

Both men hung up their phones and set to taking care of their business. Miguel told Jose that they were to continue watching the cops while Fernando looked into the address they were at earlier in the day. Fernando picked up the phone and called his contact with the Mexican Federal Police.

"Hello," came the answer.

"I need you to look into an address in Holtville for me. I need to know as much as possible about the owners. 440 Olive Street. Call me when you're done."

"Give me an hour." And the phone went dead.

Fernando sat back and relaxed. He pondered what he had been told and considered the options. He knew Rosa was important to Eme because her earnings went to them. On the other hand, he was beginning to think that this was the perfect opportunity for Los Zetas to make a bold statement in the United States. They were crossing the border whether the U.S. was ready or not. Yes, it was the perfect time to make such a statement, he thought.

TWENTY-EIGHT

Michael was explaining the various agricultural seasons to David as they drove by various crops heading back to Holtville. He had learned more than most kids not directly involved in the industry for the simple reason that his grandfather had worked for various farmers in the '50s and '60s until he took a job with the local irrigation district, and his father was an entomologist who had worked for the county agriculture department until he died. Not a day went by that someone wasn't talking about the crops or the bugs destroying them.

David was in midsentence asking about one of the fields that had something growing in it that they hadn't seen yet when Michael interrupted.

"I don't get it, it doesn't make any sense. Why would Carlos just show up at the substation, then the jail, and not do anything? He called someone, he had to. We may have been ahead of them this morning, but we have to assume La Eme is onto the Jimenez family now. We better check on them again, maybe we can get them to stay somewhere else for a couple days."

"A couple days," David snorted. "They need to take whatever they can carry and leave. I know it's a shitty situation, but they need to disappear. No matter how you slice, they're fucked. Based on what Agent Savage was saying, these guys aren't short on resources. If they want them dead, they will be. Their only chance is relocating, preferably to a different time zone, and new identities."

"All right then, we'll stop by their place on the way into town and see if we can't get them a little more motivated."

"You know this just keeps getting uglier. If they are onto the family, they're going to be onto us after we go back by."

"Good point. I think we'll stop by my mom's first. I have an idea that just might keep us a step ahead . . ."

"Well, is that it? What's this idea?"

"Just a little surprise, nothing earth-shattering, but it just wouldn't be any fun if I told you now."

The drive back to Louise's home was uneventful. It took a good thirty minutes this time, but mostly because Michael drove a lot slower. They pulled into the driveway and headed in.

*   *   *

Jose had kept his distance even greater as he followed the grey sedan. He didn't like what he'd been seeing and definitely didn't want to draw any more attention to the vehicle. He knew they had been seen earlier when the detectives came back around the corner; thus, he was being more cautious now. He wasn't concerned about the distance; with nothing but crops on the horizon, the detectives were easy to follow. The midday sun reflected off the windows, shinning like a beacon for all to see on the lightly traveled back roads.

Miguel was talking to Fernando, and it was hard to tell what was going on, listening to only half of the conversation. Jose tried listening in, but he was going to have to wait until Miguel hung up to find out what their next step would be.

Miguel finally hung up and explained to Jose that Fernando didn't want them to do anything just yet. He explained that Fernando was going to look into the address on Olive and get back to them once he knew more. In the mean time, they were to continue monitoring the detectives and waiting to see how the situation continued to unfold.

Jose was anxious; he knew it wouldn't be long before Fernando called back. "You know he's been waiting for an opportunity like this."

"What are you talking about?" Miguel asked. "This is nothing we haven't done before," reminded Miguel.

"Except for the fact that this time, it's cops. We've laid low on the cops thus far. We never target them," Jose explained, as if Miguel was blind to La Eme's operations.

"What are you talking about? We've done cops before."

"Not like this. Our carnales did what was necessary, trying to get away when they got caught, but we have never executed cops. This is big time. It's gonna be on if we have to off these pigs."

Jose explained the situation as he saw it. Miguel understood clearly that his partner wasn't so much afraid of killing the cops but rather excited about what would follow. Both men knew that La Eme's joining with Los Zetas was a big step, and thus far, it had proven lucrative. They also knew that their new partners were using them for access to the United States as they were using the Zetas for growing their trafficking enterprise. The question that remained unanswered was exactly when the Zetas would become as aggressive in the U.S. as they had been in Mexico. They would soon find out.

Jose followed the vehicle back to the Olive residence and, once again, parked in the small area at the end of the block among the other vehicles in front of the triplex units.

TWENTY-NINE

Louise Garrett was adding more lemon, garlic, and onion to the already marinated carne asada when Michael and David walked in. She had never imagined they would actually be back before dinner. Realistically, she didn't even think they'd be back for dinner; thus, she planned on just keeping the food warm. In any case, she was pleasantly surprised.

"Hi, boys, you're back awfully early."

"Sorry, Mom. We just dropped by for a change of clothes and to swap vehicles. Do you still have Dad's old shirts?"

"Hanging in his closet where he always kept them. Why?" Ever since Michael's father had passed away, the one thing Louise couldn't bring herself to do was get rid of his old Aloha shirts. She had offered them to Michael (the two wore the same size), and he had wanted them. He just never took them home when he visited.

"Thanks, we just need a fresh set of shirts. These are getting ripe." Michael responded as he motioned for David to follow him down the hall. They walked into the bedroom, which, upon entering, had two closets, one on each side of the entrance. Michael went to his father's side and slid the closet door open, revealing an assortment of Hawaiian shirts that rivaled a display at Hilo Hattie's. He grabbed an olive drab green shirt with white plumeria flowers on it and began to change.

"Grab the one you want. It's better than nothing."

David looked at Michael as he began to change. Shaking his head, he said, "This is your plan, your big surprise. Hawaiian shirts?"

"I never said it was a big surprise. In point of fact, I said it was just a little surprise. In any case, this is only part of it. So quit whining and grab a shirt."

"I can't wait to see what's next," responded David, laughing at the thought. "Who do you think we are, Five-O?" David grabbed a louder shirt, blue with bird of paradise flowers, and put it on.

Michael took the shirt David had been wearing and tossed it into his old bedroom along with his own. He headed back to the kitchen with David in tow. He stopped at the key rack, eyeing it closely. When he didn't see the one he was looking for, he had to ask, "Mom, where do you keep the keys to my old Jeep?"

Louise hadn't heard them come back from the back of the house. She turned and saw the men now dressed in the old Aloha shirts. She paused for a moment, reminiscing on the family vacations they used to take. She had tried for years to get Michael's father, Michael Sr., to go to Hawaii. He always objected, stating he didn't want to make the flight or take the time off. Finally, one day, Louise simply made the arrangements and purchased the airline tickets. When she came home with the travel package, she told her husband they were going to Kauai and gave him the dates.

Begrudgingly, he took the time off. Louise called Michael and told him when they were going and asked if he could meet them there. He did. His father enjoyed himself so much while they were on the island that the following year, he made all the arrangements to return. Except this time, he and Louise met with a real estate agent and bought a small condo in the town of Koloa near Poipu Beach and Brennecke's Beach Broiler, his favorite restaurant on the island. It had become a tradition, and every year, Michael would meet his parents for a couple of weeks in September and stay with them in Kauai.

"The keys, Mom?"

Louise was drawn from her thoughts. "You boys look nice in those shirts. Of course I think everyone looks better in a nice Hawaiian shirt. You remind me of your father, Michael."

"I know, Mom. You say that every time I wear one of these. I'll have to get them out of here someday, but for now, the keys to the Jeep."

"If they're not up there, they're in the ignition. I try to make it a point to drive it around at least once a week. I usually just take it to church on Sundays."

"Thanks, Mom. We'll see you later."

"David, you take care of my baby."

"I will, Mrs. Garrett, I will." David looked over at Michael, giving him a wry grin.

Michael shoved his friend, knowing he was goading him because of the baby comment. "Come on, we've things to do."

They walked out to the garage where Michael's Jeep was occupying the only space available. He pressed the garage door opener and tossed David's keys back to him.

"I'm going to pull out. When I do, go ahead park your car in here." Michael climbed into the driver's seat, a Baja SS by Corbeau. He checked the ignition for the keys; they were there. He pumped the gas pedal twice and turned the key in the ignition. The motor cranked a couple of times and then fired up. The rumble created by the deep exhaust of the AMC 360 was nothing short of shocking. It was not exactly what one would expect coming from the little CJ-5.

Michael stepped on the clutch and shifted into first gear. He eased out of the garage, allowing David to pull the Crown Vic in. David parked the car and hit the garage door button to close the garage. He ran past his car, squeezing between it and the memorabilia stacked in the garage, ducked his head to avoid hitting the dropping door, and climbed into the Jeep next to Michael.

David settled into the matching bucket seat and took an inventory of the vehicle. The rumbling exhaust, the shake of the vehicle that came with the slow idle that one would expect of a '50s era hot rod, and the clean interior. He noticed in the small area behind that front seats was perfectly fitted metal lockbox that the small backseat was mounted on.

"This is definitely a surprise," marveled David.

"I thought you might enjoy it. My dad and I fixed it up when I was a kid. We pulled the motor out of an old Wagoneer and added a few extras for power. Other than that and some one-inch blocks to lift the body up just enough to clear the thirty-three-inch tires, it's pretty plain."

"Plain my ass," said David. "This thing is badass."

"Well, we decided to spend what little money I had on the motor rather than other goodies, like a winch or roof racks and all that. I wasn't planning on rock hopping, and I always camp light. I just wanted to be able to play in the desert and take it hunting. My dad sprung for the seats because he didn't want me sliding off the original flat vinyl one and falling out, or so he said."

"What's in the box?"

"Two foam pads smashed in tightly so you could throw a couple of long guns in there, and they wouldn't slide around. It's how my dad and I used to travel when we went hunting."

Michael reached across the flat dash and opened the glove box. Inside were a couple of faded khaki denim caps from Brennecke's that Michael kept for himself and a passenger since the Jeep didn't have doors and only sported a slick bikini top, only covering the front occupants. He handed one to David and took the other for himself.

Michael ran his fingers through his hair, which wasn't even long enough to comb. "It helps keep the curls from getting tangled."

David laughed as he fitted the hat and put it on.

Michael eased out the clutch and gave it a little more gas, bringing the little Jeep to life. They pulled out, turned right, and headed back toward the Jimenez residence.

THIRTY

On the way back to Alvarado Street, Michael's stomach started to growl. He didn't know how long they were going to be at the Jimenezes' home or how long it would take to pick out the customs agent they were looking for. Regardless, he was hungry and needed something to eat.

"You hungry?" he asked.

"I could go for a bite. What'd you have in mind?"

"This place me and a buddy used to eat lunch at nearly every day. Mandilon's. They have this burger basket that puts others to shame. The secret is the beans. You get a little cup that goes perfect with the fries."

"If you say so," said David. "All I know is the AC in this thing doesn't work very well." David reached out and slapped the side of the Jeep.

Michael made a quick left at the end of the block. He drove past the elementary school and his mother's church. He turned right on the main road he and David had come into town on and then pulled into the parking lot for Mandilon's, which was right across the street from the Taco Shop. He grabbed the door and was holding it open for David when he noticed something.

"Hey, isn't that A-Team van again?"

David looked back and saw the vehicle go by. "Yeah. That's weird. I know this is a small town and all, but damn."

"I told you, man. That's exactly why it was so hard to get away with anything growing up around here. You always ran into people your parents knew."

The two went into the little restaurant. David saw that it only had six small bench tables, three along each side. Just past the tables were a couple of old video games, Street Fighter being one of them, and an Addams Family pinball game with what appeared to be high school-aged boys playing them. He commented on the games and how the two of them would have to return later to drop a few quarters in them. Michael was standing at the counter, ordering already. He ordered a couple of double cheeseburger baskets and extra-large 7Ups.

The food was ready in ten minutes, cooked upon being ordered. David thought it seemed to take a long time to get a couple of burgers. Michael explained that's what made the food so much better. Mandilon's wasn't some franchise chain that had a half a dozen or more orders setting up under a heat lamp until the order, nor did it have the volume of customers to do so. Everything was made to order.

The two sat at one of the benches and ate. Michael inhaled his burger as if he were being timed. It took him less time to consume the meal than it took to prepare. David was about halfway through when he noticed.

"You wanna take a breath now?"

"Hey, man, it's about filling a void, not savoring every morsel. We got shit to do." Michael grabbed his drink and headed for the door.

"You suck," complained David as he grabbed the plastic basket his food came in. "I'm eating in your Jeep then."

"That's okay, I'll hose it out later."

They walked out to the Jeep and climbed in. David set his food on his lap and kept eating. Michael fired up the Jeep, which nearly vibrated David's drink out of his lap. David looked around for a place to set the drink and quickly realized the old vehicle didn't have cup holders. He tucked the cup between his legs, closer to his body than the basket, and dipped one of his fried in the beans. "You weren't kidding about the beans. It's a weird combination, but it works."

"I told you," said Michael as he pulled out of the small parking lot back onto the main drag, once again headed for the Jimenez house.

"Do me a favor, drive a little slower. I don't think the town is large enough for me to finish my food before we get there," David mocked.

Michael looked at David who was about to take a drink of his soda. He waited for a millisecond and then quickly tapped the brakes. David's head lurched forward just as he was bringing the straw to his mouth. The straw ended up in his nose rather than his mouth.

"Come on! What the fuck, man?"

"Sorry about that," Michael said with as much sincerity as he could fake. "I was just slowing down so you would have time to eat."

David shot him a glare and ignored the sham. He enjoyed his meal as best he could despite the 113-degree wind that was coursing through the Jeep as they cruised along. Michael laughed at his friend, enjoying the moment and reminiscing as he drove through the town in his Jeep.

Shortly thereafter, they were approaching Tortilla Flats. David wrapped what was left of his meal up in the thin paper liner setting in the bottom of his meal basket. He gave it a squeeze, hoping the increased density would keep it from blowing out of the open vehicle, and then set the basket and crumpled leftovers in the back.

"I'm gonna take the first street coming in this time. We'll make our way through the neighborhood first and just check for anything out of place. If all is clear, we'll stop the second time around," Michael said as he turned onto Palo Verde, a block before he reached Alvarado.

"Roger that," acknowledged David. He began to scrutinize every vehicle parked on the road and every person in and around the various homes. Typical for this time of year, there were not many people out. It was just too hot to be outside if you didn't have to be.

Michael wound through the streets in what would be a backward *S*. Nothing seemed conspicuous. Michael was coming back around to Alvarado when he asked, "Everything kosher with you?"

"Looks good."

Michael parked around the corner from the Jimenez home on the connecting road alongside the gulch. He and David exited the Jeep and walked toward the Jimenez home. As they approached the home, Michael noticed an older-model white Ford F-150 parked out front.

"That one wasn't here this morning."

"Yeah, might be one of the kids. Didn't you say they had five or six?"

"Five according to Rosa. You watch the two side, I'll knock and cover the four." The *two side* was a reference for the left side of the building as you faced it. It was standard to number the sides of buildings, with the front or main entrance being side 1; then, counting clockwise, you had two, three, and four. This was done to ensure no one tried to sneak up on you while knocking on the door.

"You got it," David responded. He pulled his pistol from his holster and held it firm against the backside of his leg, keeping it as concealed as possible yet ready.

David stepped over the short chain-link fence at the front of the residence and approached the house from a forty-five-degree angle. Michael walked past the house altogether so he could get a look down the other side. Once he had done so, he hopped the fence and approached the house. Once he reached the corner, he stopped and listened. He could hear people talking inside but nothing alarming. He waited until David looked his way and then began to approach the door. He knocked three times firmly and then backed away from the door back to the four side.

"I hear footsteps," said David.

"I have the old man looking out the front window. I'm going to the door." Michael stepped into the view so Enrique Jimenez could see him. He waved at the man and moved to the door.

The door opened halfway. "Detective, come in, come in," said Enrique.

David heard the invite and headed to the door as well. He holstered his pistol and walked in behind Michael. It was obvious that he startled Enrique, who had not seen him coming. "Good afternoon, sir."

"I was wondering where you were." Enrique motioned to the detectives to follow him as he headed back into the kitchen.

As they rounded the corner into the adjacent room, Michael and David saw Martha and another man who strongly resembled Enrique, only about twenty years younger.

"This is my eldest son, Javier. Javier, these are the detectives I was telling you about."

"Mucho gusto, it's a pleasure to meet you." Javier extended his hand.

Michael shook his hand. "Nice to meet you as well. I'm Michael Garrett, and this is my partner, David Ross."

Javier then took David's hand. "My father said you have talked to Rosa."

"I talked with your sister last night," responded Michael. "She is doing well, all things considered. That is why we are here." Michael looked at Enrique and Martha. He explained to them what they had learned since they last spoke. He informed them of the Zetas and how they were working hand in hand with the Mexican Mafia. How Fernando, whom they previously assumed was part Eme, was actually a very powerful man in the Zeta Cartel. Michael stressed that as much danger as they thought they were in before, they now believed that to be even greater.

Enrique shook his head at the news. He told the detectives that there was no greater danger. They had lost their daughter and lived in fear of death ever since. "What could be worse?"

Javier wanted to know how this was intended to help Rosa or his parents. Michael explained that the objective was to develop a case strong enough to arrest the men involved with kidnapping Rosa and threatening the family ever since. The investigation had revealed the Eme's ties with the Zeta Cartel, whose extreme violence and barbaric ways had already been explained. He explained that they were making very good progress, but that the closer they got, the more likely Eme or the Zetas were to send someone after Enrique and Martha simply to make a point.

"So you are making things worse?" asked Javier bluntly.

"It would seem that way," responded Michael flatly, "but we are also making more headway than anyone else ever has." He then diverted his attention to the senior Jimenez. "I need the two of you to stay somewhere else for a few days. Somewhere they don't know about. Is that possible?"

Enrique looked at his wife. She shook her head, as if to say it was okay. "We can stay with my son Javier. He has a home that no one has been to. My children always come here to visit us. We have never been to his house."

"Where do you live, Javier?" asked Michael.

"I live in Imperial on a dead-end street near the fair grounds. My wife and I have been renting the home, hoping to save enough money to help pay off my father's loan and get my sister back."

"How soon can you be ready to leave?" asked David.

"We can go now. We will pack some personal items and go from there if you think it is best," replied Enrique. Martha quickly walked out of the room into their bedroom and grabbed enough clothing for her husband and herself, along with some toiletries.

Michael could see the relative frustration in Javier as well as concern in Enrique's face. "I understand things are looking bad, but I cannot even begin to explain what Rosa has gone through in the past eighteen months. I just wanted to help. I never imagined it would turn into something so colossal. I hope you know we will do everything possible to get this worked out, but if we can't, if there are just too many involved, are you prepared to move away from here?"

"What do you mean?" asked Enrique. "You want me to just leave my family, pack up, and run? I will not do that. It is my fault this happened in the first place. If failure means that I am going to die, then so be it, but I will not run and leave my family behind to pay for my mistakes."

"That's not what I meant. I will get Rosa to you. She will need to be relocated as well. In fact, take down this number." Michael waited while Enrique grabbed a napkin and a pencil. He gave him Detective Cook's phone number and told him that he would call Cook and let him know to expect their call. Cook would be able to put them in contact with Rosa so they could talk to their daughter. Michael hoped this would help keep the Jimenez family's resolve throughout the remainder of this ordeal. Talking to Rosa might be just what it takes to get them to take the next step if necessary.

"Thank you so much. We will call as soon as we get to Javier's." Enrique called to his wife, telling her the news. She came hastily back into the room, carrying a small duffel bag in each hand. She dropped the bags and gave Michael a strong hug, thanking him for the information. She looked at Javier and said, "I have enough for the next few days."

"Mama, you can stay with us as long as you need," offered Javier.

Michael had one last thought. "Just out of curiosity, whatever came of the property in Cuernavaca?"

"We have been making payments on it. Hoping that someday this would all be over, and we could still move there. My boys have all been helping. Otherwise, we couldn't have done it, but it's still ours. Why?"

"It's nothing right now, but I may have an idea. For now, you should get your things and go home with Javier. We will follow you out of the area to make sure no one follows you."

Enrique picked up the bags, and everyone headed for the door. Michael suggested they all travel with Javier as his vehicle may be less noticeable to anyone who may be waiting to see if they try to leave. Enrique and Martha agreed and rode with Javier. They would not need their own vehicle anyway. Michael and David hurried back to the Jeep. Michael cranked up the motor and quickly pulled around onto Alvarado. Javier was already on the move. Michael kept his distance and watched as Javier turned left at the end of the road, headed west toward Imperial. He and David continued to watch the neighborhood closely, waiting to see if anyone began to move with any more urgency. They didn't.

Michael slowed down some, allowing the gap to grow. He knew where they were headed. It wasn't about keeping up but rather making sure no one else was trying to. A couple of cars passed by before Michael began to follow Javier again.

*　　*　　*

Jose and Miguel had watched the detectives switch vehicles. They followed them in the Jeep when they left the house again. Jose thought he had lost the two detectives when Miguel spotted the Jeep parked in a small parking lot adjacent to a small restaurant on Main Street. Jose saw the vehicle at the last minute before he drove by. He went up the road to the next intersection and turned around. He pulled into the Del Sol grocery store parking lot across the street, and the two continued to wait.

It wasn't long before their target was on the move again. Jose followed them toward the Jimenez house for the second time today. This was all the confirmation he needed. He knew how this was going to end.

"Why do you think they switched vehicles?" asked Jose.

"I think the FBI told them more than they wanted to know. I think they are putting things together, and that ain't no good."

"You think they're onto us?"

"Not yet. If they were, they wouldn't go back to Alvarado, but I do think they know who we are and who is behind us. I think it's time we put an end to this as well."

"When they stop again, I'll keep watch. You better call Fernando back."

The two Eme thugs kept a safe distance, comfortable with the fact that they knew where they were going. Doing this couldn't have worked better. As Michael snaked his way through the small residential neighborhood, he would have noticed the van following him if not for the greater distance Jose had kept. Jose and Miguel never even entered the neighborhood this time. They parked on the edge of the road in between a couple of houses a couple hundred yards east of the small residential development.

Miguel called Fernando while they waited for the next step. He delivered the news and was shocked to discover that Fernando seemed unfazed by the information. He told them he had learned enough, and it was time to make a statement.

"I want you to take care of our problem before more people get involved. It is only a matter of time before these two stop going to the feds for information and start asking for help. I want you to take care of the Jimenez family, and I want you to take care of the cops," ordered Fernando.

"What about Rosa?"

"She's Carlos's problem. Also, I found some interesting information on the Olive address as well . . ." Fernando went on to explain that he had just received a telephone call from his source. The house belonged to a Michael and Louise Garrett. It seemed that the husband was dead, but they had a son who was a cop. Fernando further explained that his source had told him that the cop son used to work for LAPD but was now working up in the Lake Tahoe area.

Miguel was surprised at the revelation that a Tahoe detective would be all the way down in Holtville. There was only one logical explanation, and that was Rosa had told them everything. The information didn't change anything; it just made the killing easier. Miguel placed his hand over the telephone mouthpiece and told Jose what he was learning while Fernando continued to speak.

"When you are done with the Jimenez family and these cops, I want you to pay a visit to the mother as well. That's where I want you to leave a little calling card. It's time for the U.S. to know they are as vulnerable as the Mexicans. A little line on the map will not stop us from doing what is necessary. Make sure they know it was Los Zetas!"

Miguel handed Jose the TEC-9 he'd been holding in his lap and then went to the back of the van and dug an AK-47 assault rifle with a collapsible stock and pistol grip out of their war chest. He rammed a thirty-round magazine into the rifle and took an extra one out just in case. He crawled back to the front seat and slapped Jose on the leg with the magazine.

"They're sitting ducks right now. Let's just go to the house and take care of this right now," said Miguel.

"Let's do it . . . ," responded Jose. He started the van and was getting ready to pull out; he checked his mirrors and noticed a couple of cars coming up behind him. He looked ahead; that's when he noticed the white Ford F-150 pulling out from Alvarado, headed west. He watched the pickup leaving; he couldn't tell who was in it from where he sat. Just as the two cars passed, he noticed the Jeep pull up to the Stop sign. He waited to see what would happen next.

Thirty-one

Michael pulled out onto the road, following Javier. He spent as much time looking in the rearview mirror as he did watching the road. David kept vigil of all things on the roadside, checking for occupied parked cars or prying pedestrians. There wasn't much for him to do really; nothing like he was used to in the big city, but it was no less important. They were the final car in a short string of traffic headed out of Holtville until Michael noticed a vehicle behind them pull away from the road several hundred yards back now.

There was nothing unusual about the vehicle, except Michael had been watching so closely and didn't recall noticing anyone get into the vehicle. "I think we have company."

David adjusted the passenger side mirror so he could look back without being so obvious. He saw the vehicle behind them, but it was too far away at the present to tell what it was. He had already pulled his pistol out, not even realizing he had done it. "Where did it come from?"

"It was parked on the north side of the road a ways back. Funny thing is, I didn't see anyone get in it."

"Well then they must have already been there. Good obs."

Michael slowed down ever so slightly, enough to help reduce the gap between the two vehicles but not so much as to make it noticeable. It wasn't long before he could tell it was a van behind them, which he immediately voiced to David. This time, David wasn't discreet. He turned in his seat and looked back at the vehicle. He was immediately able to tell it was the same van they had seen a couple times already. "It's the A-Team again."

"Son of a bitch!" Michael exclaimed. "We should have figured that out a long time ago."

Michael accelerated quickly. The Jeep roared, the large motor propelling the little vehicle like a greyhound coming out of the chute. He tore down the road, gaining on the vehicles ahead of them. David wondered what he was doing, but before he had a chance to ask, he found out.

The two-lane road leading out of town dipped down suddenly and curved to the left shortly before rising back up and coming to the intersection Highway 115, the same road they had driven into town on earlier in the day. While Javier and the two other vehicles were stopped at the Stop sign, Michael slammed on the breaks, skidding to a stop. He knew they had dipped out of sight. He shifted into first, cranked the steering wheel to the left, depressed the throttle, and released the clutch. The tires began to screech, and the Jeep spun around suddenly. Steering into the slide, the tires finally gripped the pavement, and they launched back toward the oncoming van.

Michael continued to accelerate, not really sure what he was going to do next. All he knew at the moment was that he did not like being followed. It was better to be the predator than the prey. The road between the two vehicles closed rapidly. Jose had noticed the Jeep pulling away and increased his speed as well. What happened next is what caught him off guard.

As the vehicles sped toward each another, Michael looked at David and told him to hold on. David didn't know what his friend was about to do, but he figured it was a good idea to do as he was told. He quickly holstered his pistol and pressed his feet firmly into the floorboard while pressing his hands onto the dash. Just as the vehicles were about to pass, Michael drew his .45 and switched it to his left hand. He shoved the pistol out toward the oncoming vehicle and crossed the double yellow lines.

Jose and Miguel saw the gun; before they had a chance to react, the Jeep pulled into their lane. "Look out!" screamed Miguel, believing they were about to collide head-on. Jose instinctively jerked the van's steering wheel to the right to avoid the collision. What he didn't know was that no sooner had Michael crossed the double yellow lines, he had started to steer back, but the move had already made the desired effect.

Human reaction time is such that Jose didn't have a chance to process the fact that the Jeep was already steering away from them. Unfortunately for him, he pulled the wheel so hard to the right he found himself in the scree on the side of the road. He was steering back onto the asphalt when the road dipped and veered to the left. By the time Jose had realized the road wasn't going straight anymore, it was too late. The van was completely off the road and headed for the steep embankment that consisted of the road base for the highway up ahead.

He braked hard, but the tires on the van only slid in the gravel, stirring up a cloud of dust. The vehicle seemed to gain speed rather than slow down. Jose tried to steer back onto the road, causing the van to lose control even more as it began to slide left. Just as the back of the van began to swing around, they careened into the unyielding embankment. The impact came on the front passenger side, crushing the floorboard in and up crushing and pinning Miguel's legs and causing his head to impact the pillar between the windshield and the door. Jose slammed into the steering wheel, and his face shattered the windshield.

Javier was already safely down the road headed for home, and only one of the other vehicles remained at the Stop sign. They hadn't seen the van coming, and the occupants would later tell investigators they never even saw what happened. One second they were looking for traffic, the next there was a van crashing off the road next to them.

Michael saw the cloud of dust and quickly turned around again. He raced back to the scene, stopping shy of the van. He and David exited the Jeep, weapons in hand. They approached the crumpled van in the settling dust, each man taking his respective side. David could see the passenger in the side mirror. He appeared to be unconscious.

Michael called out to the driver, "Driver! Let me see your hands!"

Jose was badly injured but knew he was headed back to prison a failure. It was no longer an option. If he didn't die now, he would likely be murdered by his own people in prison for screwing up so badly. He reached around on the floorboard until he found the TEC-9. "No hablo, Ingles!" he shouted back.

David kept advancing slowly on the passenger side. The passenger remained motionless, his face a bloody mess. "The passenger looks out of it!"

"Roger that!" acknowledged Michael. "Chofer, ponga sus manos afuera la ventana! (Driver, put your hands out the window!)" Michael shouted. His Spanish wasn't perfect, but it had gotten him by. The driver still failed to comply, but this time, there was no response. Michael held his ground and repeated the command.

David kept inching out, slicing the pie as they put it, gaining a better view and tactical advantage over the occupants in the van. It was then that he saw the driver holding the machine pistol up near the steering wheel. "Gun! Gun!" he shouted.

Jose heard him shout gun and realized it was now or never. If he waited another second, he would never even get a chance to shoot. With what strength he had, he leaned forward in excruciating pain. Most of his ribs were broken, as was his left collarbone. He leaned forward just enough to look out the driver's side window. He thrust the pistol out the window toward Michael, jerking the trigger, sending bullets spewing wildly from the short barrel.

Michael heard David's warning. He already had his .45 trained on the driver's window. It was no sooner than David shouted when Michael saw the barrel of the gun followed by the man behind it. Michael squeezed the trigger in controlled but rapid succession, sending three 230-grain chunks of copper-coated lead downrange. The first two rounds planted themselves squarely in Jose's face, snapping his head back and scattering his brains all over the shattered windshield behind him. The third round struck the door frame to the right of the window.

David had seen the driver lunge toward Michael. He could hear the fully automatic gunfire and rapidly advanced on the passenger's window. He continued to advance, shooting on the move, placing five well-aimed shots into Jose's torso.

No sooner had the shooting began, it came to an end. The entire ordeal happened in less than three seconds. David remained on the passenger side, covering the occupants in the van. It was clear the driver was dead; David saw his head explode with the impact of the rounds fired by Michael. Although the passenger hadn't moved, David couldn't be certain if he was dead or not. "Michael, you okay?" he called to his friend.

"I'm good," came the reply. "I can't see him." Michael saw the blood but didn't know just how badly injured the driver was. He knew the sight of blood didn't mean a man was out of the fight.

"He's down! The passenger is unconscious."

"I'm coming to you." Michael made his way around the back of the van while David continued to hold his pistol on the occupants.

"On your left," Michael called out as he approached the passenger door on the side of the van. David held fast as Michael approached. When he reached the door, Michael tried to open it, but the vehicle was too damaged. He checked the sliding door on the side. It was unlocked. He opened the door and saw an array of weapons scattered on the floor. The trunk of weapons had opened due to the violence of the collision. "Holy shit! We got lucky with this one, buddy. These guys were armed to the teeth."

Michael started grabbing the guns and moving them farther back in the van so they would be completely out of reach if the passenger came to. He then saw the AK-47 on the floorboard next to Miguel's trapped legs. He grabbed the gun and set it in the back also. He could see the TEC-9 on the floor by Jose's feet. Once he got a look at Jose's head, he wasn't worried about retrieving the gun. "Clear!"

THIRTY-TWO

When the shooting started, the remaining car sped away. The driver called 911 to report what was going on, but he wasn't about to stop and wait around. What he did accomplish was getting police and medics dispatched to the scene.

Michael asked David to call it in; he called Special Agent Savage. David advised the local dispatch center of their location. He explained that there were two plain-clothes officers on scene that had been involved in an OIS (or officer-involved shooting). There was one 11-44 (or dead body) and one severely injured male as a result of a traffic collision.

Michael reached Agent Savage and let him know what happened. He had climbed back into the van and rifled through the driver's pockets, looking for ID. He found a license in his wallet and read the name off to Agent Savage, "Jose Calderon." Agent Savage took the information and told Michael he'd be there shortly to ensure he didn't get hung up by the local police.

Michael tried to get to the pockets of the passenger but couldn't. Miguel was pinned, and Michael didn't want to move him too much for fear of making matters worse. Despite the fact that this guy intended on killing him and David, it was just the way it was. You did what was necessary and then rendered aid if needed.

Medics and the fire department showed up first. Because they were outside city limits, the Holtville police couldn't respond; and since there was only one deputy sheriff for that part of the county, it could be half an hour before he arrived depending on how far away he was.

Paramedic Leah Higgins grabbed her kit and was the first one to the van. David was standing by the passenger side door, waving her over. Michael met the firemen and told them the door was pretty jammed, and the passenger was pinned. They might need the Jaws of Life to get it open. The chief started giving orders, tasking each person with something specific. They set out with the efficiency of bees. It was only a matter of seconds before each man appeared at the van with an assortment of tools.

By then, Leah's partners were assisting her in assessing Miguel and trying to stabilize his head and neck. The fire crew went to work on the door with the powerful hydraulic pry tool and had it open in under a minute. Once the door popped open, the men forced it the rest of the way, bending the hinges backward. In doing so, the mess that had become of Miguel's legs was fully exposed. The legs were obviously broken in several places; the bones were visible and protruding through the skin.

Miguel was losing a large quantity of blood from the open wounds. Leah hopped out of the van and reached into her kit, removing a three-inch-wide cloth strap with a Velcro buckle and a handle that ran through it, used for drawing it tight around a limb to cut off the bleeding. She placed the tourniquet around Miguel's thigh just above the knee. She worked it back and forth until she could slide the strap down below the knee and slightly above the uppermost trauma. She fastened the buckle and began twist on the handle, cinching it tighter and tighter until the blood stopped flowing from the wounds below.

As Leah cut off the flow of blood, Miguel came to with an agonizing cry. The pain of his legs being crushed and the strike to his head had caused him to go unconscious, and the pain from the tourniquet being properly applied brought him back. He struggled violently until the paramedics were able to calm him down. Once he realized they were trying to help him, he settled down.

Michael saw the opportunity and stepped in. "Why were you following us?"

Miguel opened his eyes again and saw the man he'd been following all day. He looked at him momentarily and then closed his eyes and looked down again.

"Hey, why is Eme following us?"

This time, Miguel looked at Michael differently. Almost as if he knew he was dying. "*Pinche bendejo*, you don't know who you're messing with. You're a dead man."

"Oh really? You and your homey are doing a bang-up job on that one so far."

Miguel hadn't looked in the driver's seat. He had forgotten about Jose. He looked to his left and saw the lifeless form of his partner slumped over in his seat with the back of his skull missing from the violence inflicted by the gunshot wounds. He was a bloody mess, much like the many people they had executed in the past.

Miguel growled and tried to spit on Michael. Michael stepped to the side, and the bloody saliva mixture missed him. Leah, not one for sympathy, realizing whom she was treating, gave the tourniquet an extra twist just to make sure it was tight enough. Miguel screamed in agony.

David witnessed the extra twist and quickly grabbed Leah, helping her up and pulling her away from Miguel. "I don't want you to get the brunt of his anger," he said sincerely. "I'll monitor this and make sure it stays secure."

Leah smiled and tossed David the other one. "Can you put this one on the other leg?"

"I think I can manage." David caught the tourniquet and smiled sheepishly. "Miguel, your other leg is bleeding badly. I need to put this on, or you may bleed to death. It may cause you a little discomfort." David reached forward to place the strap around Miguel's left leg. Miguel knocked his hands away, preventing him from applying the device. One of the other medics who was crouched behind Miguel preparing an IV saw him swat David's hands away.

"The tourniquet is necessary. Without it, you will die. We have to put it on you before we do anything else. You're losing too much blood."

"Fuck you, I'd rather be dead."

Miguel's defiance was all the medic needed to hear. He was not the first uncooperative patient they had dealt with, and he wouldn't be the last. The man reached around from behind and trapped Miguel's arms, pinning them to his chest. "Put it on, I'll hold him."

"One more thing," David said as he reached in and grabbed the bottom of Miguel's shirt and stretched it up and over his head. "This should keep him from spitting on anyone." David then forced the tourniquet under his left thigh and worked it back and forth as Leah had done before until it was just below the knee yet above the wound.

Miguel struggled, but due to his injuries and loss of blood, his efforts were weak and short-lived. He agonized with every move of the bandage, his screams penetrating the T-shirt like a siren. When David finally started tightening it to cease the bleeding, the cries turned to rage, and Miguel said something that caught Michael completely off guard.

"Fuck you, Michael Garrett. That's right, *puta* bitch, we already know who you are. I may not be the one who does it, but you're gonna die, just like your mother."

"What the fuck do you know about my mother? She died when I was a kid," Michael bluffed.

"I know the bitch lives on Olive Street, and so do the Zetas. You and your family are all dead."

David finished applying the tourniquet, giving it an extra twist himself. He looked at Michael and could see the concern. He stood and grabbed his friend by the shoulder, leading him away from the van. "Mike, we gotta get back to your mom's. We gotta get her outta here just in case."

"How did they—" Michael started, but David cut him off.

"We can figure it out later, man. We have got to go right now."

David told the medics they had to leave, and he and Michael ran back to the Jeep, headed for home.

THIRTY-THREE

Leah and the other medics continued to work on extricating Miguel from the collapsed cabin of the van. As one fireman went to work with the Jaws of Life, trying to create a gap large enough to slide Miguel's legs out, a very obvious government sedan came racing down the road, screeching to a halt next to the ambulance.

Special Agent Savage had arrived, and he made sure everyone knew it. He badged his way up to the van and told everyone he was taking control of the scene. He had expected a local sheriff's deputy to be on scene by the time he got there, but the deputy had yet to arrive. He asked the medics for a quick update and was told the driver was confirmed dead, and the passenger was in critical condition. He'd lost a lot of blood, and if they didn't get him out soon, he wasn't going to make it.

Savage started looking around for Michael and David. When he didn't see them, he grabbed Leah. "Where are the two shooters?"

"They took off when this guy"—she pointed toward Miguel—"said something about knowing where Michael Garrett's mother lived."

"You have got to be kidding me! This guy called one of them by name and threatened his family?"

"Yeah, it was obviously a surprise to them too. He said something else too, something about *setas* or *tetas*—"

"The Zetas?" Savage interjected.

"That's it, Zetas. He said they knew where she lived too."

Savage stood quickly and walked back over to the van. The roar of the jaws and the groan of the metal being pressed away from Miguel's broken legs concealed his approach. He slapped the fireman working the jaws on the back to get his attention. The man looked over his shoulder at the special agent only to see him running a hand under his chin across his throat, the universal sign to shut down.

The fireman cut the motor and was gearing up to ask who the hell Savage thought he was, but the FBI agent cut him off.

"This is a matter of national security. This guy is not likely to make it anyway based on what you have already reported to me, and I need to talk to him now. I need all of you to stand down until I get what I need."

The fireman shot back, "Listen, buddy, if we don't get him outta there now, he's gonna die, and you won't get shit out of him. You'd best get back yourself and let us do our job."

Savage didn't back down. "This is a little over your pay grade and way out of your league. Trust me on this one, go back to your truck and play with your hose for a few minutes. I can't wait for you to play superhero. There's real work to be done."

"We'll see about that." The fireman walked past Savage, crashing into him with the large metal tool he had been using. Savage scowled at the man, but he'd gotten his way, and that was what mattered at the moment. He stepped up to the crumpled passenger side of the vehicle and placed his left hand on the back of Miguel's neck and began to squeeze.

Miguel felt the pressure, but the pain was subtle. His body was slowly going numb.

"What do you want now, Michael Garrett?" Miguel taunted.

Then the shirt that had been stretched over his head was ripped away, and he sat looking into the eyes of someone he'd not expected.

THIRTY-FOUR

Michael had never pushed his Jeep harder. It was a short drive in the scheme of things and only took a couple of minutes at the speed he drove through the little town, but it seemed like an eternity. His foot had barely touched the brake pedal until he reached his mother's home. Neither he nor David spoke a word.

Louise Garrett nearly jumped out of her seat when Michael and David came bursting through the front door. "Good heavens, Michael, what's wrong with you? You're gonna give me a heart attack."

Michael took a deep breath. He knew he wasn't overreacting, but now he had to convince his mother of the same. It wasn't going to be easy since he hadn't told her anything about the case he was working.

"Mom, you have got to listen to me for a minute. You're not safe here. You have to leave."

"What have you gotten yourself into, Michael? What do you mean I'm not safe here? I've lived in this city most of my life. I still leave the doors unlocked half the time."

"You have to trust me on this. I can explain it all later, when it's over and you're safe. Just know that the case David is helping me with has links to a Mexican drug cartel, and they already found out who I am. They know you are my mother, and they know where you live. They threatened to kill you."

Louise sat staring into the face of her only child. She could see the fear in his eyes, a fear she had never seen him exhibit. She stood up and walked to her son and hugged him. "It's okay, baby, I know you will figure it out."

She let go and stepped back. "What do you want me to do? Where do you want me to go?"

"When you and Dad bought the condo in Kauai, you put the deed in the family trust, right?"

"Yes, why?"

"Well, hopefully it won't show up as easily if someone just searches for property in your name. I don't know how they found out you lived here, but they did. I mean I know we were followed, but they had no way of knowing who owned this house this soon without someone else doing the legwork."

"What are you talking about? Who followed you?"

"It doesn't matter right now. You should be safe in Kauai. We need to get you to San Diego ASAP." Michael turned to David, "You watch the front, I'm gonna get her packed and call for transportation."

David turned and headed out the front door. He stood casually at the end of the porch, leaning against the brick pillar. Despite his appearance, he was anything but relaxed. He scanned both ends of the block and quickly took note of the vehicles parked in driveways and along the curb.

Michael told his mother to call the airlines and find a flight to Hawaii that left today. While she worked on that, he was hoping to call in another favor.

* * *

"Captain Picone."

"Captain, it's Garrett again. You guys still in Southern California?"

"You know it. I told you we'd stick around just in case. What can I do for you?"

"This thing has blown up, man. David and I just dumped a couple of Eme hit men. One's dead, the other should be, but he's hanging on like a cockroach. Anyway, while medics are treating his wounds, he tells me he knows who I am and where my mother lives. He said the Zetas also knew, and they were going to kill me and my family."

"Holy shit, you really stirred up the hornet's nest on this one. Good job! So what do you need?"

"I need to get my mom on a plane to Kauai. She's booking the flight now, but she needs a ride to San Diego. I can't take her, I have to get to the bottom of this before it gets any worse or I'd drive her. I don't trust anyone else to keep her safe."

"No worries. Consider it done. Give me her address, and I'll get the crew together. We're on sight with the bird fueled up and ready to go, so we'll be in the air in no time."

"440 Olive Street, Holtville. There's a school playground at the south end of the block. It's big enough to land in, and there's no interference getting in. It's one of the local soccer fields."

"Roger that. We'll be there in a little over an hour."

Picone hung up and immediately got his crew up and running. Kate was the first one to the Blackhawk and immediately started going through the preflight checklist. Taylor and Morton took their positions in the back while the captain punched in the coordinates. They were in the air in record time and headed to their destination in the most direct avenue possible.

*   *   *

Louise had secured a seat on the first flight out Saturday morning. She had hoped to find a flight out in the evening, but the latest Hawaii-bound flights left at 1:00 PM. She had hoped for a direct flight to Honolulu but had to settle for a layover at the Los Angeles International Airport. She wouldn't have to deplane, but the stop would add an hour to the flight. Either way, at least she knew her son could relax a little. From Honolulu, it would only be a short flight on an island hopper until she landed in Lihue, the primary airport on Kauai.

"How's it going, Mom?" Michael asked as she hung up the telephone.

"I couldn't get out today. The latest flights have already departed. I'm on the first flight out tomorrow."

"Okay. I have called in a favor to get you to San Diego in style. It may not be first-class cozy, but it's the quickest, safest way to get you up there that I could think of. Besides, it'll be the ride of your life." Michael started to smile at the thought of his mother climbing aboard the Blackhawk. He couldn't wait to see the expression on her face when the big helicopter landed at the end of the street.

"What are you talking about, and why do you have that stupid grin on your face?"

Michael snapped back to reality. "We need to get you packed. Pack for a week. That gives you enough to get by and time to do laundry."

"How long do you think I'm going to be gone?" Louise asked, concerned.

"I don't know for sure, Mom, but it's better to have and not need than need and not have." Michael grabbed his mother's hand and headed down the hall to get her packing.

Louise was a great traveler. She and Michael had kept up the tradition even after his father had died and met every September in Kauai. Michael stayed for a couple weeks; she stayed for no less than a month, sometimes longer. Packing was easy; she had been going for so long she had left enough clothes there that she only ever packed for two days just in case she decided to stay the night in Honolulu before heading to Kauai.

She was packed in no time, at which point there was nothing more to do than wait.

THIRTY-FIVE

Javier had gotten his parents safely to his home. They never knew of the drama that unfolded behind them, but that was certain to change by the time the evening news was over. It was no sooner that they all got in and Martha and Enrique had put their bags in the room they would be sleeping in when Martha picked up the cordless telephone in the family room and handed it to Enrique.

"Call the detective they told you about, the one that can let us talk to Rosa."

Enrique took the phone and pulled the piece of paper that had Detective Cook's number on it from his pocket. He took a deep breath, feeling the anticipation build in his body with the hope of hearing his baby girl's voice. His chest tightened as he punched in the number. The phone was ringing.

"Detective Cook."

"Detective, my name is Enrique Jimenez, Rosa's father. I was told you could help me talk to my daughter."

"How did you get this number?" Cook asked, a little surprised but more suspicious of the caller. He instantly presumed it was Carlos, attempting another ploy to make contact with Rosa.

"I have been talking with Michael Garrett. He gave me your number and said that you could help. He said he was going to call you and tell you what was going on."

Cook looked at his phone; the caller's number had been captured by the caller ID. "I haven't heard from Garrett yet. I tell you what, I'll call him right now. If he confirms what you've said, then I'll call you back."

"Okay," responded Enrique. He hung up the phone, disheartened that he couldn't speak to Rosa, but held out hope that Michael would follow through with what he'd said.

Cook dialed Michael's cell phone. He answered on the first ring.

Michael immediately recalled he was supposed to call Cook and let him know the Jimenez family was going to call him. "Hey, Jon, let me guess, you got a call from someone claiming to be Rosa's dad, right?"

"Yeah, they said you gave them my number and that you were going to call in advance."

"I did and I was, but things got a little out of hand before that happened. In any case, can you get them in touch with Rosa? I think it'll help keep the family strong and moving in the right direction. Also, I need you to contact the local FBI officer. Tell them you're working off information I provided and have them call Special Agent Ryan Savage in the El Centro office if they have any issues. I need you to pick up Carlos wherever he is. The feds should be able to hold him for as long as needed. I can tie him to Los Zetas as well as La Eme. If nothing else, book him for conspiracy to kill a police officer and his family."

"Shit, Mike, what did you get yourself into?"

"Everybody keeps asking me that. I know you can handle it, Jon. I'll tell you the rest later. I gotta go."

"All right, brother, but you are gonna owe me big on this one." Cook hung up and retrieved the previous caller's number. He hit the Send key and waited.

"Bueno," Enrique answered the phone, sounding short of breath.

"Mr. Jimenez, it's Detective Cook. I'm going to give you a number, and I want you to call it in five minutes. When you do, just tell them who you are and ask for Rosa. They'll be expecting you."

"Okay, okay, thank you." Enrique was so excited his eyes began to well up with tears. Martha was next to him, anxiously waiting to speak to Rosa as well. She could see the emotion in her husband's eyes, and she herself began to cry.

*　　*　　*

Cook called the jail and explained the situation. The jail staff wasn't used to making such accommodations but had no problem doing so under the circumstances. Shortly after Cook called, Rosa was placed in a holding cell with a telephone. She was told she would not be able to call out, but if the phone rang, she was to answer it.

Rosa didn't fully understand what was going on, and the officers in the jail didn't take time to tell her more. They did what was necessary and went about their business. Although Rosa was currently their most popular visitor, she was still only one of about four hundred inmates who all needed or wanted something.

*   *   *

Enrique began dialing the number Cook had given him at exactly five minutes after they hung up. The phone seemed to ring forever before someone finally answered it.

"Douglas County Jail, how can I help you?"

His voice was almost shaky by this point. "Hello, I would like to speak with my daughter."

"And who would that be?"

"I'm sorry, Rosa Jimenez."

"One moment, sir." The correctional officer put Enrique on hold and transferred the call to Rosa's cell.

Rosa was sitting on a metal bed bolted to the wall, staring at the telephone. She had only been in jail for little more than half a day. She was exhausted from the stress of the situation and couldn't stop wondering if she'd made a mistake. If she should have never said a word to Michael, fearing she only put her family in danger. Had she known half of what already transpired, she would have known she'd made a mistake.

The phone began to ring. Despite the fact she'd been waiting for it, the electronic ring startled her. Rosa grabbed the phone, wholeheartedly expecting it to be one of the detectives asking her more questions. "Hello."

"Rosa, is that you, *mija*?"

"Papa?" Rosa couldn't believe her ears. In a million years, she never expected it to be her father.

Enrique nodded to Martha, indicating Rosa was on the phone. Martha hurried into the kitchen and grabbed the other telephone. "Rosa, baby, how are you?"

Rosa told her parents what had happened. None of which was new to Enrique or Martha as they had heard it all before from Michael. The story tore at the hearts of the parents nonetheless, hearing their little girl relay such a horrific saga that Enrique knew was all his fault.

Enrique explained how Michael was helping them. He explained that they were now staying with her brother Javier. They wanted to know when they were going to be able to see her again.

Rosa didn't know. She hoped sooner than later and remembered Michael saying something about Tuesday. The whole thing had unraveled so quickly; she didn't remember all the details, but for the first time since Michael had left her, she actually felt relieved. As if she hadn't made a mistake after all, and the horror that had been her life was finally coming to an end.

THIRTY-SIX

Special Agent Savage stepped away from the van and hailed the medics. They quickly returned to their patient to finish extracting him from the vehicle. They quickly resumed what they were doing until Leah announced that he was dead. She was checking Miguel's vital signs. She could tell he wasn't breathing, and she confirmed he had no pulse. She grabbed the defibrillator, but it was of no use. He had lost too much blood.

"I hope you got what you needed," she said to the federal agent. "Maybe if you'd let us do our job, you'd still be able to talk to him."

"Actually, I got exactly what I needed," responded Savage. "And honestly, you didn't really want him to live, did you? Think of the money this will save the taxpayers."

The medics gathered their equipment, leaving the two deceased men where they lay. It was the standard protocol when death occurred. They would stand by for the deputy to arrive before turning the scene over to him to conduct the death investigation.

Agent Savage stood by as well, to ensure the deputy knew what was going on. He wanted to make certain the deputy was aware the FBI was handling the investigation, and that the agency would be in charge of the bodies. No one was to notify next of kin.

It wasn't much longer before Deputy Velázquez arrived. Agent Savage met him first and quickly began to explain that he was to do nothing other than conduct the death investigation.

"I'm Special Agent Savage with the FBI."

"What's going on, Agent Savage? I heard we had shots fired at the scene of traffic collision, but no one said anything about it being the feds," Velázquez said quizzically.

"We have a couple of detectives working a case in cooperation with the FBI. It's absolutely our investigation. I'll make it easy on you. You just handle the coroner investigation, and I'll deal with the rest."

Velázquez couldn't have been happier. The last thing he wanted was to get tied up on a double homicide. He already had the largest area to cover in the county. "Thanks, I'm sorry it took so long for me to get here. I had to clear a burglary report I was taking in Winterhaven." It was the easternmost town in the valley, right on the Arizona border, and about forty-five miles from Holtville.

"No problem, Deputy. Your timing is actually perfect. I'm just going to step over here and get out of your way. I have some calls I need to make anyway." Savage walked back over to his vehicle and sat down in the driver's seat. He shut the door and turned up the air-conditioning to block out the heat. He pulled out his phone and began to dial.

Deputy Velázquez went about his business, conducting his investigation. The coroner investigation was a cinch by comparison to most. All he had to do was document the death and possible cause. It was actually up to the pathologist to confirm the cause. Velázquez spoke to medics to confirm what life-saving measures they had performed. He found it odd that they were told to stop by the federal agent, but he dismissed it quickly enough since he wasn't responsible for the homicide, and it seemed reasonable based on what the medics said. It didn't sound as if the guy had a chance.

Velázquez had all he needed and quickly called for the mortuary. The county used Hems Brothers, a contract mortuary in El Centro, for all of its body-removal needs. It wouldn't take more than about fifteen minutes for one of their guys to show up. He told the medics he had what he needed, and the mortuary was on the way.

They went back to work on the van to get Miguel's body freed up so the mortuary could get him out. Now that he was dead, much less concern had to be taken, and they had him out in no time. Leah and one of the other firemen went ahead and removed Miguel from the seat and had him out on the ground. She surveyed his injuries. There was a lot of blood, more than she had expected. Miguel's wounds were worse than she'd realized. It made her even angrier that the FBI agent was right. He never really stood a chance.

Savage stayed in his vehicle the entire time on his phone. It wasn't until the mortuary van pulled up that he hung up and returned to assert himself again. He handed Velázquez and the man taking the body a business card and told them if they had any questions to call him; then he left.

THIRTY-SEVEN

Tensions were high at the Garrett residence on Olive. Louise was packed and waiting. She watched impatiently as Michael had been on and off the phone, but he never left her alone. On one hand, she knew her son would protect her; on the other, she was terrified, wondering who would do the same for him.

Michael had hung up from his last conversation. He checked with David out front, who reported all was well for the moment. He looked at his mother sitting quietly on the couch in the living room. She'd been watching his every move. There were no words to explain the sorrow he felt for getting her involved. He had never imagined following up on this would place his mother in harm's way.

He walked over to her and sat next to her on the couch. He placed an arm over her shoulder. "How you doing, Mom?"

"I'm just waiting," she replied.

Michael could hear the apprehension in her voice, making him feel even worse. "I know this is easier said than done, but don't worry, Mom. Things are going to work out."

"I believe in you, Michael. You've always been good at what you do, but I'd sure like to know how you can be so sure this time."

Michael smiled. "It's easy, Mom. First, you are already taken cared of. You have a place to go far from here that won't be as easy to find. Second, I have a friend with a helicopter who is coming to get you so I know you'll be safely out of town and that no one can follow you. Third, once you're safe, David and I will be able to wrap this thing up, turn it over to the feds, and I can simply go back to Tahoe after a little time off spent on the island with you."

"Sounds good, everything but this helicopter. You know I hate those things. All the years your father and I went to Kauai, not once did we take a helicopter tour."

"Don't worry, this guy and his crew are some of the best out there. It's not some rinky-dink little thing. You couldn't have a safer way to travel. Besides, I can't have you on the roads right now."

Michael leaned over and kissed his mother on the cheek. He got up and checked with David to see if he needed anything. "All is well," came the response. Michael kept talking with his mother about anything and everything unrelated to the current situation. He wanted to keep her as calm as he could while they waited for the Blackhawk. It didn't take long before his phone rang again.

"This is Garrett."

"Hey, it's Picone. We're five minutes out. I'll see you at the LZ."

"Roger that. We'll be in the same gray sedan we left LA in." Michael hung up and told David it was time to go.

"I'll meet you in the garage, door will be going up shortly."

"Roger that. All is clear."

Michael picked up Louise's bags and told her it was time to go. "We're taking David's car in the garage, Mom. They'll be here in five minutes or less."

Louise followed her son down the hall and out into the garage. He seated her in the backseat on the passenger side and closed the door. He opened the garage door, and David came around the corner.

"You drive," Michael said as he climbed into the front passenger seat.

David got in and started the car. "Where to?"

"Picone is going to pick her up at the school yard at the end of the block, but I want you to go the long way around just to make sure we don't have any more visitors this time."

"No problem." David pulled out and turned to the left. He made a right at the end of the block and drove a couple of blocks down before turning again. It was late afternoon now, and the temperatures were soaring. No one was out that didn't need to be.

"So far everything is clear behind us. No vehicles, no people that I can see," David reported.

"All right, when you come to the school, there's going to be a vehicle access point at the end of the chain-link fence just before the buildings. Turn in there and pull out onto the field past the playground."

David drove past the school to the access point. Michael noticed there were a few boys kicking a soccer ball around out in the field. As soon as David was in the field and stopped the car, Michael quickly jumped out of the car and pulled out his badge.

"Hey, boys, can you come over here for second?"

They all stopped and looked at him and slowly started to walk toward him. "We didn't do anything," replied one of the boys.

"No, you didn't. My name is Detective Garrett, and I was wondering if you guys have ever seen a helicopter land up close?"

All the boys shook their heads no. While Michael was talking, the sound of the approaching Blackhawk was growing louder. Michael looked for the approaching helicopter and pointed it out to the boys.

"Well, that one is going to be landing here right now. I think you guys should watch, but I really need you to watch from the playground, okay? The pilot needs the field clear. It's an emergency."

The boys all watched the helicopter as it came closer and closer. They started talking among themselves about how cool it looked and took off, running for the playground.

Michael looked back at the helicopter and then climbed back into the car. "Mom, they'll get you to the airport. I know your flight doesn't leave until tomorrow, so just call Lilly with the condo right there by San Diego Harbor. Spend the night and have her drop you off in the morning."

Lilly was a lifelong friend Louise had gone to high school with. She stayed with her the night before she flew anywhere, as well as the night she returned. It was more an excuse to visit than anything but also proved to be very convenient as well. Louise never had to pay for parking.

"Okay, but you better stay in touch." Louise couldn't help but notice the roar of the approaching helicopter. It was both impressive and frightening to her. She gazed out the window, watching as it slowly hovered to the earth, until she could no longer see through the dust and debris it stirred up.

Another thirty seconds and the helicopter was down. Michael saw Sergeant Taylor approaching with something in his hands. Michael climbed out of the car to meet with Taylor.

"Fancy meeting you here, Detective Garrett. I have some goggles for your mother."

"Thank you. She's in the back." Michael motioned to the rear passenger door. Taylor quickly opened the door and held out the goggles for Louise.

"Good afternoon, ma'am. My name is Sergeant Jack Taylor. I'll be your flight attendant for the ride to San Diego, but before we get started, I thought you might like to put these on." He handed Louise the goggles, which she pulled over her head, covering her eyes.

"Nice to meet you," replied Louise as she took Taylor's extended hand. He helped her from the vehicle, and Michael handed him her bag.

"We'll be in touch," shouted the sergeant as he led Louise back to the helicopter.

Michael got back into the vehicle and watched as his mother was assisted into the Blackhawk. She had no sooner cleared the doorway when the massive turbine engines roared and cloaked the helicopter behind another cloud of debris. By the time the dust began to settle, the Blackhawk was in the air and headed to San Diego.

THIRTY-EIGHT

David looked across the vehicle at Michael as the helicopter grew smaller in the distance. "Time to regroup and take the next step. It would seem there's no backing out now. They know who you are. We have got to finish this now."

"Yes, we do. I'm glad you're still on board, my friend."

"You know I would never leave you hanging. So let's find someplace cozy and plot our next move."

"Good call. We definitely need to get this thing back under control. Head back to El Centro, we might as well get out of here and go somewhere a little more centrally located. Besides, there are no hotels in Holtville anyway."

David headed back through the playground, waving at the boys as they ran back onto the field. He pulled onto the roadway and headed toward El Centro. No sooner had they hit the intersection, one of the two Holtville police cruisers drove by, headed to the school grounds.

"A day late and dollar short," David said.

"Probably would have been the most excitement he had all day too. Oh well. Let's go."

David kept driving and watched the officer pull into the school yard where he had just pulled out. He turned, accelerated, and headed out of town. The drive to El Centro was anything but quiet. The two detectives brainstormed what they had learned and what they had accomplished so far. They had identified key players in the case, had Rosa's family out of the house and presumably safe, and had been identified by men they were after. They could only hope that since the two who had been following them were out of commission, they would have a fresh start and not be tipped off before they took their next step.

Michael directed David to get off on Fourth Street again. There was an old Holiday Inn there that would serve perfectly for what they needed. They exited the interstate and made the first right onto Smoketree Road. The hotel

---

was only a half block away, just on the other side of a convenient store and gas station. As expected, there was no problem getting a room. El Centro was not on the list of many tourist destinations in the middle of summer. They got a third-floor corner room. It provided them with the best tactical advantage, securing the high ground, not to mention gave them a view of two sides of the building where other rooms did not. Once they got up to the room, they each started scratching out what they had discussed. What they had learned and where they were headed. Once they completed their own notes, they began to compare and figured they'd come up with the final plan from there.

Michael went first and started with a makeshift timeline. He had been on the go since Thursday night when he got the call from dispatch. He met with Cook, got the story from Rosa, and was on his way to Los Angeles. That was at around 1:45 in the morning. He met with David around 4:00 AM, and the two of them had yet to stop.

David was listening and finally interrupted. "Where is this going? I have been with you for most of this, so I don't see the need to rehash it."

"I figure we got made the first time we showed up at the Jimenez house. Carlos probably called someone and told them about Rosa. Then they put someone on her parents' house, just waiting to see if couple guys like you and me showed up. What doesn't make sense is how they identified me so fast."

"The Internet, man, you can find anything online."

"I thought about that, but it still doesn't jive. There was no way of knowing I was linked to that address any more than the house on Alvarado. There was no reason to assume that was my home or my mother."

"I don't know, but we'll have to come back to that. It's almost five now, and we need to keep our momentum. Where do you see this going next?"

"Okay, you're right. We have to get a step ahead again. Obviously, Los Zetas and Eme know Rosa talked, and they know we're on to them. It's time to shake things up just a bit. We need to talk to that customs agent, James Elmond."

David sat back. "Fair enough, my turn. You woke me up at oh dark hundred and dragged me down to your mothball of a hometown on a case that has already proven to be out of our jurisdiction. I have had one good meal all day, am going to miss a home-cooked dinner now, and had to shoot someone. So I say we grab a bite, drink a beer, and then go talk to this Elmond fellow."

"You make a strong argument. He is supposed to be on until 10:00 PM, and there isn't much to do between now and then. Let me check in with Agent Savage and find out how things panned out at the shooting."

"Sounds good."

THIRTY-NINE

Michael scrolled through his call log and hit Send once he came to the number he was looking for.

"I was expecting you to call sooner or later."

"We had to cut out before you got there."

"Yeah, I heard they ID'd you and your mother already and have a hit on you both. I told you that's how these guys operate. You get your mom out of town?"

"Yeah, she's being relocated now. Did you get anything useful out of the passenger?"

"No, he died shortly after I arrived. I tried to talk to him, but it was too late. Where are you now?"

"We're getting ready to go eat. We're headed to Lucille's at the corner of Imperial and Adams if you want to join us."

"I could use a bite. I'll see you there."

Michael hit the End button, which was all it took to get David moving.

"Lucille's it is, but I'm driving. I've had enough of yours for the day."

Michael laughed as he and David headed out. They met Agent Savage at the restaurant. Conversation was relaxed at first as each man took turns telling tales of their careers. Michael finished his meal first; after which, the mood became more serious.

"These guys are after my family. I know those two in the van were Eme, but the passenger said the Zetas knew where my mother lived. How the hell did they piece that together?"

Agent Savage looked back and forth as the two men across from him watched while he swallowed his last bite. "You had been to the house, right? So it's most likely that they were reporting to someone. Ortiz used to work for the Mexican Federal Police. The man knows how to investigate, not to mention he is well connected."

"I should have known better. I'm smarter than that. I let my emotions get ahead of me on this one."

"Mike," David started, "I would have done the same thing. You had no reason to believe we were being watched. I still can't believe these guys were already on the Jimenez house."

"Don't be so surprised," said Savage. "The Zetas didn't get to where they are so quickly by force alone. They are highly trained and well organized. They got ahead by anticipating their enemies' moves and striking with extreme violence. Right now you two are doing well. You killed two of them and got your mother to safety before they did anything else."

"I understand the passenger died?" David asked.

"Yes, he did," replied Savage. "I wish I had a little more time to question him, but he was on his way out when I got there."

"Did he say anything?"

"No, in fact when I first went up to him, his shirt was pulled over his face. One of you had something to do with that, I presume? I pulled his shirt back down so he knew who he was dealing with. He thought it you at first," he said, pointing at Michael. "Anyway, I know it clicked when he saw me. We had met once before. I came across him in another case. His name was Miguel Rios. He was rumored to be a hit man for Eme. As with everything else we talked about earlier, I just haven't gotten enough evidence to prove beyond a reasonable doubt."

Michael looked at his watch. "I hate to cut it short, but we have a lot to do before we pay Mr. Elmond a visit."

They all dropped enough money on the table to cover their share of the bill and tip and headed out to their cars. "If you guys get into any more trouble, just give me a call. My office line forwards to my cell if I don't answer. I took the possession of the bodies from the shooting to keep your part under wraps for now and to keep the local jurisdictions from panicking, so I'm headed back to my office to take care of the paperwork. I'll be there for a few hours before calling it a night."

"Thanks for that. We'll be in touch," said Michael.

Forty

David found himself heading back to the hotel on autopilot. "What do you say we hit the hotel for a few? We have a little time to spare before Elmond gets off, and I could use a shower." David could smell the scent of blood from the man in the van. He wanted to get rid of that before he did anything else.

"Sounds good. I'll catch up with Picone and Mom. They should have landed in San Diego by now."

Back at the hotel, David immediately jumped in the shower to remedy his problem. Michael called Picone to confirm all went well with the flight. He was pleased to hear his mother had made the trip and, according to Picone, seemed to enjoy it despite her fear of helicopters. Picone told him they were headed back to the Naval Air Station in El Centro and would remain on standby there. Things had obviously heated up, and he thought it would be a good idea to get a little closer in the event they could be of future assistance. He still had contacts on Team Shadow, and with the Border Patrol down there, that may come in handy.

After talking to Picone, Michael called his mother just to make sure she didn't divert from the plan. He had no reason to believe she would, but he needed the peace of mind. He spoke with her briefly, and as planned, she was going to stay the night at Lilly's. She would catch her flight to Kauai first thing in the morning.

David finished up in the shower, and Michael decided it wasn't such a bad idea. He'd been on the go for the last day and half and was pretty sure he could smell himself. Not a bad thing on a camping trip but not ideal for the current state of affairs.

While Michael rinsed off, David tried to relax. It was six o'clock, and there had to be some local news on one of the channels. David found the news and waited to see what reports there would be about the accident and shooting from earlier. It was the lead story but very vague. The reporter announced that two men whose identities had yet to be revealed died at the scene of a traffic collision. Witnesses were difficult to find, but there were also reports of shots being fired around the same time in the same general area. The local authorities would only say the FBI was investigating the deaths of the two men.

David relayed the news to Michael. Both were pleased it had been kept so vague. With any luck, it would remain that way for a couple more days until they would have time to notify their departments. They finished the local news, taking the time to relax for the next half hour.

"Well, it's as good a time as any. What do you say we head down to the Holtville Border Crossing and have a chat with Elmond? I'm half-inclined to do it while he's on duty and just use one of their secondary check stations for a little privacy."

"Might as well," responded David, and they headed out.

David topped off the car at the gas station before getting on the freeway. As soon as he was done, the two were eastbound on Interstate 8, headed back toward Holtville. Only this time, when they exited the freeway, they turned right and headed straight for the border.

*　　*　　*

It only took about twenty minutes to get there. They didn't rush the drive this time. The two detectives felt they were setting the pace again and took their time getting there. As they headed south on Highway 7, the border crossing began to come into view. David stopped at the last posted turnaround point. He noticed there was a short road that led from the paved turn around to the customs office. It had to be employee parking. He followed the road around to the small parking lot and parked at the north end. The two exited the vehicle and began walking to the main office.

The facility was the newest border crossing in recent times and did anything but give someone the feeling of being welcome. It was a large crossing with high-tech equipment, drug—and explosive-sniffing K-9s, and well-trained staff. The problem was not the crossing itself or the protocol required to gain entry; it was the fact that of the nearly two thousand miles of border, only a small fraction of it was fenced. It was the most heavily crossed border in the world, with an estimated 350,000,000 crossings each year. A few miles in either direction and anyone could easily walk across the border into the desert. It happened all the time. People coming with hopes of making a better life; many of whom never made it as they would succumb to the harsh environment after wandering lost in the desert. Others trying to make a quick buck, illegally smuggling drugs or people into the country, were caught fairly regularly, but then there were those like Fernando Ortiz who had found a way to circumvent detection; his name was James Elmond.

As Michael and David approached the building, a customs agent came out to meet them. "If you're heading for Mexico, you'll need to cross on the other side, gentlemen."

"Actually, we were headed into the office." Michael pulled out his badge and ID, handing it over the customs agent. David did the same. "We're working a case, and I believe James Elmond might be of assistance. I understand he's working tonight."

The agent inspected the two men's IDs and handed them back. "That shouldn't be a problem," said the agent. "Let's go back to the office, and I'll let the supervisor know. Jimmy is working one of the lanes right now."

Inside the office, the customs officer left the two at the counter while he summoned a supervisor. Shortly thereafter, Vania Garcia came out. "I understand you gentlemen would like to speak with Officer Elmond regarding your case? Is there something I need to be aware of?"

"Yes, ma'am. We do need to speak with him, and it is something you should be aware of. We were hoping to speak with him privately first. After which, I would be happy to fill you in. It was actually Special Agent Savage with the FBI that pointed us in Elmond's direction."

"Let me just get someone out to relieve him, and I'll set you guys up in one of our interview rooms." Vania picked up a telephone on the counter and punched in a four-digit number. It wasn't long before someone answered. Michael could hear her asking the person on the other end to take Elmond's place in lane 2 and send him to the office. A couple minutes later, a man came in and approached Vania.

"They said you needed to see me, boss."

"Actually, it's these gentlemen here. They're working on a case and think you may be able to assist them. I would appreciate it if you would cooperate with them with whatever they need. You can use any of the vacant interview rooms."

"No problem," Elmond replied.

"If you don't mind, why don't we just take it outside? It's nothing that requires an interrogation room." Michael knew using such rooms was nothing more than a way to make people comfortable, but the bottom line was they were all set up to be monitored, and it was likely someone else would be listening in. Since he didn't really know if Elmond was the only one working with Eme and the Zetas, he didn't want to risk anything.

"Works for me," said Elmond, and the three men headed back out into the hot evening air. They started walking back out toward David's sedan but walked beyond the car into the desert so others who may walk into the lot wouldn't overhear anything. "So what can I do for you?"

Michael was sizing Elmond up. He was unimpressive, a little shorter than average and a little overweight as well. The product of sedentary life with a sedentary job. He looked relaxed, but Michael was sure that would change shortly. He wondered if this was Ortiz's link to information, the kind that would have identified his mother.

"Well, for starters, you can tell me what you know about Fernando Ortiz and how Los Zetas figured out where my mother lives?"

David hadn't expected that to be quite where the interview started. He slowly took a step back, creating a little more distance between him and Elmond in case Elmond tried something.

Elmond stood his ground, but his posture changed. It was clear Michael had struck a nerve. "Excuse me! I don't know a Fernando Ortiz, and how the hell should I know anything about Los Zetas or your mother?"

Michael knew he didn't have proof, but Elmond's change in posture and startled response was affirmation enough that he was on the right track. "Look, James, I know you're the go-to guy for La Eme around here. They use you to smuggle anything they want into the country. La Eme is working with Los Zetas, and Fernando Ortiz is the link and the man with the money. So let's try this again. If you don't tell me what I need to know, I'll send Ortiz a little message via the Café Nueva Asia and tell him how talkative you've been, or—"

Elmond stopped him. "You can't tell Ortiz. I'll be dead by morning. I don't know how you got your information, but you don't know who you're dealing with. These guys will kill us all and our families if they even think I talked."

"How did you get involved in this?" asked David.

"It wasn't like you think. It started one day when a couple guys passing through got sent to secondary for a search." Secondary was where the agents working the lanes sent suspicious people or vehicles to for additional searching. "I was the one who searched them and found they had a case of liquor. They're only supposed to be able to bring in two liters per person, so they were going to have to give it up. Anyway, one of them apologized, explaining he thought the limit was two cases, not two bottles. He handed me a one-hundred-dollar bill and said it would never happen again. Before I knew it, I had tucked the money in my pocket and sent them on their way."

"You have got to be kidding me. You got bought out for a hundred bucks over a case of liquor?" asked Michael.

"It's not that easy. I have a house I can't afford or sell. I needed the money. I never imagined I'd see them again, but the next day, they were back. This time,

I was in a lane when they came through. The driver told me he needed to talk to me and told me to meet him when I got off at Punky's Bar in Holtville."

Elmond went on to explain how he didn't know what to do. He knew they had him by the balls; if he didn't go and they reported him, he'd lose his job. So he met with the men. They told them what they needed, and that he would be compensated well for his cooperation. It started with small loads. He figured they were testing him, but as he proved to be trustworthy, the smuggling grew. He never knew for sure what was coming through, but the vehicles grew in size until they started coming on the days he was scheduled for the commercial lanes. Lanes designated for big rigs and box trucks. He had been paid well, and the payments grew with the shipments.

Michael listened to the man explain himself. It was disgusting to listen to the man justify what he'd done over one hundred dollars. "So let me ask you again, how did the Zetas find out where my mother lives?"

Elmond shook his head from side to side. "I don't know, I swear. I haven't seen anyone for about a week now. I figured they'd be calling shortly to plan the next shipment."

Michael looked at David and back at the dirty customs agent, who was sweating even more than his fat little body should have been despite the heat. "I'll tell you what, Jimmy," Michael said as he fished a business card out of his wallet. He started writing his cell phone number down on the card when suddenly, he heard a loud slapping sound. It was the sound made when high-caliber rifle round struck flesh.

Michael looked up at Elmond only to see horror and dismay on the man's face as he collapsed in a heap. The bullet had penetrated his chest and traveled through his torso, shattering his vertebrae and severing his spinal cord as it exited his body. David and Michael never heard the report of the rifle. They each grabbed one of James Elmond's arms and dragged him as quickly as they could toward David's sedan. They took cover behind the front of the car, hoping the engine would be enough to stop any more incoming rounds.

David moved to the rear of the vehicle and opened the trunk. He reached in and retrieved his M4 rifle. He began to scan the surrounding desert in the distance, but he wasn't even sure exactly where the shot had come from.

Michael tore open Elmond's uniform. He wasn't wearing a vest, not that it would have made a difference with the rifle round that ripped through his body. The entry wound was clean; it didn't appear all that damaging. It was deceptive. Michael rolled Elmond on to his side to check for the exit wound. It looked like a crater large enough to put a baseball in, and the crimson pool of blood growing in the asphalt parking lot said it all. The high-caliber round had done its job.

Michael released his grip on Elmond's shoulder, and gravity pulled him onto his back. He looked at the man's face; it was already ashen white. Elmond was dead.

"He's gone. Did you see anything?" Michael asked David.

"No. There's too much going on around here to pinpoint anything, even the dust of a fleeing vehicle."

"Shit!" Michael yelled. "Then they might be out there still."

"I know. I'll cover you, go get help."

Michael didn't hesitate. He sprinted back to the customs border station where people were looking, trying to figure out what was going on. He ran inside and was immediately passed by agents who had seen what happened. They had all grabbed M16 rifles from the gun lockers and were headed outside to assist.

"Elmond is down. He was hit once in the chest and appears to be dead. My partner has been watching the direction the shot came from but hasn't been able to spot anyone."

The agents quickly deployed to defensive positions around the border crossing. All lanes were closed immediately. One of the agents slapped the emergency fast barricade button, and a row of DSC2000 barricades sprung up from the road into place in less than a second, blocking all lanes of traffic into or out of the United States. Agents responded with the efficiency of a school of hungry piranhas on an injured animal.

No one had bothered to ask Michael any questions. It was clear their objective was to secure the border first and address the injured later. While everyone was establishing a defensive position, Vania Garcia came out to talk to Michael and find out if there was any additional information he could provide.

"What happened out there?" she asked.

"Somebody sniped him," Michael said. "We were following up on a case I've been working that involves La Eme, Los Zetas, and a customs agent on the payroll."

"That's what you needed to talk to Elmond about, he was the agent, and you didn't tell me!"

Michael could see Vania was pissed. He understood completely. "You would have never let him talk to me if I had told you everything up front. You would have wanted to deal with it yourself, and we'd still be going over details. Well, I didn't have time for that. Lives are at stake, and I needed answers today. I had to talk to him now, and I'm sorry that meant keeping information from you."

"And it got my agent shot," she snapped.

"Thus proving my point," Michael said. "Look, you can reprimand me later. Right now, we need to get an air unit headed this way to check the area. My partner is out there hunkered behind our car, hoping to see the shooter before he gets shot too. Elmond is dead, and you guys are setting up a defensive perimeter. Personally, I don't think you have to worry about an attack. They already completed their mission and are most likely in the wind."

"Well, Detective, we have protocol to follow around here. The nation's security comes first, and you're damn right, I'll be addressing you when this is over with." Vania turned and made her way back to her office where she began making phone calls and notifying her superiors what had transpired.

Michael couldn't believe the response of the agents. On one hand, he was impressed with the speed at which the border was locked down, and people took their positions. He looked back out at the vehicle where he could see David scanning the distance for any signs of the shooter, as well as the lifeless body of Elmond next to the vehicle. Michael could see three customs agents making their way out to the vehicle to assist David.

It was time to call Special Agent Savage again.

FORTY-ONE

Juan Guerra and Sammy Trujillo had been placed on standby. They were former sergeants in the Mexican army and operators in the Mexican Special Forces. They were now part of Los Zetas and lived in Mexicali. They had received a phone call and were informed that there had been a breach in security. They were told to be ready to deploy to the United States, Holtville specifically.

The phone call was nothing out of the ordinary until they were told they would be operating in the U.S. The instructions that followed were to meet with Fernando at the Café Nueva Asia immediately, and he would provide them with additional intelligence.

Juan and Sammy met each other outside the café and went in together. As the men entered the dimly lit restaurant, they took inventory of everything going on around them. The sense of awareness began with their training, increased with experience, and grew with paranoia. The restaurant was more than just a front; it was a fully operational moneymaking business. There were patrons, both locals and tourists, and of course, there was always Fernando's protection. Juan and Sammy knew the men, so there was no need to be rude. They gave each the courtesy of a head nod as they passed.

Fernando was waiting for them at his usual table at the rear of the restaurant, in a corner out of sight. The men approached Fernando and adjusted their chairs so that neither of them had his back to the entrance. There were no pleasantries among them. Fernando slid an eight-by-ten picture across the table and told the two men that this was their target. He had been identified as a potential leak and needed to be silenced before he could divulge any more of the operation.

"This man is our connection at the border. He has been very helpful for our business, and he knows too much. I have information that he is being looked at and is likely to talk. This cannot be allowed. The two men that are looking for him have already killed two men. Although they are not the targets, they too pose a threat," Fernando said clearly.

Juan tapped his finger on the photograph. "I know this man. I have not dealt with him, but I was made aware of his use to our organization. Are you sure you don't want us to simply kill the two that are looking for him?"

"It is time to send a message to the Americans. They speak of us and Mexico as if they are better than we are, as if they are stronger than we are. It is time to show them that they are more vulnerable than they think, and we will do that by killing one of their agents while he stands at one of their so-called guarded borders. The others will be dealt with in time, but I want you to start with him," Fernando emphasized by slamming his fist on Elmond's head in the picture.

Sammy and Juan both acknowledged the order with a nod. Fernando explained everything they would need would be waiting for them at a house in Calexico.

"Where is this house?" asked Juan.

"Come with me," said Fernando. "I will show you."

The three men stood, and Fernando led them to a flight of stairs that descended to a small basement. There was a locked door that appeared to lead to another room. Fernando unlocked the door and opened it, revealing the entrance to a tunnel.

"Your route to the house," he said. "There will be someone there waiting for you. All you require will be there." Fernando turned on a light switch adjacent to the door. The tunnel lights flickered to life, and the soft glow and subtle hum of the incandescent lights could be seen and heard. "You must go now. Time is of the essence."

"How do you want us to notify you when it's done?" asked Juan.

"You won't. I want you to inform your contact on the other side of the tunnel. He will relay the message to me."

With that, Sammy and Juan set off at a quick pace through the tunnel. Despite their haste, it took them nearly three minutes to reach the door at the other end. They estimated the tunnel to be at least a half a mile if not a little farther. Sammy reached for the doorknob and twisted it. He half-expected the door to be locked, but it wasn't. He twisted the knob and opened the door. He and Juan entered the room. It was larger than the one in the café and furnished.

A short stocky man was sitting in a chair against the wall. He stood as they entered. He extended his hand. "My name is Eddie." Sammy and Juan shook his hand but did not return the introduction.

"Eddie, we were told you would be able to provide everything we would need," Juan said.

"Follow me," he replied. Eddie led the men up the stairs out of the basement. He took them directly to the garage where there was a small tan standard cab Toyota four-wheel-drive pickup. In the bed of the truck was an Armalite AR-30 sniper rifle chambered in .338 Lapua Magnum wrapped in a soft case that, when unrolled, doubled as a shooter's mat. There was also an M16 with three thirty-round magazines and two Beretta 9mm handguns with extra magazines.

Juan and Sammy inspected the weapons. Each man tucked the Beretta into his waistband after inspecting the gun. Sammy was standing in front of the Armalite and slid it over to Juan. "Your turn. I'll spot you."

Juan uncovered the sniper rifle and inspected it. "Very nice," he said. "Excellent choice in caliber. We will be able to remain at a great distance with this gun."

Eddie knew the rifle would be adequate. He had recently discovered the .338 Lapua Magnum was the round used to make the longest-recorded sniper kill in combat. He had acquired the gun shortly after learning such trivia for an occasion such as this. It was a costly addition to the arsenal, but one that was easily justified with the amount of money Eme had been making since linking up with Los Zetas.

"There's a map in the cab if you need it, a spotting scope, range finder, and a cell phone with my number already programmed. Call me when it's done."

"We know our way around. We have been in the U.S. several times reconing the area. This has been in the works for some time. We just didn't know when we'd be asked to start pulling the trigger," Sammy said with a smile.

"As far as the phone goes, whose is it?" asked Sammy.

Eddie reached in the cab of the pickup and pulled out a cell phone. He tossed it to Sammy. "It's yours. Just press and hold 2 to reach me."

"We may be back here when it's done. The tunnel may be our ticket home. Make sure you have someone ready on the other end to let us back in," said Juan.

"You got it."

Sammy went to the driver's door and opened it. He pulled the backseat forward and put the M16 behind the seat. Juan wrapped the Armalite securely in the soft case and set it behind the seat as well. The two men climbed into the cab of the truck while Eddie opened the garage door. They backed out and headed for the Holtville border crossing.

* * *

Sammy drove north through the residential neighborhood for several blocks until he reached East Birch Street. He turned right onto the larger main road and continued east out of town where the road turned into Highway 98.

"How far of shot do you want to take?" Sammy asked.

"It's late in the afternoon, and the sun may be setting before we get a clear shot at this guy. I want to keep the sun behind us, so there's no chance of a reflection off the scope, or me having to look into the sun depending on how long this takes. It's hot, but not very windy, so we should be good out to 1,500 meters with this rifle easy. I'd like to be out to two thousand meters, but that's going to take a few practice shots."

"No problem, we have the extra rounds. I'll head out toward Heber Dunes. We can range a two-thousand-meter shot in the same direction and get your dope for the shot," said Sammy. *Dope* was the term snipers used for predetermined distances when shooting. Most snipers had information out to at least eight hundred meters, but some, with the recent use of higher-caliber rifles such as the .338 Lapua Magnum and fifty-caliber weapons, it wasn't uncommon for shooters to work on distances up to 1,500 or even two thousand meters. Anything beyond that was more a matter of luck mixed in with skill.

"Sounds good," replied Juan.

Sammy turned off of the highway onto Anderholt Road. It was narrow two-lane country road with mostly agricultural fields boarding both sides. Sammy followed the road for a short distance and then turned onto a small dirt road that paralleled a field. He followed the tiny road until the dunes could be seen in the distance. He stopped the truck. They were just outside Heber.

Juan got out and looked around. There was not much to be seen. The field workers had called it a day long before the temperature reached its peak. There was no one around and no vehicles to be seen.

Sammy pulled out the spotting scope and range finder. He began to seek a suitable target. He looked to the southeast, the direction they planned on shooting. He spotted a trailer parked in the distance. It had an oval white tank on it. It was anybody's guess as to what it contained—fertilizer, pesticide, or weed killer. Such trailers were a common sight in the area and used for all types of chemicals. Sammy held the range finder to his right eye and depressed the button. In an instant, the device fired an undetectable laser to the intended target, measuring the distance.

"1,783 meters. We need to back up a little." The men climbed back into the truck. Sammy backed down the dusty road approximately two hundred meters. He exited the vehicle and checked the range again.

"2,008 meters," he said. "This will do." He pulled the spotting scope out and set it on the hood of the Toyota.

Juan was unraveling the Armalite. He paced eight meters toward his target and spread the shooting blanket out on the ground. He set the rifle at the front of the blanket and took a prone position behind it. He pulled the bolt of the rifle back, verified the rifled was empty, and closed the bolt. He adjusted the twenty-four-power Zeiss scope to its maximum power. He settled in behind the rifle and centered the cross hairs on the oval tank. He could see the fluid level of the chemical in the tank. He used the line as a reference. He took a breath, exhaled halfway, and stopped. He gently placed his finger on the trigger and began to apply smooth, consistent pressure. The trigger broke, and the crisp metallic snap of the firing pin could be heard. The trigger was smooth; it was nearly perfect. Juan would work on it if it was his rifle but only a little. He liked it.

Juan knew he would be pushing the scope close to its limits, if not beyond, with such a shot. He reached up to the elevation dial and adjusted it to the maximum elevation. Once he dialed the scope to its max, he reached out and pinched the dirt with his right thumb and index finger. He raised his hand and rubbed the two fingers together, watching the dust as it drifted from between his fingers. The wind was with him; the dust blew toward his target and slightly to the right. He knew it was likely to change directions twice before the bullet would actually reach its destination, but it was a good start.

Juan pulled a couple of cartridges from the box of ammunition Eddie had given them. He pushed the first round into the magazine then the second. He pushed the bolt forward, catching the lip of the top round and chambering it. He settled down behind the rifle.

Sammy watched patiently. He began looking through the seventy-five-power Burris spotting scope. He dialed the scope in so he could see the oval tank and the earth in front of it. If Juan's first round hit low, he wanted to be able to let him know how short the shot was.

"Shooter ready," said Juan.

"Wind is steady, slight right now, slight left at target."

Juan considered the change. He was just getting set, so he decided to hold dead center on the tank, just as he had done when testing the trigger. He squeezed the trigger; the rifle recoiled firmly into his shoulder. Without thinking, he worked the bolt action, loading the second round. He had never taken his eye away from the scope.

"Impact about forty meters low, and five meters left," called Sammy.

Juan adjusted the scope's windage right two clicks. There was no adjusting the elevation; he would use the elevation bars built in to the reticle. Juan peered through the scope again; he held the cross hairs high. He centered on the oval with the horizontal reticle held on the fluid level. He then raised the point of aim to the third elevation mark. He squeezed the trigger again.

"Hit!" called Sammy. "Center trailer a quarter of the way up."

Juan ejected the spent casing and gazed through the scope. He watched as the liquid in the tank arced out from the bullet hole. He was a few feet lower than he had aimed but close enough to know the shot was going to be easy. He needed to be sure. He retrieved one more cartridge from the box and loaded the rifle. He located the leak through the scope again. He took aim at the leak, placing the fourth elevation mark on the leak. He squeezed the trigger.

"Hit!" called Sammy. "One foot low of hole."

Juan looked for the second leak. He found the second leak, right where Sammy called it. It was not as easy to see in the rifle scope; it was only a third the magnification. Once he saw the point of impact, he knew he was ready. He loaded the rifle with five rounds; it was all it would hold. He placed the rifle in the soft cover and rolled it back up. He gathered the three spent casings and tossed them into the field. As he headed back to the vehicle, Sammy gave him an approving nod.

"Two thousand meters, not bad, my friend."

"Now for the money shot," replied Juan.

The men put their respective equipment away and climbed into the vehicle. They returned to Anderholt Road and headed south. Sammy followed Anderholt until it dead-ended into Carr Road. He turned left and followed the road until the border could be seen in the distance. Sammy followed Carr Road as it began to veer away from the border back to the north.

He finally saw what he was looking for. There was a large area of sage he would be able to hide the pickup from view of passing motorists. Looking to the southeast from the sage brush was a clear view to the U.S. side of the border crossing. Sammy and Juan had been to this exact location numerous times before, but in the past, it was where they had met Elmond to pay him for allowing their vehicles to pass without inspection. The area provided a clear view of the U.S. side of the border and the inspection stations.

Sammy paralleled the brush until he estimated the distance to be close. He stopped the vehicle and got out with the range finder. He pointed it at the crossing lanes and depressed the button. The laser range finder read 2,176 meters. He was close; he got back in and drove forward. When he knew he was close, Sammy turned the truck around so the bed was facing the southeast toward the border. He quickly took the range again—1,988 meters. He pulled forward twelve meters and stopped.

Having positioned the truck so the bed faced the border gave Juan an elevated platform to shoot from, keeping low-growing desert grass and flowers out of way. Juan quickly went to work, getting set up. With the rifle loaded, he only needed to grab the rifle itself. He carefully unsheathed the rifle from the case and then positioned the dual-purpose blanket in the back of the truck. He climbed in back and positioned himself on the blanket. The bipod of the rifle forward on the tailgate, his body prone behind it.

"Shooter ready," he said. "I just need a target."

Sammy had pulled the spotting scope and range finder out and was setting up on the bed of the truck next to Juan. He quickly climbed in and began to scan the lanes. Elmond was nowhere to be seen. Sammy began to broaden his search, checking around the buildings and also the parking lot. That was when he found him.

"Shit! Those two are already here and talking to Jimmy."

"Where are they?" asked Juan.

"North of the parking lot in front of the grey sedan." Sammy grabbed the range finder and held in on the sedan. "Range is 2,086 meters to the vehicle. Jimmy is the one in the middle."

Juan swept the rifle to the north end of the parking lot. Peering through the scope, he quickly identified the three men. Although he would not have been able to identify Elmond at this distance through his scope, he only had to shoot the man in the middle. He considered the added distance and held Elmond's head in the fifth elevation bar on the scopes reticle. "Wind?" he asked.

"Same as before," Sammy replied.

Juan watched through the scope. He would lose sight of the men every once in a while with the passing of a big rig. "Trucks block the target," he said as he settled down for the shot. "Am I clear to shoot?"

Sammy dialed out the magnification on the spotting scope. He checked the traffic. It was clear. All but one vehicle was currently stopped, and the one was a small two-door coupe. "Clear, clear, clear!"

Juan slowly exhaled and then held his breath. He had already begun to apply gentle pressure on the trigger, taking up the slack. As soon as he stopped breathing, he increased the pressure smoothly until the firing pin was released, striking the primer of the chambered cartridge, igniting the gunpowder and setting the bullet free. The .338-caliber piece of copper-coated lead sped across the desert at nearly 3,200 feet per second. The round flew true and, in a matter of seconds, impacted its intended target.

Sammy zoomed in on James Elmond once again and watched closely to confirm the kill. He heard the rifle go off and waited. He knew it would take the round close to three and half seconds to reach the target. He waited. "Hit!" he declared as he witnessed a large red mist explode from Elmond's back. "He's not getting up."

Juan immediately sprang to his knees and rolled the rifle up in the case. Sammy had already jumped out of the bed of the truck and grabbed his equipment. He tossed both items behind the seat. Juan did the same with the rifle half a second later. They climbed back into the truck and slowly pulled back out onto Carr Road. Once on the road, they drove west, never leaving the road until it merged with Highway 98 just outside of Calexico where it turned into East Birch. It didn't take more than twenty minutes, and they were pulling back into the garage where Eddie was waiting after receiving the call.

Forty-Two

The sun was setting. Michael had called Agent Savage and told him what happened. He knew things couldn't go as smoothly as before when he and David got into the shootout with the two gunmen in the van. He was right; Agent Savage told him he would be on the way, but they were going to have to stay put this time.

David had been relieved from his position at the vehicle. He was brought in immediately and kept separate from Michael. Vania was furious that the two men had intentionally kept information she felt was pertinent to her command from her. She was not about to let them try and get their story straight now. As far as she was concerned, their lack of professional courtesy is what got her agent killed. Anything she could do to make them uncomfortable was going to be done. She had no way of knowing there was nothing that could have saved James Elmond.

While David and Michael were locked in separate interview rooms, awaiting their own interrogation into the shooting of Elmond, dozens of customs and Border Patrol agents had responded to the Holtville Border crossing from all around. There were agents from the Algodones area; the Yuma, Arizona, office; as well as the Calexico and El Centro offices. Among the agents on the ground were Robert Porter and the regional BORTAC unit.

They scoured the area in four-wheel-drive vehicles, looking for any evidence as to where the shooter was hidden, while others hovered overhead in helicopters, doing the same. All was for naught as the two Zeta snipers had long since fled the area and were casually driving through the residential district in Calexico, headed back to their origin before the searching really got underway. Juan and Sammy would be sitting comfortably in the living room with Eddie watching the search unfold on live local news feeds.

Special Agent Savage arrived as the sun dipped behind the sandy horizon. He identified himself to the perimeter guards and asked to speak with the on-scene commander. He was directed to the building where the two detectives were being held in and where Vania Garcia continued to receive updates on progress (or the lack thereof).

Vania met the FBI agent at the door. He could tell she was incensed at his arrival by the intensity on her face and the manner in which she approached. He presumed that she thought he was there to take over; he was right.

Vania had been notified that Agent Savage was on his way to meet her by the agent whom he had checked in with. She was not about to let him pilfer information about the incident until she found out what he was even doing there. She had heard his name around before and knew that he was the SAIC (or special agent in charge) of the local JTTF. She was not about to give up the murder investigation of one of her agents to the FBI without a fight.

"Agent Savage," she said as she approached. "As you can imagine, we have a lot going on right now. What do you need?"

Savage could hear the tension in her voice as she tried to remain calm. He wanted to assure her that he was only there to help, not take over. He knew what she was thinking and why. It was always the same when the FBI showed up to another agency's crime scene; they took over.

"I am sorry to hear about your agent," he said. "You must be the supervising agent. I wanted to offer my assistance."

Vania was taken aback. She had never dealt with the FBI in such a capacity. It was not the norm. She relaxed a little, thinking that the higher-ups were finally figuring things out. She was fully capable of handling this, just as most other agencies could handle their work without outside interference. The whole concept of open communications that was supposedly put into place following 9/11 never seemed to work anywhere but at the ground level. The top-level brass in every federal organization still played the same games they always had, vying for positions based on what their agency was capable of and what they brought to the table rather than simply cooperating with one another.

"Thank you," she said. "Right now we have the area search covered. I have agents checking every possible location for the shooter and any evidence that may have been left behind. I also have two detectives that seemingly lured my agent out into the open being held in separate interrogation rooms as we speak."

"Let me guess, Detective Michael Garrett and Detective David Ross." It was a statement, not a question. Savage knew as soon as he dropped their names he would have her off guard.

Vania was surprised, and her face showed it. She knew there had to be more with the FBI's arrival than merely offering assistance. "Yes, and I find it more than a little interesting that you know that." Vania turned and motioned for Agent Savage to follow. "You need to come with me." She led him back to her office so they could speak privately. Other agents in the building had been watching as the two began to talk. They all wondered who was going to win as they too believed Vania was about to be relieved of command.

Once they had reached her office, Agent Savage replied, "Certainly, you can't believe they were part of this."

"I find it suspicious. They said they needed to talk to Elmond about a case they were working. They told me he may have information for them. I indulged them by pulling him off his post and offering them a room. Instead, they took him outside into the open, and now he's dead. Then they tell me he may have been linked to Eme and the Zetas. That's bullshit!"

Savage wondered how much she had been told. Now he knew. "It is what it is. I can't say I would have done anything different. Do you mean to tell me that you would have let them talk to him if they had told you what it was about up front?"

"Of course not, at least not alone. Elmond had rights, and he should have been given those rights as an employee of the government and a citizen of this country. If they weren't involved in the shooting, they sure as hell violated his rights, and he's dead because of it."

She was getting herself ramped up. Savage knew timing was critical, and he knew now was the best time to make his offer. "I couldn't agree with you more. In fact, that's the reason I am here. I knew you would have your hands full with the investigation of the shooting. Trying to keep up with all the agents, where they are and what they find, are daunting tasks." Savage took a casual breath, letting his comment sink in. He continued, "The last thing you need is to worry about the detectives and their rights. Let me deal with them. I am already familiar with them and the case they're working. They came to my office earlier asking a bunch of questions about La Eme and human trafficking. I can get them outta here for you and get full statements. You have enough to worry about right now. Has anyone even notified next of kin yet?"

Savage was right. She did have her hands full, and if he was already familiar with the two, he may have a better rapport. Besides, the last thing she needed was to have another customs agent get into a heated interrogation with them. Emotions would be running high, and they were the only current link to the dead agent. It would be assumed they had a part in it. "Fair enough," she said after some thought. "But I want you to keep me in the loop. If they have any information of value, I need to know the second you do."

"I wouldn't have it any other way," Savage lied. The last thing he wanted was let her know that he was the one who turned them on to Elmond in the first place. She was mad enough already; if Vania had known another federal agency had knowledge of a potential dirty agent and had not shared it, she would have gone through the roof. "If you'll just show me where these two are, I'll take it from there."

Vania called a passing agent over. "Take Special Agent Savage to the interrogation rooms where the two dicks are being held. He's going to be handling their questioning."

"Yes, ma'am," responded the agent. He led Savage to the rooms and quickly went back to what he was doing.

Savage opened the door and went into one of the rooms. He saw David Ross sitting quietly with his head back and his eyes closed. "Mr. Ross, you two have had a busy day."

David sat up and looked at the FBI agent. "You're not kidding. All I can say is, *what the fuck* . . . That crazy bitch locked us in here like we're a couple of fucking suspects. Doesn't she get that we are the only two fucking witnesses she's got? We should be out there helping direct the search."

"I know, she's affirmative action at its best. But don't worry, you couldn't have made a difference. Whoever did this was clearly professional. You guys are just lucky to be alive. Personally, I'm surprised they didn't cap you too."

"This is twice today. Michael has definitely started barking up the right tree—"

Agent Savage interrupted, "Anyway, I need to get you and Detective Garrett to my office for statements. You may still be able to provide some valuable information."

Savage knew Vania would likely be recording everything said in the room, if not listening directly. He didn't care about the affirmative action comment; he meant what he said, but if asked later, he would merely say he was trying to buddy up to the interviewee. Find some common ground that they could relate to ease the conversation. He figured David had already said enough to screw her over though because everything he said about being a witness and able to guide the search was 100 percent accurate.

Savage got up and signaled David to follow him. They walked out and over to the adjacent room. Savage just opened the door and motioned for Michael to come with him. "You're with me, Detective. Let's go."

Michael got up and exited the room. He caught up to David and asked what was going on.

"I'll tell you in the car," David whispered.

As the three proceeded to head to the door, Vania reappeared in the main lobby. She was fuming mad, and everyone could see it. David and Agent Savage both knew she had been listening. Agent Savage reassured her he would keep her in the loop while David concealed his satisfaction that she knew how he felt. He had little sympathy for the dead agent. As far as he was concerned, it was instant justice. There was no telling how many thousands of pounds of narcotics he had let pass, let alone how many people he allowed to be smuggled into the country who were now taking advantage of the system or, worse, being abused like Rosa. Michael never even bothered to glance; he was deep in thought as to what their next step would be. He was already devising a plan.

The men walked out to their cars. Agent Savage asked them to follow him back to his office. They still had some things to sort out before calling it a day.

FORTY-THREE

"Can you believe the audacity of that . . ." Michael stopped before he finished his statement. He still wasn't sure how Agent Savage was going to handle this. He and David had talked on the way back to his office, but neither was really sure what was going on. David couldn't tell exactly what Savage was up to. He knew he was trying to piss her off, which they both succeeded at.

Agent Savage looked at the two men. "You guys have accomplished more in the past twelve hours than I have been able to in a year. You opened up Eme's sex trade, drawn Los Zetas into the United States, and closed the file on a dirty customs agent."

"Don't forget getting my family and friends placed on a hit list," Michael said. "This is not going exactly according to plan."

"You think," David said. "But it is definitely getting more interesting."

"So what happened exactly?" asked Agent Savage.

Michael and David proceeded to explain what had happened out at the border. They covered everything from Elmond's admission to taking money and working with La Eme and Los Zetas to his sudden death in explicit detail. Agent Savage recorded the conversation and took notes about particular details. Everything was handled officially. Once Savage concluded the interview and turned off the recording, he contacted each man's department and advised the department head what was going on. He also expressed his gratitude in advance for the agencies allowing the two detectives to continue working with him as liaisons with the FBI's JTTF until the conclusion of the case.

Both Michael and David sat and listened while Savage expertly managed to finesse his way to the top of the food chain in each department and then get approval for each of them to be placed "on loan" to the FBI with assurance that their contribution to the case was invaluable and would not go unrecognized.

"Thank you," Michael said when Savage finished. "You just saved me a lot of explaining. I may still get an ass chewing, but at least I know I'll get an attaboy first."

"So what's next, gentlemen?" asked Savage.

David looked at Michael, wondering what he had in mind. He knew his friend well enough to know he had something up his sleeve.

"Well, our first order of business has got to be sleep. It's late, and both of us need some rest," Michael said. "Tomorrow, I think we should grab a little lunch at the Café Nueva Asia."

David's mouth dropped. "Are you kidding me? We can't go into Mexicali. They know what we look like, they have already tried to hit us once. Who knows why they didn't cap us when they got Elmond, but I think it's safe to presume they are the ones who did it."

"I would have to agree with your partner on this one," said Savage. "If you go into Mexico, I won't be able to help you."

"I know," responded Michael. "Here's how I see it. The two that have seen us up close and personal are dead. Whoever killed Elmond had the chance and didn't even take a shot. He was clearly the intended target. They are going to be looking for us here. That being said, I figure on going to Mexicali tonight. We'll get a room and start fresh in the morning. No one will know where to start. We'll simply set up obs on the café until we see Fernando."

"Then what?" asked Savage. "Are you just going to walk up and grab him? Drag him back across the border?"

"Michael," David started, "I know you're pissed and I understand. Coming after us was one thing, but going after your mother is crossing the line. But how does this help solve the case?"

"Simply," Michael said calmly. "It's not just about prosecution anymore. It's about survival. Fernando is the key. He is the one pulling the strings. He's gonna feel safe there, confident. I walk up and introduce myself. We'll talk while you"—Michael glanced at David—"make sure I don't get stabbed in the back. I'll tell him about my case and plead with him to release Rosa, explaining that she's paid her family's debt, and that they only want to move to their property in Cuernavaca, but can't do it until Rosa is free."

"I think I see where this is going," said Savage, "but I don't see how you think you're just going to walk out alive."

"He won't have me killed there. That's his haven, and it'll draw too much attention, even in Mexico. He probably won't go for it, but who knows, he might even agree. Either way, I get it all recorded, and you will finally have something on him that we can proceed federally on. If our government can present enough evidence on Ortiz to the Mexican government about his involvement in human trafficking, there is no way they won't cooperate with us by assisting in his apprehension and exporting him to the U.S. as long as it's not a death penalty case. Right?"

"I think you are on to something," Savage replied. "That still leaves one question. You walk in, meet Ortiz, and have a nice little chat. He will be comfortable and will likely brag and indulge you by answering questions. He may even agree to release Rosa, but it'll be a lie. When you're done, you have to get up and walk out. What makes you think you'll make it back across the border?"

"I haven't figured that part out just yet, but I will," Michael said confidently.

David looked at Michael. "I can't believe the shit I let you talk me into."

"I think it's a suicide mission. It has merit on the surface, but it hinges on you returning with the evidence. I don't like it, and I'm advising you against it," cautioned Savage. "However, from what I've seen of you so far, I know you're going to try. So good luck, and don't call me if it gets ugly over there. I can't do anything this time."

"Duly noted," Michael said. "Well, we've got to hit the road. We've got some packing to do."

The men all headed out. Agent Savage escorted them to the door, wishing them luck and explaining he needed to wrap up a few things before calling it a night. The truth be told, the paperwork generated by David and Michael's escapades would take Savage a solid week to finish.

FORTY-FOUR

David waited until they were safely in the privacy of his Crown Vic before he started asking questions. It had been a long day, and there had been too many coincidences for him to let go. "Are you sure about this plan of yours for tomorrow?"

"What do you mean?"

"I'm just saying, these guys have been ahead of us every step of the way. I just don't want to walk into a trap. Our nine lives are gonna run out pretty soon."

Michael slapped his friend on the shoulder. "Truer words have never been spoken, but the Café Nueva Asia will not be where it happens."

"I wish I shared your optimism."

"Here's how I see it, David. As soon as Rosa got pinched up in Tahoe, the wheels were set in motion. Carlos called in and put his people on standby down here. These guys are professionals and wanted to cover their bases. We expected this. I had hoped we could stay ahead of them because we made good time. That's where I was wrong."

"Exactly, and they were waiting for us. So what makes you think they won't be waiting for us again?"

"Because so far, we have acted exactly like cops following up on leads. These guys are aware of our tactics. They study them, and some of them have no doubt used them in the past. They probably wanted Elmond dead anyway because he was the weak link, just like they sent those others after us earlier. In their plan we were supposed to be dead, and I'd bet that Rosa's parents were on the list as well. They weren't following us to border. They were already there. They had to be waiting to take Elmond out. We just made it easy by walking him into the open."

David agreed. It was a plausible explanation, and the more he thought about it, the more he believed Michael was correct. "You're right, but you are forgetting one thing. They still want us dead."

"I know, that's why we get in, get out, and get the evidence back to the feds. My case is closed, and they can do the rest. I'll tell my mom to stay in Hawaii awhile. In fact, we should join her for a couple weeks after this. It'd be fun, and we're gonna need the break."

"Sounds like you have it all planned out," David said, laughing. "I hope it's as easy as you think it will be."

"Me too," said Michael honestly.

It wasn't long before the two were back at the Holiday Inn. They gathered their belongings and headed out for the night. *So much for a peaceful night,* David thought as they walked back to the car. They tossed what little they had in the backseat and headed for the border. It wasn't long before the iridescent orange glow that could be seen to the south grew brighter. David asked Michael as they drove down Highway 111 through the middle of Calexico if he wanted to grab a bite to eat before they reached the border.

"Sure, in fact, it's the perfect plan."

"What is?"

"While we eat, we'll call a taxi. We'll have him take us across the border so you don't have to leave your car parked over there. It'll stick out like a sore thumb. Then we'll have a cab pick us up in the morning and drop us off near the cafe."

"Works for me," replied David. "Where do you wanna eat?"

"Don't know the choices in Calexico. We'll just have to find something close along the way."

As the men drove into the busy border town, they kept their eyes open for the right place. Somewhere the car could be parked inconspicuously while still offering some degree of security. The last thing either of them wanted was to hide it in a dark corner or alley. Although it wouldn't be easily noticed, it was also where the less savory part of society tended to lurk for the same reasons. Such a vehicle would be a prize to them, and hidden in such a location would simply give them time to strip the vehicle bare. A twenty-four-hour restaurant would be best. Some place that vehicles were expected to be parked all night long. No one would know for sure if the vehicle's owner was still inside or not.

"There." Michael pointed as they approached an all-night gas station located on the corner of Highway 111 and Third Street. There was a taco shop in the gas station mini-mart that would be perfect, Tacos El Rey.

David turned into the gas station parking lot to look for a place to park, but the lot was full. "Must be a popular place," he said.

"It's Saturday night and summer. A lot of the local kids between eighteen and twenty-one all head south of the border for fun. The drinking age is the same, but getting carded down there really just means getting asked if you're twenty-one. So a lot of them stop at places like this to grab a bite before they get started drinking, and of course, others hit the place on the way back, hoping to sober up."

"Nice, so I take it the DUI rate is a little higher around here for that age group."

"I don't know about that, but rumor has it a little courtesy and a jackson will pretty much take care of a traffic stopover there. You just have to present it like you're paying the ticket in advance, not bribing the officer."

"There's a difference?"

"Nope, but if you simply call it what it is, the officer is likely to take offense. Call it paying the ticket to avoid a hassle, and no one gets their pride hurt, and you get a free pass, or so I'm told." Michael grinned.

"It's no wonder people fight to get into this country. If the cops are paid off that easy, who knows what else they'll be willing to overlook."

"It's no secret that corruption is off the charts over there. You remember they told us stories about that in the academy. Didn't they even throw out some statics, like studies have shown at least 80 percent of Mexican police have accepted payments that would constitute a bribe at least once," Michael recalled.

"Yeah, but it's funny to hear stories firsthand."

"Whoa, whoa, whoa, my friend," Michael said, feigning offense. "I never said I did that. That's just what I hear."

"Yeah, whatever." David laughed while rolling his eyes. "I'm gonna pull up to one of the pumps and wait for a space to open up."

He pulled up to the first open gas pump and left the vehicle idling. While the men waited for a parking space, Michael pulled out his cell phone and dialed information. He got an automated answer, as was the case when calling just about any business anymore.

"What city and state?" said the automated voice.

"Calexico, California," Michael said, overly deliberate. "I hate these things," he whispered to David. "They always get it wrong."

David listened to one side of the call but could easily tell how it was going.

"Business . . . Go Back . . . Business . . . Taxi . . . No . . . Taxi . . . NO! Taxi . . . Yes . . . Number 2 . . . NO! NUM-BER 2!" Michael emphatically punched the End button on his phone. "Sometimes I think phone books were easier. Definitely less aggravating."

"You get a number?" David asked. "Or was that all for show?"

"Yeah, California Cab Company. I am supposed to receive a text with the number." As Michael was talking, his phone chimed, indicating a text message being received. "And there it is now." He looked at the message and quickly dialed the number. As he was on the phone setting up the pickup, a parking stall came available, and David pulled in.

"Taxi should be here in fifteen or twenty minutes. Let's go grab some tacos."

"Sounds good to me," David said, and he turned the car off, and the men walked inside.

The taco shop took up the left side of the business. It was as clean as any twenty-four-hour truck stop, which didn't say much, but the volume of business said enough. The food had to be good. Michael ordered three carne asada tacos with everything, which meant diced onion, pico de gallo, and cilantro, and a Dos Equis. David stepped up next to him. "I'll have the same." Michael paid for the food, and a few minutes later, each was handed a paper plate with the three tacos on it and an ice-cold bottle of beer.

They walked out front and over to David's car. They set their plates down on the hood and popped the top off of the beer. "Here's to things going better tomorrow," David said. They raised the bottles, clinked the long necks together, and took a long drink.

The tacos tasted even better than expected. The men were hungrier than they had realized. It wasn't long before each had scarfed down all three and was looking at an empty bottle as well.

"What do you say, one for the road?" David said wryly.

"Any other day I'd say make it two, but tonight, we better make it a sixer and go from there."

"I like the way you think. I'll grab the beer, you wait for the cab."

David ran back inside and grabbed a six-pack while Michael watched for the taxi. It wasn't long before the taxi driver pulled into the parking lot. Michael flagged him down and walked over to the driver's side. "My friend and I need to get to a hotel near the Café Nueva Asia in Mexicali. Are you familiar with the area?"

"Si, señor, vivo en Mexicali. El restaurante es muy bien (*Yes, sir, I live in Mexicali. The restaurant is very good.*)"

Michael knew the drill. The driver was testing him to see if he understood. If the fare didn't understand, the cabby would take advantage of the false language barrier to earn a little extra. Most people would end up overpaying out of frustration. "Bien, bien," Michael responded. "Usted sabe que es un hotel cercano tambien (*Good, you'll know of a close hotel as well.*)"

The cabby looked at Michael; he was slightly irritated as he realized he would not be gaining anything on his latest fair. "Yes, of course. You get in."

"You speak English, excellent. My friend's Spanish is not good, so he'll feel better." Just then, David walked out and approached the taxi with the beer in hand.

"Get in," Michael said. "We are good to go. I'll grab the bags."

David climbed in and slid over behind the driver while Michael grabbed their gear from the backseat of David's car and locked it up. He tossed their things in the backseat between them and climbed in the passenger side. "Let's *vamos*," he said to the driver. Slang or Spanglish as referred to in the area for *let's go.*

The driver pulled out and headed for the border. He wasn't much for small talk, which suited them fine. Michael asked him to drive by the restaurant first and then take them to a nearby hotel. Café Nueva Asia wasn't far from the border. They passed by it in a matter of minutes despite the traffic. This is where passing the test came in. The driver knew not to take too many scenic routes because he was likely to be called on it.

Michael pointed out the café and took note of the building and its surroundings. David did the same. It was cross between the two cultures, with a Technicolor banner of the Virgin of Guadalupe hanging next to a red paper lamp bearing Chinese characters all in front of a rundown stuccoed shopfront, painted a light green with a sign that read Café Nueva Asia. The men would map what they had seen as soon as they got to the hotel. It was near the corner of Colima and Ignacio Manuel Altamirano.

"Good enough, sir?" asked the driver.

"That'll do," responded Michael. "Thank you."

The driver headed for a hotel. "I'm going to take you to the Hotel del Norte. It's only about a quarter mile from here headed back to the border. I pass it on my way to work every day. If you need a ride tomorrow, I can pick you up. You just call, okay?"

"Thanks for the offer. We may just take you up on that."

Traffic was much more congested headed back toward the border. It took twice as long to get to the hotel as it had to get to the café, but soon enough, they were there. The driver pulled up in front and told Michael it would be $13.00. Michael handed him a twenty, said he could keep the change. The man smiled graciously and quickly wrote down his name and number on a small notepad. He tore the paper off and handed it to Michael.

Michael read the note out loud, "Ignacio, 686-552-9050, correct?"

"Si, señor, buenas noches."

David and Michael grabbed their things and stepped out of the taxi. The hotel was a white four-story building right on the corner of Fco I. Modero and Adolfo Lopez Mateos, and it was every bit as close to the café as Ignacio had said. Ignacio Manuel Altamirano Road was three hundred yards away at best. A right turn and few hundred yards farther and you were there.

Hotel del Norte was extravagantly lit with lights over each window, floodlights illuminating the column entrance, and a grand neon sign on each side. Michael and David walked into the lobby of the hotel and headed for the registration desk. The hotel was not exactly what either man had in mind; it was very nice. The fact that the hotel had a foyer was not the only giveaway; the floor was beautifully done with marble tile, and the restaurant bar resembled something one would expect at a Marriott or Hyatt Hotel.

Regardless, Michael wasted no time getting a room and asked for one on the top floor. High ground was always best, no matter what. He was a little surprised when the hotel clerk gave him the room price, but he didn't care at this point. He handed over his sheriff department credit card and paid for the room. As soon as he had the key, the two headed up. The elevator ride was slow but smooth.

The room faced south of the hotel and had a view of the city lights that stretched to the night sky. The accommodations were very nice. The room was small but clean. It had two beds separated by a nightstand and a bathroom that would get the job done. It was clear the money was spent on amenities rather than accommodations, but all they needed tonight was a place to sleep.

"Not exactly what I was expecting when you said a hotel in Mexicali," David admitted. "I'll have to think about coming back here for a little R and R."

"Yeah, I'm sure accounting is gonna flip when they get the credit card statement on this one. $259 for the night in this city is a rip-off, but I'm not really in the mood to haggle."

"Holy shit, man, I missed that part. That is a bit steep, but it would cost that much or more in California. Shit, I've paid more for less."

"Tell me about it. Try getting a room in Monterey when the MotoGP races are in town. If you can find one, you're lucky, and if it's under $300, it's gonna be a shit hole."

They each tossed their things on a bed, and David handed Michael a beer. He opened one up for himself, and they started planning for the next day. A couple beers later and they were ready for bed. Michael looked at the clock; David didn't bother; it was the next day.

Forty-Five

Neither man bothered setting the alarm. At this point, time was not critical; sleep was. David woke up first. He didn't bother waking Michael; he just went straight for the shower. Michael woke up to the running water. He glanced at the clock. It was a little after nine in the morning. He picked up the phone and ordered a couple breakfast burritos and pot of coffee.

It seemed as if David was in the shower forever before the water finally stopped. He opened the door, and steam came rolling out like a thick fog on the coast. He saw Michael sitting up on his bed.

"Good morning, sunshine," David said. "You ready for another fun-filled day?"

"If by that you mean getting shot at a couple times and being placed on another Mexican cartel hit list, then absolutely," Michael responded sarcastically. "I have a couple burritos and some coffee headed up. So don't be surprised when someone knocks on the door."

"Good thinking. I hope you put that on the county's tab as well."

"Of course, it's well within my per diem allowance anyway."

David laughed. Michael got up and headed for the shower while David got ready. He took half as long, not by choice but rather because he ran out of hot water. He came out of the bathroom slightly irritated but was pleased to see breakfast had not yet arrived. So at least he would get his share of the coffee.

He was getting ready to put on yesterday's clothes when room service arrived. David got the door, and a petite woman, probably in her early thirties, promptly wheeled in a small cart with a covered tray, two cups, and a thermos on it. "Buenos dias," she said, smiling at David.

Although not fluent, David knew enough for casual greetings. "Buenos dias," he responded.

It was then that the woman glanced over at Michael, whom she had not yet seen. He was as embarrassed as she was, caught midway through pulling on his boxers. He quickly tried to pull them up, but only having one leg in made it difficult. He lost his balance and had to hop a couple of times before getting his other leg in and himself covered.

The young woman blushed and began to apologize. David began to laugh hysterically; Michael looked at his friend and then the woman.

"Thanks a lot, buddy. You got the tip?" Michael said pointedly.

"After your performance, I don't think I can cover it," David responded, still laughing. He reached in his wallet and handed the woman five dollars. She graciously nodded her head and left the cart. Both could hear her chuckling as she walked back down the hall.

"Asshole!"

"What, I didn't know you were gonna try and get a date. And for future reference, you might try a little warmer shower first," David advised.

"That's why you're an asshole, the water was already cold. I'm not worried about her, I'll never see her again."

"No, you are probably right about that, even if you wanted to."

"Fuck off, dickhead."

David laughed even harder. "Come on, we have serious business to address."

Michael finished getting dressed. David rolled the cart between the beds. Each man sat on his bed, eating a burrito and drinking coffee in absolute silence. It was almost ten o'clock, and Michael was finishing his second cup before he spoke again.

"The café isn't far. You wanna walk or give Ignacio a call?"

"I think we should walk. Maybe hit a couple of little vendors on the way and grab a couple of T-shirts and hats. Something a little less conspicuous than our current attire."

Michael looked at David's Aloha shirt and then down at his own. "Yeah, that's probably a good idea. Not to mention you're a little ripe."

Michael picked up the phone and hit the Call button for the concierge. David couldn't understand the conversation but knew it had to do with the café. Michael hung up a few minutes later. "Okay, she said the café isn't open for breakfast. They generally open for lunch around eleven and stay open till ten, but sometimes go as late as midnight if it's busy."

"Good to know. We should get there a little early and try and find a place to keep watch. It'd be nice to know what we're walking into."

"Agreed."

FORTY-SIX

The two men finished up the coffee. Michael grabbed his wallet to see how much cash he had left. He always tried to keep at least $100 cash on him when he was traveling, but this trip wasn't exactly a vacation or planned in advance. He only had $18 in his pocket.

"How much cash do you have?" he asked.

David grabbed his wallet off the nightstand next to the bed he was sitting on and counted his money. "Twenty-seven bucks."

"Perfect. Between the two of us, we should be able to cover the cost of a couple shirts and taxi ride back to the States."

"We can always walk if we have to," David responded.

"No really. I think customs might frown on us crossing the border with firearms," Michael pointed out.

"Holy shit! That never crossed my mind. I got so wrapped up in the day's events I never even considered taking it off before we came over."

"Nor should you have. We are about to walk into a meeting with the one guy who wants us dead more than anyone else. He needs to know that he is not as well protected as he may think, and I guarantee he'll know we're armed when we get to the restaurant."

"How's that? I thought we were going to try and be inconspicuous?"

"We are, right up until we sit down with him to have a chat. That's where I suspect the guns will come out."

"I hope you have a better plan than that. This isn't some Hollywood bullshit where the good guy only gets a flesh wound and walks away free and clear."

"Don't worry, David. It's not going to be like that, but I guarantee this guy has operated with impunity around here. If he doesn't know we are armed, he'll think we underestimated him, and we'll be dead. Guns equal respect. That being said, we'll be able to talk. Probably not for long, but we'll see if we can't end this thing."

"What, you expect to negotiate a truce?"

"Something like that. Come on, we better get moving." Michael grabbed his go bag and rifled through it. Everything was just where it had been. It wasn't as if he expected something different, but he always checked it before heading to work. It was habit, and in some manner, it comforted him, knowing he was prepared. He grabbed his belt and ran it through the loops of his pants and then slid his holster on, securing his .45 to his hip.

David was doing same. "We checking out, or do you think we'll be back before heading across the border?"

"I'd like to think we'll have time to come back, but we better be ready to go just in case our meeting requires a rapid departure."

David laughed. "That's one way to put it," he said and then began gathering all his things. "At least we travel light."

Michael and David were ready in a matter of minutes. They each gave the room one last glance and then headed out. They didn't bother checking out. If they made it back in time, they could drop in; if not, the hotel already had what they needed to charge the county credit card Michael had given the receptionist when he checked in.

It was nearly ten thirty when they stepped outside for the first time. It was already heating up outside. Despite being only blocks from California, with all its emission regulations, the smog was thick. David couldn't believe how bad it was having come from Los Angeles. Old cars and trucks motored down the roads with black smoke belching from exhaust pipes.

There were pedestrians and beggars crowding the sidewalks. The men hadn't made it more than ten yards before a young girl approached them, holding up a box of Chiclets, a Mexican gum. "Chiclets, Chiclets," she said in a soft, touching voice. Michael couldn't help but feel for her, to be forced into begging at such a young age. She couldn't have been more than eight years old, and already she was forced to try and earn money, no doubt to help her family put food on the table.

Michael retrieved a few dollars from his wallet and handed it to the girl. She tried to hand him several packets of the gum in return. He graciously declined, and the two men kept moving.

It wasn't long before they came to Ignacio Manuel Altamirano Road. They made the right turn and found exactly what they were looking for. There were several small shops that lined the road; a number of which had a variety of T-shirts to choose from. All of the vendors did their best to get their business, but Michael and David ignored the relentless vendors until they found what they were looking for. David grabbed a dark blue shirt with *FBI* in large print across the front, with smaller print between each letter spelling the words *Female Body Inspector*.

"Really?" Michael asked. "Of all the shirts to choose from to memorialize our little vacation and you grab that one."

"It makes me official."

Michael grabbed a pirated Mexicali Harley Davidson shirt and held it up.

"At least mine isn't a trademark violation," David said sarcastically.

"Whatever, you don't know that this isn't official merchandise."

"Keep telling yourself that."

It was then that the man selling the shirts approached them. "You like? $25 for both," he said.

Michael looked at the man and shook his head. He pulled his wallet out and made it a point to let the man see the cash inside. He pulled out the last two bills. "Fifteen for both and you have a deal."

"Twenty, you give me $20, and you can have shirts."

"This is all I have. Fifteen or no deal," Michael said pointedly.

The man reached out and grabbed the money. There were too many other shops that carried the same shirts down the road. He knew if he passed on the offer, the next guy down probably wouldn't.

The two continued toward the café but ducked into the next open shop. It was a leather goods store with jackets, vests, pants, and purses packed in so tight it was hard to see from one end of the shop to the other, which was exactly what they needed. David went first while Michael talked with the woman working inside. David quickly changed into his new shirt and took over where Michael left off. Michael then slid between a couple rows of stitched cowhide, keeping his gun concealed as best he could by keeping the woman on his left in case she walked by David to see what he was doing. He unbuttoned the top two buttons on his shirt and pulled it over his head. Just as quickly, he put the T-shirt on and stepped back out. As soon as David saw him, he left the woman standing there, and they headed back out. Michael stuffed both shirts into his go bag, and the men continued to weave through the pedestrians and vendors.

It was eleven o'clock when they reached Café Nueva Asia. Michael and David had made a point to stay on the opposite side of the street, walking among other pedestrians as a cover just to make sure they weren't recognized. Michael didn't think anyone else would know what he and David looked like, but at this point, he couldn't be too cautious.

The men watched from across the street. The restaurant was not open yet. It wasn't uncommon for shops to open late in Mexicali. Everyone was on fiesta time, which meant they weren't late until they were over twenty minutes late. Fortunately, it wasn't that long before someone came to the front door and unlocked it.

"Let's go," Michael said as he stepped between a couple parked cars and out into the road, quickly heading across the four lanes of traffic toward the restaurant.

"What are you doing?" David asked. "I thought we were going to wait for Fernando?"

"Five bucks says he's already there."

"Nobody's gone in yet."

"And yet someone unlocked the door from inside. Trust me on this one, he's there. If he wasn't, those two guys watching the road from the second-story balcony wouldn't be there."

Michael and David made it across the street, working between a couple passing cars. They reached the front door and walked in. The two men Michael had referenced watching from above never gave them a second thought, and he was right about them. They were Zeta guards who lived in the hotel above the café.

The restaurant was dimly lit. The darkly tinted windows were also covered with sheer drapes with Asian designs inside, which added to the lighting effect and ambiance for the restaurant. The men were quickly met by a slender Asian woman with acne. She attempted to seat them, but Michael walked past her and headed toward the rear of the café. There was a short wall that seemed to separate the front from the rear. That had to be where Fernando worked. It had to be.

Michael sped up. It was only a few more paces, but it seemed so much farther. He could feel his heart pounding; he was scared. He was smart; he knew what he was doing, and it still scared the shit out of him. He hoped he was right. He had a way with people, suspects. He was good at reading them and predicting their actions and reactions, but he generally had more to go on than simply what someone else had told him. This time, he was trying to make such forecasts without any personal knowledge of his suspect. A task generally left to criminal psychologists who specialize in human behavior and offender profiling.

David kept right behind him. As they approached the back of the room, David slowed down a step and began to watch everywhere Michael wasn't. He looked for potential threats.

Michael reached a point in the café where he could see everything except one corner. He knew that's where Fernando was. Even though no one else had gone in before them, he saw two men sitting at a table in the opposite corner. It was also clear that they were watching him intently, yet neither had moved yet.

David picked them up as well. He kept an eye on them while Michael rounded the corner. They were only a few steps away, and David already had the advantage. Having slowed down, the men hadn't picked up on him as they were locked in on Michael.

Michael rounded the corner. He knew instantly he had been right. At the table in the corner with his back to the wall sat a lone man with a laptop in front of him, Fernando Ortiz. Michael discounted the men behind him. He trusted that David would do his job. He had to deal with the man before him, a much more immediate threat.

David did not let his friend down. At the same moment Michael was approaching Fernando, he distracted the two guards who were starting to move. David was quicker. He closed the distance in the blink of an eye, delivering a sudden powerful kick to the table the men were sitting at, driving it into their stomachs. At the same time drawing his pistol and ordering both men onto the ground. The two were slow to respond, taken completely by surprise. They had always been there as a show of force when Fernando did business; they never imagined someone would actually walk into the café so brazenly, posing a threat.

David didn't let them recover. He stepped in and pistol-whipped the man closest to him on the side of the head. "Get on the fucking ground, NOW!"

The woman who had met them as they walked in quickly disappeared. Michael now stood before Fernando, who did not react to his men being bested so easily.

"Mind if I join you, Mr. Ortiz?" Michael asked. "You are Fernando Ortiz?" He let the question linger.

"Of course, who am I to argue with a man like you?" Fernando replied.

Michael tossed his bag off to the side of the table. He pulled out a chair and his gun. He placed the two-tone .45 directly in front of him. Fernando glanced at the sidearm; it clearly caught his attention, but he did not react further. Michael had made his point, he had the man's attention.

"This won't take long," he said.

"I hope not, Detective Garrett. I am a busy man."

"So you know who I am too."

"Of course I do. My men sent me pictures they took of you at your mother's house. How is she anyway?"

Michael knew Fernando was trying to take control of the situation. He wasn't about to let that happen. "Here's the deal, all I'm trying to do is close a murder case and free Rosa. From what I have heard, she has more than paid off her father's debt. I'm not trying to save the world, or take you in. I just want you to write off the Jimenez family."

"I already have," Fernando said coldly. "They will be dead before the end of the day, and you will wish you were."

"It's unfortunate you feel that way," said Michael. "I was thinking we could work something out. I understand you're down a man at the border."

"I don't know what you're talking about."

"Sure you do. You had some of your boys whack a United States Customs agent yesterday. I was there talking with him when it happened."

"He's only one of many," Fernando lied. "Hardly a concern."

Michael didn't want to get into a debate. He was losing his advantage with every passing second. He had to cut to the chase. "Here's the deal, like it or not. I have gotten farther in two days than anyone ever has where you're concerned. You tried to kill me, and the men you sent are dead. You need to let this one go, let Rosa go and forget about me. If you don't, I'll keep digging until you won't have anywhere to hide. You'll be the most wanted man in two countries with a bounty so big one of your own men would kill you to collect it." Michael picked up his .45 and pressed the thumb safety down. He pointed the gun at Fernando's head. "You have failed, you lost the battle, and now you're losing the war. This is chess, not checkers, motherfucker, and if you come for me again, I won't give you the same courtesy next time. Let it go."

Michael stood and grabbed his bag. He backed away from the table, never taking his eyes off of Fernando, keeping his pistol aimed at the head. "David, time to say good-bye."

David began backing away from the two men on the floor. As soon as Michael had cleared the corner, he turned and headed for the door. David continued to walk backward, never taking his eyes off the two men on the ground. They never took their eyes off of him either. Michael opened the door slowly and looked up. The balcony shielded them from the two men he had seen there while crossing the street. He holstered his pistol and grabbed David by his belt, guiding him through the door.

"Time to make haste, my friend." He pushed the door open and headed out, pulling David behind him.

David quickly turned and holstered his pistol as well. No need to show the rest of the world what was going on. Michael instantly started to run. David fell in behind him.

"Hug the wall, use the awning as cover."

The two sprinted to the end of the street. Fortunately, every shop along the way had some kind of shade out front, allowing the men to remain invisible to the snipers they suspected would be watching from above. They reached the corner and rounded it quickly. They were running down Benito Juarez Road.

"We need to get off the street," David said.

"Over there." Michael pointed to a bar. "Follow me."

"Like I have a choice."

The two ran across the street and headed for El Campesino Bar. Michael reached the door first and didn't wait to go in. David caught the door behind him and took the time to look back. No one was coming. He let the door go and followed Michael into the bar. There were several people already there.

The men found a place to sit at the end of the bar. Michael ordered two Dos Equis and two shots of tequila.

"That went well," David said sarcastically.

"I think so," responded Michael.

"You can't be serious?"

"I am. You should have seen the look on his face after you took out his protection, and I set my gun on the table in front of him. It wasn't much, but we definitely had his attention."

"Okay, I may not have seen his face, but I was there. I heard the conversation. I don't care what he looked like, he pretty much told you you're gonna die a slow and painful death."

"You read too much between the lines. We had the upper hand and still do," Michael declared.

"Is that why you just ordered a couple shots and a couple of beers?"

"No, those are so we can blend in again. We can change back into our Hawaiian shirts. We'll stink more like alcohol than BO, and then we'll call a taxi and head back to the States. No one at the border will give a second look."

"Fair enough, but I still say we're fucked as far as Fernando and the Zetas go. Thanks for that by the way. Next time you need help with a case, don't call me."

"Hey, at least we're one step ahead again."

The bartender delivered their drinks. Michael grabbed his shot glass and the lime that came with it. He held it up. David did the same. The men tipped back the shots, bit the lime, and chased both with a long drink of Dos Equis.

"I'm gonna call Ignacio. We'll wait here for him and go from there."

"You better order a couple more beers just in case," David said.

"Just in case what?"

"Just in case they find us before he gets here. The more we drink now, the less we'll feel then."

Michael laughed. "Good idea on the beer, but for all the wrong reasons . . ." Michael pulled out Ignacio's phone number and began to dial. "Oh yeah, I spent the last of my money on the shirts, so pay for the drinks, would ya?"

"Of course you did." David rolled his eyes. He flagged down the bartender and held up two fingers. It wasn't long before each had two more bottles in front of them.

Michael finished his call and finished his first beer. "Now we wait."

"How long?"

"He said he was still at home. He should be here in about twenty minutes."

The two men sat in the corner and casually drank their beer. Each man deep in thought yet neither let down his guard. David watched the back of the bar while Michael watched the front. Both ready for trouble but silently hoping it didn't arrive.

FORTY-SEVEN

Fernando watched the man before him slowly back away. It had been years since he found himself at the mercy of another, particularly someone pointing a gun at him. Looking down the business end of a .45-caliber pistol was fantastic motivator. He had used the exact same tactic more times than he could count, and there were other times where he simply pulled the trigger.

His rage was growing with every step. He looked over at his so-called security specialists lying on the ground. He was disgusted how easily they had been caught off guard. Clearly, they had grown too complacent in their positions. It had been a very long time since they found themselves on defense rather than offense.

Fernando had lost sight of the men from his corner seat. He rose from his chair, continuing to watch his guards. He knew the men were still there based on his guards' continued failure to react. He slowly walked in a large arcing motion toward the opening Michael and David had vanished through. The restaurant came into full view one step at a time; the men were gone. The only evidence remaining that someone else had been there was the single tinted glass door swinging shut.

"Imbeciles!" he shouted. "How could you let this happen?" Fernando had kept his composure long enough; his rage exploded from within. He turned toward the men charged with his protection. They were both getting up, but only one would succeed. Fernando stepped forward as if approaching for a penalty kick in soccer. His wrath erupting from the blood boiling in his veins, he unleashed a kick into the head of the man closest to him, striking him solidly on the left side of his face. The guard's jaw was crushed. The breaking bones could be heard throughout the café. It was a sickening crunch; had the man survived, it surely would have left him drinking his meals through a straw for months to come, but that would not be the case. Fernando followed through with his kick as if the man's head wasn't even there. First, it was the jaw, but in the following milliseconds came the worst. His face was shattered, and as his head snapped back and to the side, the vertebrae in his neck reached the breaking point as well. The last resounding snap of his neck couldn't be distinguished from the crunch of the jaw. It happened too fast, but it happened. The vertebrae gave, and the jagged shifting bone fragments in his neck severed the spinal cord as it exited the skull.

The guard dropped back to the floor lifeless; his partner of more than decade stood next to him. Fernando didn't give the man a chance to make excuses. "Let this be the lesson. You will not be forgiven for your incompetence, but unlike this stupid *bendejo*, you will have a chance to avenge yourself. If you fail me again, you will meet with the same fate."

The remaining guard did not hesitate. He quickly began to pursue the men, determined not to let them escape. He pushed the door open wildly as he bolted from the café, only to catch a momentary glimpse of them rounding the corner a block away. He quickly gave chase, but by the time he reached the corner, they were out of sight.

They must have had a car waiting, he thought. Surely they would have had a ride. He scanned the vehicles driving away. He could not see them, but he knew they were out there and where they were headed. He pulled a cell phone from his belt and quickly dialed.

"Bueno," came the answer on the other end.

"Eddie, are Juan and Sammy still there?"

"Yeah, what's up?"

"I need to talk to Juan or Sammy right now."

"Hang on, I'll get them." There was silence for what seemed like an eternity. The man stood in the street, watching as the vehicles ahead of him began to disappear amid the traffic. "Come on!" he yelled at no one.

"Eh, this is Sammy."

"It's Santino. We have a problem. Those two cops that have been snooping around just left the Café Nueva Asia. They were supposed to be dead already."

"What? Nobody said shit about taking them out. Me and Juan were told to take care of Jimmy, and we did. That's it."

"I know, I know. A couple guys with Eme, Jose and Miguel, were supposed to do it. Apparently, they failed, and I think they're dead."

"So what happened?"

"These two guys showed up at the café this morning right when it opened and walked up to Fernando like they knew he was there. They got the jump on us and then threatened Fernando."

"No shit . . . so what do you need us for?"

"They got away, but they have to be headed back to the border. I need you to pick them up. Follow them and keep me posted."

"Yeah, no problem, but how are we supposed to pick out two white boys crossing the border? Thousands do it every day," Sammy pointed out.

"No shit, but you have seen these two. The one talking to Fernando said he was there when you shot Jimmy."

"Son of bitch. That was Garrett. I could have hit them all. We're gonna have to set those fucking Eme pussies straight. They need to learn how to handle shit. This ain't the '80s anymore."

"Tell me about it, but for now, can you handle it?"

"You got it, Santino, we'll be there. I'll call you as soon as me and Juan are in place."

Santino hung up. He clipped the cell phone to his belt and began walking. He wasn't about to go back to the café until he had Michael Garrett's head in a sack. As for David Ross, simply dead would suffice, but it would be agonizingly slow.

*   *   *

Michael nursed his second beer. Although David's thinking was sound, he found it more satirical than foretelling. Michael had no intention of getting them caught, let alone killed. He had hoped the meeting would go better, but the bottom line was that he got under Fernando's skin. He could tell by the man's posture. He may have acted cool, but his was rigid. He was nervous.

He probably thought I was going to pull the trigger, Michael thought to himself. Michael quickly returned to reality when David slapped him on the leg.

"That's our ride," David said as he took one last drink from his beer. He too had been nursing the bottle. Michael noticed as he placed it back on the bar that it was still over half-full.

Michael glanced to the back of the bar. Ignacio had come in the back door. "Hey, you made good time."

"Always for good tippers," Ignacio replied. He had been tipped more than 50 percent the night before and hoped for the same today.

"Let's go," David said as he led the way.

Michael grabbed his bag and set his beer down on the bar as well. David slowed at the back door and let Ignacio go first. "How far is your taxi?"

"It's close."

Ignacio headed out. David watched closely for any unusual movement. He knew he couldn't be sure; it was the middle of day, and there was too much going on. He finally just stepped out and was thankful to see that Ignacio had parked within ten yards of the door. He was already getting in to the cab.

Michael and David quickly climbed into the backseat of the vehicle. "How did you say it?" asked David. "Let's *vamos*."

Ignacio accelerated away from the bar and headed down the alley. "Where to?" he asked.

"Same place you picked us up last night," Michael responded.

Ignacio simply nodded his head in acknowledgment. Soon he came out onto the main road only a block and half from the Café Nueva Asia. Michael and David slid down in the seat as low as they could get without lying down. Michael pulled the Hawaiian shirts they had been wearing earlier out of his bag and handed one to David. They each pulled off their T-shirts and tossed them on the seat of the cab. As they put their colorful-print shirts back on, David started to think it just might work.

Both men stayed low in the car until they reached the border. It only took a few minutes before they found themselves in line for the border crossing. Fortunately, traffic wasn't bad. Early morning and late afternoon vehicles could be stretched for miles, waiting to enter the United States, as thousands of Mexicans drove to work every day in the U.S. Midday was a different story; traffic was minimal, and the vehicles only stretched the length of a football field at the moment.

The closer they came to the border crossing, the more comfortable they began to feel. "We better sit up. If the customs guys see us like this, they'll think we're hiding something, and we don't need to give them any more reason to hate us."

"Good point," said David as he sat up. He began breathing a little heavier, filling the car with the scent of beer.

Michael grabbed the T-shirts off the seat and stuffed them in his bag. He tucked the bag under his feet.

The cab was next in line. The customs agent had just waved the previous car through and was now motioning for Ignacio to pull forward. He did as directed and stopped with the agent next to his window. Ignacio presented his green card; it was what allowed him to pass freely into the United States.

The agent glanced at the card and handed it back to the driver. He looked into the backseat at the two men sitting there. He took a step back and aligned himself with the rear window.

Michael rolled the window down. "How are you today?"

"American citizens?" asked the agent.

Both men responded, "Yes."

"Where were you born?"

"Modesto," said Michael.

"San Pedro, California," Davie replied.

The agent looked at each man closely. He was checking for telltale signs of nervousness, a visible pulse in the neck or temple area, profuse sweating, clenching of the jaw, and rigidity or frequent flexing of muscles. "What's your purpose for visiting Mexico?" he finally asked.

"Pleasure. My friend and I came over for lunch. There's a little shop that makes a seafood cocktail you just can't get in the States," responded Michael.

The agent stepped back and waved them through.

Ignacio slowly moved through the border crossing and continued to his destination. It would only be about five more minutes, and they would be back at Tacos El Rey where he had picked them up the night before.

FORTY-EIGHT

Sammy hung up and told Juan and Eddie what was going on. It didn't take long before Eddie had each man outfitted with a couple of Berettas with extra magazines again; except this time, instead of tack-driving long guns, he gave them an AK-47 with a collapsible stock and a couple of thirty-round magazines.

The men went to the garage. Juan climbed into the driver's seat of the Toyota this time. "You drove last time, this time you can have the fun."

Sammy smiled and grabbed the AK from Eddie. He climbed into the passenger seat and pressed the barrel of the rifle into the floorboard between his legs. He ejected the magazine and tapped it twice on the dash, seating the bullets to the rear of the magazine. He inserted it back into the rifle and pulled the action back. He let go once it reached the end of its travel, and the spring launched it forward, capturing the top round in the magazine and seating it in the chamber.

Juan started the little truck while Eddie opened the garage. As soon as the door was raised, he took off. They were only blocks from the border, and Juan knew the perfect place to wait. It didn't take long before he pulled in front of a small shoe store on the corner of East First Street and Paulin Avenue. The corner parking placed them within one hundred feet of passing motorists entering the United States. Paulin was the first right turn they could make in the U.S.

Juan didn't worry about a parking spot; it was both metered and handicapped, but he didn't care. They wouldn't be there long enough to matter. If the two men he was looking for were truly headed for the border, they would already be in line. He kept the truck running while Sammy pulled out a set of binoculars that was left in the glove box. He began to scan the vehicles in the border lanes. It didn't take long.

"There," Sammy said, pointing to a beat-up taxi. "The two we are looking for are in the backseat. Shit, they're even wearing the same shirts they had on yesterday."

"This is going to be too easy. I can't believe those Eme guys fucked this up," Juan said seriously.

"We need to work on communication. I know they have their protocol and everything with Fernando, but if we had been in the loop 100 percent, we could have prevented all this yesterday," Sammy pointed out.

The truth of the matter was simple. Just like any organization, communication is critical and generally the problem when things go wrong. Unfortunately, for the Mexican Mafia, they were the underlings when it came to their dealings with Los Zetas, and they would have to change their tactics as directed or suffer the consequences. Despite hating to take second seat to the Zetas in operations, the enhanced power and unlimited financial gain made it worth it.

Juan made a mental note of the discussion to bring it up with Fernando in the future. For now, they had a mess to clean up. Truth be told, both Juan and Sammy were ecstatic to get to keep working in the U.S. They would be leaving a mark on local law enforcement that wouldn't soon be forgotten. This was the type of action that created guttural fear. Fear that lasted. The kind that earned the Zetas the respect in the world they operated in.

Sammy kept watching the taxi as it crept forward and finally across the border. Juan pulled away from the curb and turned right onto Paulin. He didn't want to lose the taxi, but he couldn't risk jumping the small divider or traveling the wrong way on the road to get behind them. It would draw too much attention. He quickly headed down to the next block and then turned left on Second Street.

"There they go," he said as he saw the taxi go by. He accelerated and made the left onto Highway 111. He was just settling in to follow the taxi when the vehicle pulled into the gas station on the corner of Third.

Juan made the right onto Third and continued past the gas station. He pulled into the alley past the gas station and quickly took advantage of a bank parking lot that would give them full view of the gas station.

Sammy was calling Santino to update him. The phone rang and was answered before the second ring.

"You found them?" was the immediate question launched from the other end.

"We found them. They are in taxi right now, but stopped at a gas station at the corner of Third and 111."

"Stay with them. I'm on the way. I'll catch up and—"

"Wait, they're moving. They just got out of the taxi and are getting into a grey unmarked cop car," Sammy interrupted.

"Great work. I'll call you back in a few. I am headed for my truck." Santino hung up and began running back toward the café. He had been walking around the block waiting for just such a call. He knew he was a dead man if Garrett and Ross got away. His luck was taking a turn for the better.

Sammy put the phone down while he and Juan watched the two men get into the grey sedan and back out of the parking stall. They pulled out onto the highway and headed north. Juan shot down the alley, coming out on Fourth Street. He made a quick left turn and then came to a stop, waiting for an opening in traffic. He gunned the little truck at the first chance and fell in behind the detectives a few cars back. Yet again, he wondered what kind of amateurs Eme had sent after these two.

"This is going to be fun."

Sammy agreed.

Forty-nine

Michael was glad to be back on the California side of the border. He knew they had taken a big risk going to meet Fernando on his turf, but it had to be done. If nothing else came from the meeting, at least Michael now knew what he looked like. It was important for him to put a face behind the name; it made his enemy less enigmatic and more real. Michael stood before him and lived. Fernando was not nearly as elusive or deadly as Agent Savage had made him out to be. He was just like every other criminal Michael had known, a coward who was hiding behind something. A gun, a knife, or, in this case, a couple of thugs in the corner on the other side of the border where lawlessness prevailed.

Not anymore, Michael thought. He had not only stood before the man, he could have easily taken him out right then and there. If he wasn't on the side of righteous, he would have killed Fernando and one of his goons. Leaving the other to tell the world what happened. If he had only known then what was to come, he just might have; as it was, he and David were headed rather aimlessly for the moment, neither really aware of what their next step would be.

"Well," David began, "now what?"

The words snapped Michael out the reverie he was in. The morning had been a little surreal, and he found himself wondering just what Agent Savage was going to say when he told him what had happened.

"I've gotta check in with Cook up in Tahoe. I want to let him know what's going on and have him get ready just in case Fernando tries to make a move on Rosa," Michael said.

"She's in custody, right?"

"Yeah, but only until Tuesday morning. That's as far as we could stretch the arraignment, and the DA's gonna cut her loose because they don't have anything to file on. It was self-defense. We held her for her own protection so I could come down here and try and figure things out."

"Nice job, Ace," David harassed. "We kind of stirred up a hornet's nest in my opinion."

"Maybe, just maybe, Fernando will realize I was right and that she's just not worth it. Head to my mom's house. I want to check things out, and we can get some fresh clothes before taking our next step. I'm gonna call Cook."

"You got it," David replied. He kept driving north, regularly looking back, trying to pick out a tail just in case they were being followed. It wouldn't be easy. There were only a few places anyone could turn off once you got out of the city, making it impossible to determine if someone was following you or just headed in the same direction. David realized he was going to have to take a more indirect route to see if anyone followed.

Michael pulled out his cell phone and looked at the remaining power. He was down to his last bar. It was the one thing he had forgotten to do, and now he was hoping to have enough juice left to at least warn Cook to get prepared. He quickly punched in the number and hit the Call button. The phone rang a few times before being answered.

"This is Cook."

"Hey, Jon, it's Michael. I've got some news for you."

"That doesn't sound very good, brother. What've you been up to in the last twenty-four hours?"

"Nothing good, I can tell you that much," Michael quipped, trying to lighten his mood more than anything. "Here's the deal. I met with the man pulling the strings this morning in Mexico, and it's not good."

"Mexico . . . Are you outta your mind? You don't have any authority down there. What were you going to do?" Cook retorted.

"I hit a bit of wall yesterday. I don't know how much you may have seen on the news, but there was a U.S. Customs agent killed last night."

"I know. It was on the news. The story is said to have gone international. What do you know about it? The news reports were pretty vague."

"I was talking to him when he got hit. Someone sniped him with me standing there, not one hundred yards from the customs building on the border."

"Holy shit, man, are you doing okay?" Cook asked sincerely.

"That's not the half of it, Jon. A few hours before that, David and I were following Rosa's parents to her brother's house. I had convinced them to leave their home for safety purposes and put them in touch with you."

"Yeah, I remember. They called right after you did, and I arranged everything for them to speak with Rosa."

"Well, right after we talked, two guys with La Eme tried to take us out. I don't know if they were after me, or Rosa's parents, to be honest with you, but either way, they're dead."

"Michael, you need to throw in the towel on this one, man. You've done more than you should have. Our responsibility was to Rosa up here. We investigated her story, she's cleared, and she'll be out on Tuesday morning when the DA refuses to file. I know it's fucked-up, but the world is what it is, and we can't save it. You do your best, but you have to realize you can't fix everything."

"Look, I don't have time for lectures, my phone's about to die. Like I said, I talked to the man, and told him to let it go, let Rosa go. I don't think it went over very well, and I want you to be prepared. I think that Carlos might try to make a move on her when she gets released, and I need you to be ready."

"Ready for what, Michael? We can't follow her around from now on," said Cook.

"I know! Just trust me on this. I don't think it'll take very long. These guys don't seem to waste much time. And get the U.S. Marshals on line with witness protection. Tell them I'm working the case with Special Agent Ryan Savage out of the El Centro FBI Office. They can confirm with him what I've told you. Find out what it will take to get Rosa and her family protected. This case should be big enough to meet their criteria."

"I'll give them a call, but I don't know what I'm going to be able to accomplish on a Saturday. Charge your phone, I'll be in touch."

Michael hung up as David was turning onto Ross Road.

"Isn't this the way you went yesterday?" David asked.

"Yeah, but why are you taking it? The freeway would have been faster," Michael pointed out while he looked back at the power on his phone. The single bar remaining wasn't blinking yet, but he knew it was close.

"I had to do it for namesake." David laughed. "I couldn't tell if anyone was following us, so I wanted to take a less-traveled route to see if anything jumps out," he finished more seriously.

"Good call," Michael extolled while looking over his shoulder to take in the vehicles behind them.

Of the many cars, trucks, and minivans that lined the road, only a few made the turn. It was still impossible to tell if any of the vehicles were following them, but David had narrowed down the possibilities. It would be much easier to keep track now.

FIFTY

Santino wasted no time. He had reached his truck and headed for the border; there was no time to spare. He fired up the black Ford F-150 and drove as fast as he could only to be stopped in traffic at the border. Fortunately, the line was short, and it only took a few minutes before he reached the crossing. The customs officer looked at him closely and inspected the bed of his truck. It was empty. "Where are you from?" he asked.

"Mexico," Santino said proudly. He fished out his papers and handed the officer a green card. The name on the card identified the man as Juan Guerra Ortiz. The card was real, issued by U.S. immigration, but the documents used to get it had all been counterfeit.

Los Zetas never used real names when traveling. Although they had not begun working in the U.S., it wasn't uncommon for them to travel there for other reasons. Because false birth certificates were so easy to come by in Mexicali, they always used such documents to ascertain IDs. It wasn't a new concept. It was more the norm for Special Forces soldiers and criminals around the world. In the Zetas' case, it was also necessary as all of the former Mexican army soldiers who now called themselves Los Zetas had been placed on international watch lists. The irony was that several of them had entered the army using false names in the first place, trying to elude the law for one reason or another.

The officer inspected the card and quickly flagged Santino through. He accelerated steadily away from the border until he was traveling faster than most down the highway dissecting the city. He called Sammy back and asked for an update.

"We're a little more than ten miles north on 111," said Sammy.

"Good. I'm just leaving Calexico headed your way. I should be able to catch up soon."

"Wait a second, they're slowing down. They just turned right on Ross. It'll be your first right past the freeway."

"Okay, keep the phone on and let me know what's going on."

Juan was now directly behind the gray sedan. It wasn't long before another car turned and was behind them. He closed the distance slightly, hoping to lull the two detectives into a false sense of security. He assumed that they would be watching for a tail, and by closing the distance, it would look much more as if they were simply in a hurry rather than trying to be discreet.

Sammy kept Santino apprised of their location. Santino was closing in. He could feel the anger caused from being humiliated by these men in front of his boss raging inside of him. His partner, the man he had worked with for years, who had become one of his best friends, was dead because of them. They were going to die, and he was going to kill them.

Sammy's voice crackled from the phone. "Passing Bowker."

Santino didn't need to respond. He just kept driving. He crossed over the interstate; he was gaining on them. It wouldn't be long.

Juan just kept driving. He and Sammy had their orders, and for now, everything seemed to be going smoothly. The sedan hadn't deviated out of the norm of daily travel. So far, it seemed that all was going well. Juan checked his rearview mirror to see what was going on behind him. The minivan that had been there before turned as they passed the last road. The road was clear; if the cops were going to get suspicious, now is when it would happen.

It wasn't much longer that the gap began to grow between the two vehicles. The sedan was speeding up.

"You think they made us?" asked Juan.

"I don't know, but something's up," said Sammy.

Santino could hear the conversation in the background on his phone. "What's going on?"

"They're speeding up. We're keeping a safe distance just in case they're just testing us. We have a good visual out here. There's nothing to worry about."

"I'm turning onto Ross now. I'm almost there."

Fifty-one

Michael had been watching more closely now that he was off the phone. He wasn't overly concerned by what he'd seen so far, but the second car back was a van. It made him nervous. There was no reason for it other than the men following them the day before also drove a van.

"You see the van back there?" he asked.

"Yeah, it's been there for a while. Came out of Calexico with us."

"That's what worries me," said Michael.

David continued straight while Michael watched the vehicle closely. He was approaching a Stop sign. He slowed down while Michael kept vigilant.

"Turn or straight?" David asked.

"Straight, the van is signaling."

"Roger that." David proceeded through the intersection of Bowker Road and continued east on Ross headed for Holtville. It was another thirty seconds when he felt an unsettling churn in his lower abdomen.

"Mike, I gotta go."

"What? What are you talking about? We are going."

"No, I mean I gotta go. Something about breakfast isn't agreeing with me. How long to your mom's from here?"

"Depends on you. We can probably make it ten or less if you step on it."

David wasted no time. He smashed on the gas and accelerated down the road, stirring up swirls of dust as the vehicle careened through the hot air.

"What's the quickest way?"

Michael could hear the urgency in his friend's voice. "A straight line."

"Come on, man, you know what I mean."

"I thought you knew the way. What if this was life and death, partner? What if I was injured, what would you do?" Michael was enjoying watching his friend's face contort while he began to control his breathing. He knew David was never going to make it.

"This is serious, man! What's the fastest way?"

"I know, I was just getting you back for the hotel incident. The fastest way is straight ahead, but you're not looking so hot already. You have any paper in here?"

"What the fuck do you need paper for?"

"Toilet paper, you know, ass wipe. Don't you keep a roll in your car just in case you're stuck on surveillance and need to take care of business?"

"No! I work in the city, Michael. If nature calls, I use a bathroom."

"Well then, I suggest you better start thinking about which sleeve of your FBI T-shirt you wanna cut off then."

"You're enjoying this way too . . . Oh man!"

"You drank the water, didn't you? Never drink the water or use the ice." Michael was watching for something that would do when he saw just the spot rapidly approaching. "There." He pointed. "Right there."

"What are you pointing at? There's nothing out here but field and a haystack," David said, concerned.

"Exactly. Pull over behind the haystack." Michael pulled David's T-shirt out of his bag, snapped the blade open on his Benchmade. He quickly sliced off one sleeve and then the other. "Here you go, now you can show off the pipes down at muscle beach."

David never heard a word. He pulled the car off on the dirt road separating two fields. He swerved at the last minute, not realizing there was a drainage ditch there as well. Such drains were commonplace in the valley; this one stretched nearly thirty feet across and descended no less than twelve feet before it reached the murky brown water running through it; the banks lined with deceptively tall tule grass. He accelerated again, his haven just over a hundred yards dead ahead.

Michael tossed the sleeves between his friend's legs. David snatched the cloth and slammed on the brakes. He threw the car in park and bolted from his seat, leaving the door open. He quickly disappeared between a break in the hay.

Michael got out of the car and stretched, standing between the open door and the body of the car. He looked around; they were relatively alone except for a couple of vehicles in the distance. Michael looked at the crops on either side, reminiscing briefly of old times spent with his father hunting for dove and pheasant amid the crops.

Michael was drawn by the sound of the vehicles. Far away they were nothing more than a shimmer, their windshields gleaming in the sun. As they drew near, he could hear the motors. They were racing.

"How's it going over there?" he shouted, not taking his eyes off of the rapidly approaching vehicles. Michael wasn't overly concerned until he realized it was the same tan Toyota that had been behind them earlier, now followed by a black Ford, and they were slowing down.

Michael reached back into the car and quickly turned it off, extracting the keys from the ignition. He hurried to the trunk and opened it, immediately retrieving the M4 rifle and Remington 870 police shotgun David carried there. He sprinted the short distance to the haystacks, just as the vehicles turned onto the dirt road.

The man in the Ford accelerated wildly, causing the vehicle to drift sideways. It looked as though the driver was going to end up in the field, but that was far from reality. He maneuvered the vehicle with the precision of a desert racer, maintaining control and guiding it forward until it smashed into the tons of bailed hay where Michael disappeared. Bales of hay toppled from the top of the stack as the truck pushed even more out from under them. Where once there had been a gap was now filled with hundreds of pounds of hay and two tons of Ford truck.

The men in the Toyota stopped behind the gray sedan in line with the hay. As Juan and Sammy exited the truck, they could each see down one side of the haystack.

Michael had reached David with the guns. He had seen and heard the trucks coming as well. He did what was necessary and was buttoning up when he saw Michael run around the corner, long guns in hand.

"Here!" Michael said as he handed the M4 to its owner. "Follow me!"

David grabbed the gun and hotfooted it behind his friend.

Michael tore across the small patch of earth that remained between the haystack and the drainage ditch. He led David away from the approaching vehicles and away from the only concealment they currently had. At the edge of the ditch, Michael leapt. David did the same, never skipping a beat. The men landed amid the weeds at the edge of the water. They could hear the impact of the truck as it rammed into the hay.

Michael stepped into the murky water. It was moving deceptively fast; fortunately, the mud his feet sank into kept them from being swept out from under him. He crouched as low as he could get without having to use his hands for support. He kept the shotgun pointed up toward the ditch bank, trying to spy any movement through the tule reeds that extended well over their heads. David stayed on his heels, rifle at the ready.

"Where the hell did they come from?" David whispered.

"I don't know. One of the trucks was behind us earlier. I don't know about the other one. They must have called someone."

Michael and David could hear one of the men shouting.

"They went this way! They must be in the ditch!" shouted Santino. He then began firing blindly into the ditch with a 9mm Glock pistol that had been modified to fire full auto that he kept in a cutout compartment under the front seat. Santino burned through a thirty-round magazine in mere seconds. The bullets ripped through the tall grass like a nuclear-powered knife.

"That was a little too close," David said. "We need to keep moving until we can get a shot."

Michael agreed, but he also knew that if they moved any quicker, the movement in the reeds would give them away. They didn't stand a chance if that happened. He moved farther into the water with David in tow. It was up to their waist now. They continued to move back toward the road. They knew there was no escape; they merely needed to gain a tactical advantage.

Michael and David were moving as fast as they dared; the tall grass seemed sharp as knives. They looked for a sliver of a man through the reeds in hopes of reducing their foes' numbers. Neither really knew how many men were above them on the bank. Only one had spoken. It didn't matter; they were out of time. Santino reloaded and began firing madly into the ditch again. This time with larger side-to-side motions, hoping one of the bullets would find the men lurking below. It did.

David felt the impact in his right forearm. The small copper-jacketed round ripped through the flesh near the elbow. The round went through and through, missing the bones in his arm, but then entered his right side. The bullet penetrated the large latissimus dorsi muscle.

The hollow-point bullet expanded to its maximum potential almost immediately upon hitting the dense muscle. It spiraled into David's body, sliced flesh and blood vessels until it impacted a rib. The rib absorbed the remaining energy of the bullet, preventing the wound from being mortal. David stumbled into the water with the impact. He growled in agony, doing his best to keep from giving them away.

Michael pulled his friend up and pressed him into the weed-covered bank of dirt that rose above them. The grass moved above, but nothing more than it had with the barrage of fire coming from Santino. The men lay flush again the ditch bank until the shooting subsided.

"Where are you hit?" Michael asked in a hushed voice.

David raised his right arm. He noticed he couldn't move his fingers well; no doubt one or more of the tendons had been severed. The wound itself didn't look that bad. The entrance was no larger than the size of the bullet, a red circle that should be there with a pink flesh filling it in and a small trickle of blood flowing from it. The exit wound was roughly twice the size, with the flesh erupting out like the whites of an overboiled egg. There was more bleeding but nothing that appeared arterial.

"I got hit in the side too, but I can keep going," David declared.

"You sure? You can lie low and I'll lead them away. If I can make it to the culvert, I can get to the other side of the road and ambush them."

"The road is one hundred yards from here. You'll never make it without getting caught."

"Okay, then we need to take the fight to them. Are you ready?"

"As I'll ever be."

Michael laid out a down-and-dirty plan of attack. It would have made any marine proud. Back-to-back, he and David inched up the steep embankment. David facing in the direction Santino had been shooting. After the shooting, he could be heard reloading again. Michael facing the unknown. The men were at the point of no return; they were at the edge of the sheet of grass that had concealed them.

Michael waited for David's mark. They would move when he was ready. David took a painful breath and began the countdown. "Three, two, one . . ." And the men launched themselves out from the cover of the weeds.

David immediately spotted Santino, who was now reacting to the movement on his right. It didn't matter; he was too late. David squeezed the trigger on his M4 in rapid succession, firing left-handed to ensure he had the strength to do it. The bullets found their mark. Santino was struck three times in the chest. One of the rounds pierced the upper part of his heart and the ascending aorta. Santino, whose heart was racing, collapsed and died in a matter of seconds as the blood pumped furiously from his heart.

Michael wasn't as lucky. He scanned energetically for the others. They were not as brazen and farther back from the edge than Santino. They stood back, watching the crest of the ditch, waiting for the slightest sign of movement. This way, they would not be surprised by a blast from within like Santino had been.

The two Zetas had a rough idea of the shooter's location. They separated and began to approach the edge, triangulating on their quarry. Michael and David had remained as far back in the weeds as they could, only protruding far enough to see clearly. The tactic had worked.

Michael saw Juan first. The Zetas had slightly miscalculated, and both men were on the same side, rather than coming in from opposite angles to Michael and David. Michael drew Sammy into the ghost ring sights on the twelve gauge and pulled the trigger in an instant. Twelve lead pellets each the size of a small marble exploded from the end of the barrel; eleven of which impacted Juan's upper body; two of which penetrated his face and skull.

Sammy was farther down, and Michael had not seen him yet. Armed with the Ak-47, Sammy squeezed the trigger and held it back. The weapon fired over and over in rapid succession. Although not as accurate as David had been with his M4, Sammy's rounds were on target.

Michael had seen Sammy the moment he began firing. The bullets were striking the dirt in front of him and climbing with every shot as the recoil caused the rifle to rise. Michael adjusted his aim and began firing back.

David turned to engage the shooter as well.

Michael's first round was off. He racked the action and acquired another sight picture, placing Sammy in the center of the ghost ring sight. Everything was happening so fast, yet it seemed like an eternity. The dirt stopped erupting in front of him. The bullets were tearing through his body. Michael pulled the trigger.

David came around 180 degrees. He identified his target and brought his M4 up on target. He began to squeeze the trigger as Sammy just held the trigger of his Ak-47 back, letting the automatic weapon cycle through every round in its magazine. The rifled continued to climb. The bullets now traveled over Michael and into David.

Michael's next round had been on target. The round of double-aught buck had done its job. Sammy was mortally wounded but would not die immediately.

David managed to fire two rounds; one of which struck Sammy in the center line of his body. The bullet severed his spine, and Sammy fell immediately to the ground where he lay until he died.

David had been hit twice more, both in the gut. He fell back on the dirt in excruciating pain. Blood seeping from his wounds.

Michael had been hit in the left ankle, hip, and the right side of his chest. His ankle was broken; the round that hit his hip struck at an angle, but it still fractured the large bone. The round into his chest punctured his lung and exited cleanly out the back.

Michael fell back next to David. He looked at his friend who was laboring to breathe a little more with every breath.

"David, you gotta hang on. I'm gonna call for help. You gotta hang on." Michael pulled his cell phone from his pocket, hoping the battery would survive long enough to make one last call. He looked at the phone to dial and realized it had been submerged in the water. The phone would not work.

He tried to roll over and crawl to the surface. The pain in his hip was excruciating. He forced himself to do it. David's life depended on it. Once to the top, Michael crawled over to the closest body. He shuffled through his pockets, searching for a phone. He found none. He had to move faster; he tried to stand, but he couldn't physically do it. He fell to the ground. He dragged himself over toward Sammy.

"David, you're gonna be okay, buddy. Help's on the way. You gotta hang in there."

There was no response. David was too weak to speak. Both of his lungs were filling with blood.

Michael could feel the pain in his chest increasing. The chest wound was allowing air to collect in the pleural cavity of the chest between the lung and chest wall. The pain was increasing and causing Michael to suffer shortness of breath with the exertion of trying to reach Sammy.

It took every ounce of determination he had, but he made it. He went through his pockets and found what he was searching for. He pulled the cell phone from the pocket and dialed 911.

"911, what's your emergency?"

"There's been a shooting. I'm an undercover officer, and my partner and I have been shot." Michael was struggling to speak. Every breath grew more painful. Getting enough air to talk was a challenge.

"What's your location, sir?" the emergency operator asked with complete control.

"We're just off of Ross Road somewhere east of Bowker," was all he could manage.

Michael spoke his last word, fading into the darkness and peace of the unconscious world.

He and David lay in the sweltering heat, unknown to the world passing by, dying.

EPILOGUE

Detective Cook had taken every precaution with the information Michael had provided. The plan went off without a hitch. Rosa was to be released Tuesday morning following the district attorney's dismissal of the murder charge. The information was given to the local press, who ran with it on all the local news channels.

Rosa cooperated fully and called Carlos, asking for a ride when she was to be released. He was waiting for her in his Buick outside the jail when a swarm of Douglas County sheriff's patrol vehicles swarmed in like a pack of wolves, surrounding him, trapping him. Carlos was arrested without incident. He was marched into the jail while Rosa was escorted out by a pair of U.S. Marshals.

Detective Cook had contacted the U.S. Marshal's office and arranged for witness protection just as Michael had suggested. It was simple enough. Once the marshals had the information about the case, it was clear the Jimenez family was going to be needed to testify when Carlos went to trial. The charges against him spanned the entire spectrum—murder, rape, kidnapping, conspiracy, and terrorism. Rosa and her father's testimony would be critical, and it was no doubt both Los Zetas and La Eme would want them dead.

The U.S. Marshals reunited Rosa and her entire family in northeast Nebraska on 580 acres of tillable farmland twenty miles from the town of Creighton. There was nothing more than a three-bedroom, two-bath modular home on the property, but it would have to do. It wasn't quite the dream her father had of moving back to Mexico, but it was a farm nonetheless. The federal government had acquired the property when the previous owner had died and had back taxes exceeding the value of property. With no next of kin to fight the seizure, the property sat awaiting auction. The marshals came across the property and, with the knowledge of the family, decided it would be put to better use for the Jimenez family.

There was but one last detail—new names.

* * *

Michael was startled awake by someone forcing his eyelid up. The light in his eye pulled him from the coma he had been in. The pain began to set in. He felt it in his chest with every breath he took. His hip and leg ached; the pain was constant but not throbbing.

His vision was blurred at first; then slowly, his eyes began to focus. He could now see a man dressed in a white smock holding the small light that had recently been shined in his eyes. The name badge hanging from his smock read *Dr. Yang.* Next to him was a woman in floral scrubs. Michael couldn't see her name.

"What's going on? Where am I?" Michael asked.

"You're in the hospital, Mr. Garrett. You've been shot. You had a collapsed lung and two fractured ribs. Your lung was filled with blood, and you most likely lost consciousness due to extreme oxygen deficiency and blood loss. You almost died, Michael. If it hadn't been for the flight medics, we probably would have lost you," replied Dr. Yang.

It all came flooding back. Michael had a vivid memory of what had taken place. It seemed like only moments ago.

"Where am I? How long have I been here? Where's David? I—"

The doctor held up his hand. "Michael, you need to try and calm down. Getting yourself worked up right now isn't going to do any good. You're at Scripps Hospital in La Jolla. You were brought here by Life Flight. You've been here for four days, and you're going to be here for at least that many more."

Michael tried to sit up, but the pain intensified. The nurse quickly stepped forward, placing her arm behind his shoulders, helping him ease him back down. Michael noticed her name tag now, *LVN Jen Kassel.* She was beautiful, tall with long copper-colored curly hair. Her face gleamed, and the corners of her mouth curled up slightly as she laid him back on the hospital bed.

"Thank you," Michael said as he couldn't help but notice her emerald green eyes and porcelain smooth, lightly freckled cheeks.

"No problem, it's my pleasure," she responded. Her voice was kind and gentle.

"I have to finish my exam. You can ask Nurse Kassel any other questions you may have when I'm done. I have to finish my rounds, then I'll be back to check on you again. We'll have a lot to cover now that you're out of the coma," said Dr. Yang.

The doctor examined Michael's injuries, removing bandages and wrappings, checking the sutures and drain tubes on his chest from the surgery to repair the pneumothorax. Once finished, Dr. Yang left the room, leaving Michael and the nurse alone.

Michael had many questions, but only a few were answered. His zest for knowledge ended when the nurse informed him that David Ross had died. "He was already dead when the medics found you. He had lost too much blood."

Michael couldn't believe it. It was his fault. He should have just let it go, but now because he couldn't, one of his closest friends was dead. Michael raged within; he could not rest; his mind raced. What could he have done differently? How had they found them? What about Rosa and her family? He would not stop until he had answers.

32200174R00135

Made in the USA
San Bernardino, CA
11 April 2019